All That Soars

A. N. Horton

Veil & Valor Books

To my own little dreamers. May you reach for the stars even when they fall around you.

Contents

PART ONE
HELL

Chapter One

A Sacrifice

The edges of my pain burned away until I felt nothing. Darkness swarmed in, encompassing me in its familiarity, soothing my mind with blissful nothingness. But it, too, blinked away a moment later and left me standing in a strange foyer that I had never seen before.

I blinked, staring around at my surroundings. Vibrant purple damask wallpaper clung to the outer edges of my vision and flowed into a beautiful cherry wood floor beneath my feet. Paintings and little pieces of art were scattered about almost haphazardly as if they'd just been moved into the area and the occupant of the home hadn't yet decided where to put them. A set of stairs ran along the far wall and led up to rooms that I could not see. But it was the door that drew my attention; the one leading, presumably, outside of the home. It was made entirely of pure silver. I stared at it for a moment and then took a step forward.

My head snapped sideways in the direction of the approaching footsteps that emanated suddenly from somewhere off to the right. I hesitated, eyes flicking to that silver door, calculating an escape route should my mother appear in this strange place. But the person who finally emerged in the threshold of the foyer was not my mother at all.

"Uncle," I breathed in awe.

"I have to say I'm surprised about the choice of meeting place," he replied, striding forward and pacing about the foyer in that familiar studious way of his, hands clasped behind his back, polished shoes glinting in the light of the silver chandelier hung far above us. It was such a familiar sight that my heart ached. "I thought for sure you would have chosen Hadley."

"How are you here?" I asked him, my brow furrowed in confusion.

He continued his pacing, glancing up at me with head cocked slightly to the side, so close to how I remembered it. Close, but not quite. There was something about his eyes. I caught it as he turned and they caught the light. Something glinted in them. Something wrong. They were the same hazel that I remembered, wizened and wrinkled at the corners, but now they burned with something... older. Something that was not Xavier Belling. I blinked in shock at the realization.

This wasn't my uncle.

I backed away suddenly, pressing myself against the wall as my eyes shot rapidly about my surroundings once more. My curious observation turned suddenly to anxious threat assessment. Something was wrong. Some part of my subconscious was screaming that fact at me but the panic felt distant, so far away, like a version of me was calling out in warning but was muffled by something, some other sense that felt foreign.

"You need not worry," the thing that looked like my uncle called out, raising a hand in a gesture of goodwill. "Nothing happens here unless you want it to."

I frowned, brow furrowing again in even more confusion.

"You—you're not my uncle," I accused.

"I am not," he agreed, picking up a little statue of a goldfinch and examining it. "I am the projection of his image into your subconscious. I'm a conversational piece. I'm not him but I am of him. I know everything about him. I have his motivations, his memories. I know Xavier Belling, perhaps better than the man himself."

His eyes flicked to mine and my heart pounded against my ribs.

"What are you?" I gasped.

"I have no name or, rather, I did but men have forgotten it," he replied with a shrug, setting the figure back on the shelf and pacing again. "For our purposes, let's say I am the elixir. Or, rather, the force within the elixir. And I'm here to help you understand."

"Understand what?"

"Your father's choice of setting made far more sense. His childhood home where he grew up with your uncle. That, I understood, but this. Tell me, where are we?"

He turned his gaze onto me and I leaned off of the wall, examining him anew. It wasn't my uncle, I knew that, but the likeness was uncanny. Everything was the same. Everything.

"Seren," he said my name and I blinked at him.

"I—I don't know," I confessed, glancing around at our surroundings myself. "Where are we supposed to be?"

"Home. Wherever you believe your true home to be, that's where we go. For your father, it was his childhood home, the place where he lived his most pleasant memories. But you don't know where we are?"

I shook my head.

"Curious," he mused, hand on his chin. "Perhaps you haven't found it yet."

"Yet?" I asked. "So I'm going to live?"

His eyes snapped to mine again.

"It doesn't work that way," he told me. "I had suspected your clairvoyant friend, the one touched by Rhene, would have told you that had she had the time to explain. The future is not preordained. It's not a set stream of events. It's constantly changing, always shifting, based on whatever decisions you make. When you came here, your future was one thing. Perhaps now, it is another."

"You speak in riddles."

"Allow me to clarify. If you wish for eternal life, you may enter that silver door and I shall grant it. The pain is excruciating as everything against nature is. If you wish to die a mortal death, head up those stairs and be spared from pain for all eternity. The longer you remain in this foyer, the more of your demons will come to haunt you until you've made your choice. I will warn you, Seren Dawnpaw, that the elixir does not give without taking. You will be required to make a sacrifice should you choose immortal life."

"What sacrifice?"

"That, I cannot say. Only the elixir knows."

"You said you were the elixir?"

"I said I was the force within the elixir. These are not the same thing. You must learn to listen, Seren Dawnpaw. You hear, but you do not listen, much like so many men and fae."

He spread his hands wide and offered me a sad smile before turning and striding for the door.

"That's it?" I called after him. "You're just leaving me here?"

"You know the rules. You know the risks. Your destiny is your own now, Seren Dawnpaw."

Just like that, he was gone. I was alone in this empty foyer, surrounded by those purple walls and all its gleaming artwork. What a pretty tomb, I thought morbidly and then hated myself for it a moment later. I couldn't think like that, couldn't give up so easily. I had a choice to make, if the elixir who was not the elixir was correct.

"Seren," someone said suddenly and I jerked back to attention to find Cass entering from the hall on the opposite side from where my uncle had vanished.

I blinked at her, stunned to find her here, heart soaring at the opportunity to see her again. But then a swarm of visions flashed through my mind and I stumbled away from her.

I saw Cass tossing her head back, laughing at that gaudy dinner table in the center of the Court of Wanderers. I saw her watching me tentatively as she picked through the produce I'd gotten from the market when we had been alone in that apartment. I saw her smiling over her shoulder as a bright bulb of magic light shone from her hand. Then I saw the moment she appeared on that snowy road and pulled me away against my will. I saw her begging for her brother's life, throwing mine at the heels of her vengeful father. I saw her weeping as they hung an imitation of Lark, wincing when I screamed at her to get out of my room, fleeing in the night when I needed her most. I saw her sobbing on my mother's floor, hands covered in Lark's blood. And then that look, that sad, pained expression she had offered me before she left with Lark and Rook to hunt the gorgon.

Because she had known.

I came spinning back to the foyer with a gasp. The accusation was out of my mouth before I even righted myself.

"You knew," I spat at her. "You knew she would catch you. Maybe you even knew what she would do to me!"

Cass stopped a few feet from me, cocked her head to the side, and blinked.

"Premonition," I hissed, recalling the way she had shot shadow at Medusa's magic so fast, too fast. "You saw it."

She lowered her face, her eyes darkening, her smile vanishing. She looked like a cruel imitation of herself, not like the glowing, radiant Cass that I had come to know.

"You could have stopped it," I snapped. "Why didn't you stop it?"

She just stared at me.

"Tell me why!" I screamed, lashing out at her.

But the moment my hand reached for where her shoulder would be, she vanished into a puff of smoke. I stood still, breathing hard, chest heaving. The feeling of betrayal rose up within me, crashing against my mortal heart in a wave of confused fury. Cass had lied to me? Cass?

From off to the right, I heard footsteps again. I closed my eyes and shook my head.

"No," I sighed. "No, no, no."

I wasn't ready. I was still reeling from the revelation of Cass' betrayal. I couldn't take a similar assault. Not yet.

But the elixir wasn't inclined to wait for me. When I opened my eyes, it wasn't my uncle standing there. Nor was it Cass. It was Wyn Kendrick and he wore a scowl to rival that of any he had given me before.

"You never told us about them," he barked, furious, as he crossed the room in a few strides and pushed his nose up against mine. I felt him there, solid, real. I looked down at my hands against which Cass had just vanished and my brow furrowed in confusion. "You were supposed to be one of us. You were supposed to have chosen us. But you kept their secret. You kept them safe. And for what? What had they done for you? Mortals raised you. Mortals gave your your academic standing, your professionalism, your values. Is this how you repay Xavier Belling? Calling yourself Seren Dawnpaw and becoming one of them?"

My eyes snapped up to his, my lips parting slightly in surprise.

"You do this and she wins," he snarled.

I looked past his shoulders, at the stairs behind him.

"You're right," I murmured, my voice soft.

"You do this and you become one of them. Forever."

"You're right."

"Would you really give up on us so completely? Would you really cast the mortal realm aside? Cast your home aside?"

My gaze snapped back to his and then to my surroundings. My home...

"You do this," he repeated, his voice already blowing away like leaves on a stiff breeze, "and Ariadne wins."

Then he was gone, faded completely, and I was alone again. I hung my head, tears streaking down my cheeks. I reached up and felt them there, wet, real. How? How did this feel so real? What magic was this that was so capable of solidifying a dream, some kind of out of body experience that felt lucid in a way nothing ever had before? I shuddered. This wasn't possible. This shouldn't be possible.

The force within the elixir...

I looked toward the stairs, then to the door. Immortal life or mortal death. What would it feel like, to die? And more, what would it feel like to live? I took a step forward, then another. I whirled around, searching for the next memory, the next shadow person who would come to convince me to die, to convince me that my life wasn't worth whatever sacrifice I would have to make, wasn't worth my mother's victory.

I didn't hear him come. I just felt his breath on my neck a heartbeat before he spoke.

"Ren," Lark whispered against the shell of my ear and my breath hitched as I was assaulted, yet again, by that onslaught of memories.

It started with the kiss. I felt the memory like the ghost of his lips upon my own. The moment we met, the way he leaned toward me as he sat across from my desk. Our jaunt down that arctic mountain. Healing the rift and the moment he pulled me through it. All of the little looks and glimpses we took, we cherished, in the Court of Light and Life. Our conversation in the garden and the way he had laughed. Then when he broke that fae male's bones, when he was captured, when we begged his father for his life only for him to receive a sentence of death. His execution. His second kidnapping of me, the knife fight we'd had in the snow. Training and travel. Juicy peaches, crisp tea shirts, and hot tea.

I fell to my knees, tears flowing freely down my cheeks.

"My love," he breathed in a way that seemed more like a hiss, circling me. "My gift. My bonded."

I heaved in a shaky breath and opened my eyes to find him standing before me, watching me with that same strange tilt to his head that Cass had done.

"She broke you," I gasped because that was the last memory I was given. Lark, broken and bloody on the floor of the Bronze Throne.

"Because of you," he snarled.

I sobbed, chest heaving, body shaking.

"All of this, because of you," he growled. "My exile. My execution. My torture. You. You. You."

"We are bonded," I choked out my argument.

"I am bonded to pain," he roared, lip curling in disgust as he stared down at me. "I am bonded to death."

"Lark, no. Please."

I shifted forward on my knees, reaching for him, but he pulled out of my grasp, glaring down at me with such hatred that I felt it in my bones. It was the same way I'd looked at him, all those weeks ago, when he had pulled me into that frozen wasteland and begged me to hear his end of the story. When I had spent weeks despising him for all that I believed he had done. He was repaying it to me now. Tenfold. And my heart was shattering to pieces at the truth of what he was saying.

"I'll never save you," he hissed. "I'll never come for you. You knew that already, didn't you? I would never pull my people into a war. Not for you."

"Lark, I don't—"

"Come back to me, Seren."

It was his voice, the same as the one before me, but different. It was quieter, softer, and somehow, more real. I blinked through my tears, looking up to find that other version of him just as stunned as I was. That imitation Lark, it blinked in surprise, and then vanished. I reached out for him, the real him, and felt him solidly on the other side. But he didn't speak to me again and I wasn't even sure he could. Part of me wanted to beg him to, to cling to him as the only bit of my sanity I had left. But I couldn't. I knew I couldn't.

The longer you remain in this foyer, the more of your demons will come to haunt you until you've made your choice.

I looked up at the stairs. It would be easy. So easy. No sacrifice, no pain. No war to fight or mother to fear. She would lose something she loved. I could ensure that. I could make sure she felt my death in every part of her cold, cruel heart. I could make sure it haunted her until the day she died, knowing she killed me out of her own selfish desire to keep me. Something about that was satisfying.

But there was no satisfaction in death. Not really.

I turned slowly to that silver door. Immortal life. And a sacrifice.

What would the elixir take from me? What would be the price it demanded for my eternal life, for an immortality I didn't even want?

I rose to my feet and took a step forward. I wiped the tears away with shaking hands. If I were going to face eternity, I would do it with my head held high. I would meet its demands with fearlessness in my soul and Lark's words in my heart.

Come back to me, Seren.

I took a deep breath and reached for the doorknob. I twisted it until the mechanism clicked into place, until it gave at my touch and was pulling backward with a quiet groan.

I gasped into the blinding white light on the other side.

Seren Dawnpaw has chosen to live, a voice boomed within my skull. I winced, hands going to my temples as it softened and was echoed again by a thousand other voices. The price for life anew is a surrender of the old... of the old...

I blinked into that light, squinting, but saw nothing.

To be immortal, one must relinquish the mortal... the mortal... Seren Dawnpaw must promise never to set foot in the mortal realm again... never again... again...

I felt the command like a blow to my soul. Wyn Kendrick had been right. I had chosen them. I had always chosen them. And now I was to be one of them. Forever.

Pain ripped me out of that place, pulling me back into the world of the living to the sounds of my own agonized screaming. My consciousness joined my body and continued that crying out. But not just for the physical pain, the burning of my insides as if I were on fire with no way to douse the flames, but for what I had lost as well. For what I would never have again.

Chapter Two

A Rebirth

I was delirious.

My body contorted. Breaking and reshaping itself, reforming into something ethereal, something unnatural, something immortal.

That beauty that all fae possessed, it came with a cost. And the price I had to pay was the shattering of every one of the bones in my face, the breaking of my skull. My brain cried out in agonized misery as its cage of bone and tendon shrunk and then stretched, resizing and reforming. My cheekbones rose, my nose straightened, my neck became smoother, longer. My eyes stayed the same piercing violet but gained that divine shimmer. My hair kept its shade of honey blonde but grew out longer, stronger, silkier. My nails sharpened, my waist slimmed and tightened, my legs lengthened.

I felt as if I were being smashed and stretched over and over on the outside and my organs were being tactfully rearranged on the inside. My lungs burned, my stomach hollowed, my head ached. I grit my teeth so hard my gums bled and some healer had to shove a strip of wood between them to keep me from grinding them right out of my head.

I cried for days. Through the pain and the long hours of the night when it finally receded. My pillow was soaked through from the tears. And when it all finally, mercifully, stopped, I could do nothing more than lie there, staring up at that cold russet ceiling and gulping in air like it was the first time I'd ever breathed before.

"I knew you'd be strong," someone said.

I didn't have to look to know it was my father. And I couldn't have looked even if I wanted to. I could barely move.

"I'm glad you chose to stay."

His voice was a whisper. I just closed my eyes and inhaled a shaky breath.

"After what I saw in that throne room, I thought you might take the exit just to deprive her of her win," he said and I frowned, remembering having that very same thought in that strange place the elixir had taken me to. "I considered it too."

"Why didn't you?" I croaked, my voice hoarse, raw.

"Because I deserve to live more than she deserves to lose."

I didn't answer that and he said no more. We just remained in one another's company for a time. Him waiting, me breathing.

"Is it worth it?" I asked after a long period of silence. "The sacrifice?"

"No."

I breathed in, closing my eyes. I had expected as much.

"Maybe it would be," he told me, changing course, "if we had wanted this."

"And if she wasn't on the other end of it."

More silence at that. I took the quiet as his agreement.

"Did he make sure you were taken care of?" my father asked, so quietly.

I closed my eyes again because I knew what he was asking.

"Professor Xavier Belling raised me," I told him and heard the inhale though he tried to hide it. I couldn't imagine how greatly my father missed his brother. It had been over sixty years since they had seen each other. My uncle believed he was dead. And now, with my sacrifice, I might never be able to tell him the truth. "He's better than I could have ever asked for. He taught me to be inquisitive, fierce. He taught me never to accept my limitations. He taught me to challenge everything and not to fear the unknown."

"That sounds like Xavier."

I pretended not to notice the way his voice cracked at the words, the near silent sniffling now coming from where he stood. I just raised my eyes to the ceiling and tried to will the tears away.

"I love him," I whispered.

"Me too."

The silence descended between us once more. We hung suspended within it, so many words to say and never the time to say them. Ariadne would know I was awake by now. She would be coming herself any moment. He knew that as well as I did. Even as I thought it, I felt the shift in the emotional state of the room. Wrath squeezed in, shoving itself up against our sorrow. Impatience to combat our numbness. She was here. Or rather, she would be soon.

My father seemed to sense it as well. Something about our immortality giving us senses we hadn't had before, strengthening ones that were already there. For him, it wasn't magic. Maybe it was instinct. Survival. My gut clenched as he turned away from me, schooling his features back into that aloof mask he always wore in her presence, the one through which he never let that vulnerability show.

"Whatever it took from you," he started, speaking over his shoulder without turning to face me, "don't try to get it back."

I opened my mouth to question him but was cut off by the quick snap of the door as it opened. The sharp clicking of my mother's heels filled the cavernous space of the bedroom they had placed me in. I stared up at the high ceilings to avoid looking at her for as long as possible.

"I'm told you survived the elixir," she said simply, no trace of emotion in her tone, but I felt it emanating from her all the same.

Pleasure, swift and delicate, lingering below a mask of rage, fury angled towards my pain, towards what I had gone through to live forever. It was some macabre impersonation of maternal instinct that had my lip curling in disgust. In timely fashion, I flipped to my side and wretched over the edge of the bed, spilling the contents of my stomach onto the soft carpet below.

Servants rushed forward to clear the mess away, waving hands to magically clear the bile, replacing it with a linen fresh scent that filled my nostrils and made me feel queasy all over again.

"Dinner," my mother said, clapping her hands together with a grin.

I just shot her a glare, wiping my mouth with the back of my hand as my sweat soaked hair fell around my shoulders.

"Get her ready," she added to the hovering servants, waving a hand in my general direction as her own lip curled in disgust. "Richard, with me."

My father offered me one last glance before striding from the hall behind her, hands clasped behind his back. I couldn't help but consider his final warning to me once they were gone, the door swinging behind them as they departed.

Whatever it took from you, don't try to get it back.

Cryptic. And unhelpful.

"Princess—" one of the servants tried, reaching for me as if to help me up.

"Don't," I snapped, thrusting out an arm to keep her away from me.

Then, gritting my teeth against the pain, I pushed myself up on the bed, swinging my legs over the side. Every muscle in my body screamed in agony. My bones harbored the memory of the splintering, the fracturing. My tendons and joints ached from the strain. A deep, throbbing pain waited patiently behind my eyes, released by my every movement. My head ached every time I tried to formulate a coherent train of thought. I closed my eyes for a moment and heaved a breath. I felt one of the servants step forward and held another hand up in warning. Then I rose, slowly and shakily, to my feet.

My legs were strange, longer than they had been before, and stronger. I tested the new muscles, bending them slightly, bouncing on the balls of my feet. But I was rewarded for my efforts with a sharp shooting sensation from my left calf to my thigh. I winced and stopped myself, making a note to explore my new body at a later date when it wasn't still struggling against its transformation. I took a step, then another. Every footfall was a new torture, a nightmare of agony. But I pushed forward, made myself move, keep going.

I let the servants help me out of my clothes, some faded old dressing gown they had put me in while I writhed in pain. It was filthy with my sweat and other stains that looked suspiciously like blood. I paled at the sight of them as one of the servants carried the gown away. All of those feelings of fragmentation, of my body being broken in order to be made anew, perhaps I hadn't imagined them at all. I felt sick again and only had time to motion for a nearby bucket before I was vomiting onto the marble floor at my feet. It splashed up my bare legs onto the hems of the dresses they had brought for me to choose from but neither of my servants said a word. One just put her hands on my shoulders and helped lower me into the bath while the other attended to the mess.

I couldn't stop shaking. Even in the scalding hot water that they had drawn to help ease my aches, my teeth were chattering. My fingers and toes were numb, twitching. I couldn't fend it off, the cold, no matter how low I sank into that hot water. It had settled into my very bones, a reminder of that icy fire that had burned me from the inside out. I ducked my head under the water and stared through the lapping pool at the magical bulbs of light above me. I held my breath until my lungs burned again, until my heart started beating faster, until my instincts to survive kicked in, until I felt mortal again.

Then I rose up, gasping for air, as my servants ran to me, worry plain in their wide eyes. But I pushed them aside and stood from the tub, dripping onto the marble, feeling sturdy for the first time since I had awoken. Because even fae had to breathe. Even fae could die. So I was immortal now. But maybe there was no such thing as immortality.

"The Queen requests your presence for dinner," a new voice spoke and my head whipped in the newcomer's direction, my wet hair slapping against my chest as my two attendants dabbed at me with fluffy brown towels.

I examined the messenger from head to toe. She was a servant as well but one who thought entirely too highly of herself. One of my mother's then. Leave it to Ariadne to pick the most ambitious women for her own personal service.

"My mother is no Queen," I drawled, channeling my best impression of Lark, that cold, callousness that he exhibited to everyone but me, Rook, and Cass. The cunning, cruel prince that everyone thought him to be. I could be that too. I could act that part.

I sent a feeling to him, a caress, just to let him know I had survived, that I was alive. I waited a breath, then two, but felt nothing in return. Panic gripped me. Had the elixir taken him from me? Had it done something to our connection, to the bond?

"The Queen requests your presence—" the servant started again, narrowing her gaze.

I threw up a hand and the door slammed shut, locking her on the other side. My servants froze, exchanging wide eyed glances. I tried not to show my own surprise as I lowered my hand, hiding my fingers so they wouldn't see them shaking. That power, that magic, it had rose so quickly to my fingertips, had flown from me far easier than it ever had before. Was that the result of the elixir or something else?

Survive, some voice inside me called in reminder. And survival here, in this wicked court, meant strength. Power. I could at least pretend to have those things.

"I can do that," I snarled, grabbing the towels out of my servants' hands that they had begun to use to dry me off.

I stormed out of the bathroom to the door opposite the one to my bedroom, a closet. I dripped upon the marble the whole way, not bothering to care. They'd clean it off with a wave of their dainty hands anyway. Cleaning meant nothing to them here. Nothing meant anything to them here.

I let them select my gown. Some chocolate monstrosity with layers of chiffon more fit for a grand gala than dinner with my narcissistic mother and devastated father. I let them dry my hair too, using their magic to dry and style it when it became clear I wasn't going to bother with it myself. When I was presumed ready enough, they walked me down the hall and toward the dining room, stopping short so the guards could open both of the enormous double doors to admit me. I just clenched my jaw and strode inside, holding my head as high as I could as I made my way to the table.

I felt it as I sat, my answer from Lark. Quiet and fleeting but there. Relief, happiness, affection. It was difficult to bite back my smile as I scooted my chair in closer to the table, letting the legs scrape loudly against the marble. Ariadne winced but waited as I settled myself, staring down at my plate to avoid looking up at her, into her eyes.

"A celebration," she told me with a smile, gesturing widely at the table before us.

My eyes flicked down and I ran my gaze over the surface. She had really gone all out. Three different types of meat, ten plates piled high with the freshest vegetables, noodles drenched in butter and herbs, potatoes mashed and creamed, even pastries sat on a separate table nearby, beckoning the end of our meal, waiting to be consumed. I stared at it all in silence and then looked back up to her where she sat, waiting. Waiting for what? For gratitude? I huffed. Her smile fell.

"You could at least pretend to be gracious," she groaned and I winced. Had she read my thoughts again? "No. I didn't read your thoughts. I hardly have to, Seren. They're written all over your face as it is."

She wasn't looking at me now, just digging into the food already piled high on her plate with a shining copper fork. I glanced to my father who was focused on his own plate and sighed.

"So this is how it's to be for all eternity?" I asked, raising a brow. "Silent, tense family dinners where we don't even have to speak because you already know every thought that enters our heads?"

My father's jaw tensed. My mother paused, looking up but not at me. Instead, she seemed to focus on a singular point on the wall opposite her in an effort to reign in the annoyance overwhelming her.

"Preferably, no," she answered, cocking her head to the side. "But I suppose that will be up to you."

"Because you bear no part of the fault, obviously."

Her gaze narrowed and she opened her mouth to argue but then her lips snapped shut and her eyes darted to the door behind me.

"We have a visitor," she said.

I sat up straighter, every muscle tensing. I wondered briefly which of her sentries' minds she was invading in order to know that someone had arrived, which of her own soldiers' thoughts she was reading to be alerted to her visitor first, and if that was how she had sensed mine and Gemini's presence so easily. But then my thoughts snagged on what she had said. A visitor. Someone she hadn't been expecting if the frown on her lips was any indication. It was too much to hope, and too soon, that it might be one of my friends, my newfound family, come to rescue me. That Rook or Cass or Lark had found some way around the vow I had made to my mother. That even Gemini—

The doors flew open and the visitor strode inside. My lips parted at the sight of her, windswept and harried, more distressed than I had ever seen her.

Ariadne leaned back in her chair, smiling her signature wicked smile at her guest, lips curved upward unnaturally, bright eyes sparkling, clear. When she spoke her name, I felt a chill go up my own spine at the sound of it.

"Ursa."

Chapter Three
A Traitor

"Ariadne," Ursa answered, her gaze flicking to me briefly before landing on my mother in that way of hers that I had become accustomed to, the way she used when she was assessing a threat.

Subconsciously, I reached for my dinner knife. It would be hopeless against those spinning obsidian blades but the memory of their cutting through my skin, my blood coating the Bone Court's floor, had me clinging to any weapon I could find. Ursa saw the movement, her eyes snapping to the knife and back to my mother once more, having decided, probably correctly, that Ariadne Dawnpaw was the more credible threat.

"You actually came," Ariadne spoke, lifting her goblet to her lips and drinking deeply, savoring both the wine and Ursa's discomfort. "I must admit, I wasn't sure what to expect from you. Not after that little stunt your brother pulled. Not after I caught your most favorite aunt."

And lost her, I thought it so hard that my mother had to have heard it. And I knew she did from the way the corner of her lip twitched in irritation.

"Tell me," Ariadne continued, examining her nails as always, feigning boredom to disguise her true interest. It didn't work. It never worked. But she was conceited enough to keep trying. "Am I at war with the Bone Court?"

Ursa's eyes widened a fraction.

"Of course not," she said, shifting slightly on her feet.

I noticed it then. The familiar, soft blue gleam at her chest. I stopped breathing.

"I'm going to need it back, you know," my mother droned, still examining her nails, "if I'm going to continue what we started."

I froze, my grip on the knife going slack in my shock. What we started. My gaze flicked to Ursa and I understood. Her coming here, being summoned here, the way she stood in front of my mother, sheepish and afraid. That blue glow against her chest, that cord around her neck, it was an amulet. Ariadne had said it herself in the throne room while she tortured my bonded and threatened my friends. She hadn't stolen Perseus' power. Ursa had.

The legs of my chair scraped loudly as I leapt to my feet, enraged.

"You," I snarled at Ursa, rounding the table to meet her.

She had the grace to look ashamed, bowing her head as she took a step back, away from me. My mother only watched, amused grin on her lips as if she had not only been expecting this but had eagerly awaited it. The moment that I realized my teacher, the person who had taken my training upon themselves, whose very soul I had invaded time and time again with her own permission, had been working with my mother all along, against her own father, against her own court, and especially, against me. It all clicked into place. She had been the one who told my mother that Lark and our friends were in the Court of Peace and Pride. She had been at the Bone Court when Cass and Rook appeared to tell their father about the gorgon, about their mission, to seek his approval. She had known and she had sold that information to my mother. She was the reason they had been captured.

I roared with rage, raising my hands to use my magic against her, to hurt her worse than she hurt me. But she speared me with a feeling, and not one I had been expecting. Anxiety, fear. I hesitated. Ursa wasn't one to expose any vulnerability, least of all to me. Her wide eyes flicked down to my hands and I understood what she was trying to convey. She hadn't told my mother about my magic. She could have. She had known more about it than anyone. But she had kept that secret to herself. I cocked my head to the side, lowering my hands. She had helped me in that small way and yet sold out her family to their enemy as captives. Why?

"Well, that was rather anticlimactic," my mother intervened, rolling her eyes in boredom as she glanced between Ursa and I. "I was hoping my daughter would kick your ass so this part would be a little easier."

Before Ursa could question what she meant, my mother flicked her wrist and the amulet snapped from Ursa's neck, floating across the room and landing in Ariadne's palm. She weighed it for a moment and then shrugged.

"Guess that was pretty easy anyway."

"You said it was mine," Ursa said, pleading.

I crossed my arms and backed away from her, watching her closely but keeping my distance.

"And now it isn't," my mother replied with a shrug, running a finger over the amulet's smooth surface as she stared down at the swirling blue magic within it.

"You said it only worked for me because he was my father," Ursa begged, "my blood."

"No, I said it would be better for you to have it because he was your father. It still works for me. The only difference is, while you felt that connection to him enough to know when to stop drawing his power out of him, I have no such awareness."

Ursa visibly paled.

"So you won't know when—" she started.

"When I've taken too much?" my mother asked, already putting the amulet on around her neck, new cord made that easily, with a wave of her hand. "Not until he dies from it, I suppose."

I grit my teeth. It was killing him. It wasn't just stealing his magic, it was stealing his life as well, his very essence. And when it was drained away entirely... I gulped. Immortality wasn't real, indeed.

"Please," Ursa squeaked. "Please don't—"

"It's a shame, really. I never hated Perseus. Just his petulant son and that altruistic daughter. But if I am truly to be at war with your court, dear Ursa, I can think of no finer way of throwing it into chaos than killing its monarch, thereby thrusting all remaining heirs into some absurd fight to the death. It's brutish, really, your succession."

"Better than limiting the royal family to one child their whole unending lives," my father muttered.

My gaze flicked to him.

"I need it," Ursa was begging now, a moment from getting down onto her knees. It was jarring, seeing this strong, fierce warrior of the Bone Court brought so low. "I'll never defeat my brothers without it. You know that."

A few more pieces of the puzzle clicked into place at her words. She couldn't beat Lark or Taurus, not without that extra, ancient magic, not without her own father's strength, the power of a king. She had learned that first hand months ago when she had tried to kill Lark while he still remained in the mortal realm, went after Taurus in the Court of Rivals. Was that what had pushed her here, to my mother, to this?

"You need me on the throne," Ursa continued, her tone becoming firmer, more desperate. "Taurus would never listen to you. He'll bring war before he bows to your court. And Canis—"

"Do not speak his name," my mother snapped, knuckles turning white where they gripped the amulet around her neck.

Ursa fell silent, her gaze falling to the smooth marble floor.

"You can have it back," my mother said then, the fury vanished from her tone, replaced with something sickly sweet, sinister, "if you retrieve my father."

Ursa froze, her gaze sweeping the room again until it landed on me.

"But I—they have him," she spoke, her voice quiet as though she didn't want to mention them in front of me.

My lip twitched as I clenched my fists to rein in my fury. How dare she speak of them. How dare she even think about them after what she did.

"And who better to know where they might be keeping him?" my mother asked with a sigh, her tone beginning to sound almost bored. "Well, besides Seren here."

Her gaze flicked to mine, narrowing, and I felt it, the invasion. It was like that foreign piece of me that I had found all those months ago, the part belonging to Lark, the part of him embedded into my soul. But she was in my mind instead, poking and prodding around with malice, searching. And I realized what for an instant later. I willed my thoughts away from that place, that unassuming little orange apartment in the Court of Wanderers far away, my friends' chosen hideout, the only place they seemed to feel at home. She could find it if she saw it in my mind. I knew the way well enough from all my trips to the market and back. She could trace my steps all the way to the door, map out the inside. She could take that from me, those memories, she could use them to hurt the people I cared the most about.

Ursa was staring at me, her eyes having gone wide once she realized what Ariadne was doing, that this mother was invading her own daughter's mind. But looking at Ursa reminded me of that wall. That high, impenetrable fortress the royal fae had built around their souls, entrapping what was most precious, what mattered more than anything. I closed my eyes, envisioning it, copying it, brick by brick. I fell to my knees, remembering how it felt to sort through myself, to invade my own emotions. I knew myself better, I had more experience within myself. Ariadne was starting with nothing, sifting through the memories of my uncle, my childhood. I flooded her with more of them, thinking as hard as I could about any part of that time with Xavier so that she was drowned with it and could access nothing else while I used what little was left of my mental capacity to build that wall.

"Ariadne," my father's voice spoke in low warning somewhere far away.

I ignored him. I thought of the time that Xavier took me to the NASA space convention, all the times we spent at the observatory, the way he jotted down notes in his ever present notebook while I danced and ran in the little garden outside of the university, tended by the students of botany. Every smile he had ever given me, every time he had squeezed my shoulder, hugged me, taught me something that no other eight year old would have ever learned.

Tears streamed down my face at the memories as they filtered past, at the realization that I would never see him again, would never hear him laugh, or receive a hug from his arms. But that was the price I had paid to survive. The cost of getting back to Lark. And I would get back to him.

I gritted my teeth until they ached, clenched my fists until my nails dug firmly into my palms. My wall was up. It was shaky and new, still unsettled on its foundations, but it was something. I locked that apartment inside of it and any knowledge of that piece of Lark within me as well. Those bits of information, they became dulled somehow, even to me. I took that to mean it was working.

When I was certain enough that they were secure, I rose to my feet, new legs shaking, and I leveled a finger at my mother. Then flicked it.

Ariadne went sprawling back in her chair, legs flying over her head as she tumbled onto the marble behind her. I advanced, narrowing my gaze, my stride purposeful, unhurried.

"Get out," I growled at her, summoning my best impression of Lark once more.

Strictly speaking, I hadn't necessarily intended to knock her right out of her chair. I'd only meant to sweep her back a bit, show her that I meant business. But my immortality seemed to be making the magic I had wielded before more powerful, easier to wield, perhaps too easy. I didn't know my own strength. Not yet, at least.

"Seren," my father said my name now, turning his warning gaze upon me. It calmed me slightly. I hesitated, cutting off my advance, and then turned back to my mother who was scrambling back to her feet, smoothing her skirts and her hair as she tried to reclaim whatever dignity she had lost in her tumble.

"Stay out of my head," I snapped once and then whirled on my heel and strode from the dining hall.

I did my best to take my time, holding my head high and swinging my hips in the way I had learned from, of all people, her. If she wanted me here, she would have me. But I wouldn't make this place my home and I wouldn't make my presence easy to bear. If Ariadne Dawnpaw wanted unquestioned power more than anything in the world, I would challenge her for it, rival her. Her younger, half mortal daughter, the only other person in all the realm also in line for her precious throne. If she was to make me stay here, live in her court, among her people, I would make her regret it. I would make her wish for the days when she, alone, reigned over this court, the unquestioned heir, the obvious sovereign. Not anymore.

I gritted my teeth as I strode through the halls, trying to remember the way back to my room. There was more urgency in my step now as I glanced desperately at the doors I passed, looking for the one most familiar. I might have stopped to ask for help if the servants I passed didn't retreat into dark corners and abandoned side halls just to clear out of my way. I almost felt a pang of guilt for the fear I seemed to inspire in them but kept my face that cruel mask, knowing it would be better for me here if I was feared than if I became someone weak enough to prey upon. Perseus had told me that himself.

You're not that little rabbit anymore.

I turned down another hall, breathing a sigh of relief to have finally found something a bit familiar. An enormous painting of a harvest, bowls of fruit and stacks of grain laden on a long mahogany table. I'd seen that before, not long ago, as my own servants led me to the dining hall. This way, then.

I found my room at the end of the hall and pushed inside without warning.

"Leave me," I snapped to the same attendants from before.

They lowered their heads and scurried away without question, shutting my door tightly behind them as they went.

I paced to the desk on the opposite side of the room as the bathing chamber and started frantically searching through its contents, opening drawers and rifling through everything inside, leaving it strewn about and disarrayed as I slammed it shut and went for another. I found what I needed quickly enough and set the empty scrap of paper atop the desk, reaching for a pen with a shaky hand.

Ariadne knows. Sending Ursa for Alban. Don't stay anywhere I know.

I set down the pen, rereading my warning message once, twice, three times. It was enough. He would understand. He would know what to do. I only had to get this to him. I only had to warn him.

I took a step back, wringing my hands and rolling out my shoulders. I'd seen Cass do this before. It looked so simple, so easy. I took a deep breath, released it, and held up a hand. I thought as hard as I could about that apartment, that place where I had stayed for so long, ate, trained, slept. I closed my eyes and waved a hand. Nothing.

I reached for the note, remembering she had been holding it at the time. I mimicked the move I remembered her making, the stretching and curling of her fingers. Nothing. Maybe it wasn't a place. Maybe it was a person. I tried again. Nothing.

Time and time again, I tried to send that note. I focused with every ounce of my magic, every kernel of thought, of feeling. But still, that scrap of paper remained in my hand, on my desk, taunting me. I was just about to switch tactics all together when I heard the rhythmic tapping of heels on marble echoing in the hall outside my bedroom door. I took a second to send a feeling of panic to Lark on the other side of our connection, hoping that just that little something could be enough for him to understand, and then tossed the note back into the bottom drawer of the desk, slamming it closed just before my door swung open and my mother stepped inside.

Chapter Four
A Familiar Foe

"My arrangement with Ursa Morningstar is a precarious one," Ariadne started speaking before the door even closed behind her, striding forward into my room with all the confidence of someone who owned this house and went wherever she wished. "What you did could have unraveled it."

"I think you've mistaken me for someone who cares," I drawled back, sliding in front of my desk to shield it from her view, to hide what I had been doing when she burst in uninvited. To keep her attention from drifting to my awkward standing position, I blurted out, "I don't see that it matters. You got what you wanted anyway."

I nodded in the direction of the amulet hung around her neck and her lips stretched into a wicked grin as she looked down at it, holding it out to peer into that strange, swirling blue magic once more.

"Indeed, I did," she beamed, pleased.

I just crossed my arms and perched on the edge of my desk, hoping the stance looked more natural than the one I had opted for before.

"What do you want?" I quipped.

"You know where they are," she said, narrowing her gaze as she raised it to meet mine once more. "You can either tell me or I can shatter that hastily constructed wall in your mind and discover it myself. Trust me when I say that the former option is far less messy."

"You can try," I growled, standing up straight, fists clenched at my sides. I began preparing for her invasion once more, readying my magic and feeling it coursing through my veins. I built that wall back up in my mind, brick by brick, and readied it for an assault, despite how hastily constructed it might be.

"Enough," someone spat and we both turned to see my father entering.

His face was gaunt but his eyes were firm, unyielding.

"Richard—" my mother started, her tone something between exasperation and pleading.

"We're supposed to be a family now," he snapped, walking forward until he was standing in front of me, between us.

I gaped at him, stunned by his sudden intervention. He'd hardly so much as looked at me that day that she tortured and threatened my friends in front of me, had barely spoken to me at all after all the pain I had suffered at her hands, and had merely shook his head each time we sniped at each other over dinner. But now he was getting involved. Now, he wanted to play hero. I crossed my arms and clenched my jaw as I glared at the back of his head, wondering if I could stare so hard he could feel it.

"Isn't that why you did all of this?" he addressed my mother, imploring. "Isn't that why you went to such great lengths to keep me around, to get her here? So that we could be a family. Together forever."

The word forever made me flinch but both of them ignored me as they stared one another down, the silent argument that I imagined only occurred between parents. Not that I would know. And not that any of those arguments were ever as pathological as this.

"What's your point?" my mother finally barked but I saw it. His argument had shaken her, drawn away some of her resolve. She wasn't as firm, as menacing, as she had been before.

"If you want that, Ari, truly want it," he said and I blinked at the nickname, caught off guard by the loving tone, "you can't let it start out this way. You can't crack open her mind and rifle around inside it every time she is withholding something from you. You've seen what that can do. She's your daughter. Our daughter."

My mother's eyes softened as she met my father's and something that I didn't understand seemed to occur between them. He reached out a hand and she barely hesitated at all before she took it. She never voiced her agreement, never promised to refrain from invading my mind, but she did give his hand a squeeze and turned away, striding toward my door and the hallway beyond.

I stared after her in stunned disbelief. She was actually leaving. And she was doing so without invading my mind and reading my thoughts, without violating that very precious sense of privacy. At least this time.

"When you're ready to tell me what you know," she called back to me, "come and find me."

I stuck my tongue out at her back as she pulled open the door and left. It might have been childish and certainly unfitting behavior for a sixty year old professor turned princess but it felt good in the moment.

"It's too late to warn them," my father said, his eyes falling on the desk behind me, to the pen I'd left atop it.

I frowned down at the evidence of my attempt, mentally scolding myself for the carelessness of it. He was already walking to the door himself when he finally called that final announcement over his shoulder and made my heart stop cold.

"Ursa is already on her way."

***

But I tried.

I tried again and again until I was curled into a ball, sobbing in my desperation, gripping that paper with white knuckles and muttering a string of curses I wouldn't dare to repeat in my uncle's company.

"Please," I begged nothing and no one. "Please find Lark. Just find him. I have to warn him. I have to. Whatever deity created this place, this power, hear me. Help me. I beg you. I will do anything. I will—"

My door opened again and I leapt to my feet, sliding that page behind my back as my servants entered.

"I thought I told you to leave me be," I snapped, attempting to regain that cold, cruel demeanor. However, the tears I wiped from my cheeks were a dead giveaway that I wasn't the strong captive I pretended to be.

"We are to ready you for breakfast, princess," one of them spoke.

My eyes flicked to the windows. Sunrise. I had been at this all night.

Shoulders slumped, I nodded my assent.

"Very well," I said and watched as they strode away, toward my wash-room.

Once they were gone, I hid that note away again, deep within the bottom drawer of the desk. I had searched for the key to this lock before, praying I would find it and some semblance of privacy but, of course, my mother would never allow even that small bit of liberty. I would have to make do with hiding it among the clutter and hoping no one would even think to look. I wasn't sure it even mattered if they did. My mother had to know that I would attempt to warn my friends, would try to thwart her plans once she had revealed them in my presence. Undoubtedly, she believed I was incapable of doing so. It infuriated me to know she was right.

"Princess, the bath is ready."

I padded across the carpet to join my attendants in the washroom. I let them strip my clothes from my body and help me into the hot water. I soaked until my skin wrinkled and pruned and they begged me to get out. When I finally did, I merely stood as still as death and allowed them to dress me and do my hair and makeup. When the smaller one began dabbing powder onto my nose, I turned to face her with a raised brow.

"This is all a bit much for breakfast, wouldn't you say?" I asked, gesturing toward my painted face, soft, textured curls, and gaudy brown dress.

"Lord Koa Oaksky is here, princess," she answered me, blushing the way she always did when spoken directly to. "We were told to make you fit for his presence."

Lord Koa. I clenched my fists at my sides and turned my reflection back to the mirror in front of me. Fury ignited within my sharp, violet eyes. Lord Koa of the Court of Friends, the man who had come to treat with the King of the Bone Court only to threaten him and lecture him and later try to kidnap me against my will, likely to bring me here, likely for his own alliance with my mother. His was one on my ever growing list of names belonging to those that I would ensure felt pain inflicted upon them in equal measure to that which they had dealt me by the time this was all over.

Rage welled up within me as I remembered those last few moments in the Court of Blood and Bone, the way Ursa and I had been on our way back from Gemini's, the way those soldiers in deep, velvety green had emerged from the shadows and lunged for us, for me. The way Lord Koa himself had tried to entrap me in his vines. My jaw ached from how badly I was gritting my teeth.

Then a cool caress, soft and gentle against my soul. Lark. A reminder. Cruel, cold, cunning. Right. I snapped my mask back into place and peered at my servants' reflections in the mirror.

"What do you think of him?" I asked, my tone careful, measured. "Lord Oaksky?"

They exchanged a glance and hesitated.

"The lord is wise," the second one, the more careful of the two, told me. "He treats his servants well."

I turned to her, cocking my head to the side, and then glanced to the other.

"What are your names?" I asked because I never had before.

Another exchanged glance. I almost rolled my eyes. Did they need confirmation to tell me their names too?

"Fern," the blushing one answered first, giving me a tentative smile as she resumed her task of blotting my cheeks.

"And I am Tilda," the other one answered, pulling tight on my curls to get them to stay in place.

I winced but slipped that cool mask back into place.

"You do not have to hold your tongues in my presence," I told them and saw the way they glanced at one another yet again behind me. "If you breathe, you have opinions. I will not command you to leave them unspoken. You are living beings with just as much worth, just as much value, as me, as my mother."

I turned my gaze upon them and they seemed to shrink away, despite my attempt at offering them an olive branch.

"I'm willing to bet," I started again, turning back to my reflection and tucking a flyaway hair behind my ear, "you know more about the happenings of this court, and most others, than we do. So I'll ask again. What do you think of Lord Oaksky?"

"He is... smart," Tilda tried again.

"A snake, you mean."

Fern snorted. Even Tilda's lips quirked up into a conspiratorial grin.

"When did he start sniffing around my mother?" I asked, turning away from the mirror entirely now and pinning them each with my gaze. This time, they did not shrink away. Though they did still exchange that infernal glance, as if neither one could speak without seeking the approval of the other.

"Five years ago," Tilda answered with a shrug, having apparently decided I couldn't do much damage with the information she provided. "It was all pleasantry at first. Small talk, friendly invitations to each other's parties, dinners and gifts."

Five years. That was when the first rift had opened in the mortal realm. I highly doubted the timing was coincidental.

"And then?" I asked, crossing my arms and waiting.

Another glance.

"Then he stopped," she told me and I cocked my head to the side. "It went from weekly dinners to never seeing him again. We all assumed it was because of how busy the princess suddenly seemed to be. King Alban had started to become ill and she was running things in his stead. She didn't have the time for all that she had done before."

"Sick," I repeated, leaning forward with interest. "I didn't think immortal beings could get sick."

They exchanged a much longer glance this time.

"The King was very old," Fern interjected now, her eyes settled on her fellow servant as she cut in. "He's the oldest living fae. None of us are... certain what happens to the body after a couple millennia. He would not die. Not from sickness. But, well, even we get colds from time to time, little bouts of illness here and there. Maybe it's worse when you're two thousand years old."

It was her turn to shrug, as if the issue of an ill immortal was of no consequence. But I could tell it wasn't the first time they had discussed it amongst themselves and this nonchalant approach to the matter wasn't the one they favored in private. I watched them for a moment longer before turning back around to face my own reflection.

"Very well," I told them because I didn't want to push my luck, not when I was just starting to gain some of their trust, not when I had this cold facade to maintain with everyone else at this court. "Am I ready, then?"

They nodded at once, helping lift the elaborate folds of my gown in order to squeeze me through the door and then the other beyond. They followed me down the hall, holding that ridiculous train aloft so that I could walk unencumbered. I cursed as I tripped on an errant bunch of chiffon and stumbled to right myself while Tilda muttered her apologies and gathered it up in her fists.

I flipped the hair that had fallen into my face away and held my head high once more as I strode on. I missed the thin, simple fabric of the Bone Court. Maybe it had been a tad too revealing for my taste on an occasion or two but at least I wasn't suffocating in a cocoon of chiffon whenever I dined with nobility.

The guards on either side of the dining hall opened the doors without question as I approached. My attendants dropped my skirts and stepped smoothly aside to avoid being seen as those doors opened wide and I was revealed to those waiting beyond.

My mother and father were already seated in their usual chairs. Mine was left empty and waiting, my goblet already filled with the sweet wine my mother preferred, my silverware arranged delicately on either side of my empty plate. And across from that setting, on the other side of a copper candelabra and basket of fresh, juicy fruit, sat Lord Koa Oaksky, eyeing me with a predatory smile that made that ball of fiery rage snap right back into place around my heart.

Chapter Five

A Roaring Rain

Every step of my hard-bottomed flats echoed along the cavernous walls of the enormous dining hall as I strode forward, making my way to the seat I normally occupied on one end of the table between my parents. I avoided Lord Koa's gaze as I pulled out my chair, letting its legs scrape noisily against the marble as I did. I did not miss the irritated quirk of my mother's jaw and delighted in the momentary satisfaction her annoyance gave me. But then I felt hard, bright, wise eyes upon me from across the table and couldn't help but allow my gaze to flick upward to him.

He was resplendent as always in a deep emerald velvet waistcoat and matching breeches. The Court of Friends, apparently, preferred something along the lines of the colonial style for their more formal engagements. I wasn't sure if it was a warning or a sign of respect that he had chosen to don such attire for this evening's meal. Either way, I didn't give him the satisfaction of too long of an observation as I reached forward for my napkin and busied myself with draping it delicately over my lap, the picture of royal grace that my mother so desperately wanted to paint. I felt a wisp of her approval in the air around me and refrained from curling my lip in disgust.

"It is nice to see you've made your way home, princess," Lord Koa spoke boldly.

I did not remove that cruel, icy venom from my tone when I replied.

"How disappointing for you that it wasn't your attempted kidnapping that did it," I mused.

He bristled, that friendly smile snapping instantly from his lips.

"Lord Koa is an old friend," my mother interjected before I could deal any further damage to her relationship with this man, whatever it may be. Her eyes flicked between us, warily, as she chose her next words very carefully. "When I received word from Persues that he held you captive at the Bone Court, I couldn't go myself. He never would have granted me an audience."

"Whyever could that be, mother?" I muttered under my breath.

"So Lord Koa went in my stead," she spoke over me as though she hadn't heard but I noticed the way her fingers curled tighter around the goblet in her hand. "I would have trusted no one else with such an important job; the bartering for my daughter's life."

"Is that what you did?" I asked, turning my gaze blandly to him, affecting that cold disinterest I'd learned from Ariadne Dawnpaw herself. I might have even inspected my nails if utilizing her signature move wasn't a task that made me ill to even consider doing. "From what I remember, it was less bartering and more posturing."

"That's all it ever is with the Bone Court," Lord Koa waved away my remark with a sigh, ignoring me completely as he turned to my mother. "It's always so dreadful dealing with them. Their souls are as black as their court."

"They aren't," I snapped, losing my temper, forgetting my mask momentarily.

My mother's gaze shot to me and I retreated, withdrawing within myself and sitting back against my seat, crossing my arms with a clenched jaw. Patience. Pure, cool patience seeped into me. A gift from Lark in response to the anger I'd unleashed. I gripped it tightly and held on, wondering if he knew just how much those rare flashes of emotion from him meant to me and how grateful I was for whatever magic made it possible for me to feel him even so far away.

"At any rate, it's done," Lord Koa said, smoothly ignoring my outburst as he leaned forward casually and dug into his meal. "As long as Sophierial holds up her end of the deal, that is."

I could tell my mother was holding his mind before either of them even said a word. Lord Koa's eyes widened. His mouth opened and then closed again as he turned to her in surprise. There was a beat of silence in which they simply looked at one another, my mother's gaze narrowing as if she were communicating with him in the quiet. I wondered if she could speak to someone, in their mind, and shivered. Could she send someone thoughts the same way that Lark and I could send each other emotion? And how did that work, without the bond? I frowned. There was still so much we didn't know about what my mother was capable of. And every new possibility seemed even more horrifying than the last.

But I filed away the information that Lord Koa had already let slip. Sophierial was involved. Whatever they were planning, the Queen of the Court of Light and Life had a hand in it, an important one if Lord Koa's comment were any indication. I needed to get that to Lark too. Perhaps I would amend my note when I returned to my room, try yet again to send it careening through space and time to find him. Try and fail likely.

My father cast a quick glance in my direction as if he could sense the direction of my thoughts. I schooled my face into a careful mask of cool indifference and busied myself with eating my vegetables like a good little daughter while my mother and her noble friend discussed trade routes and resource stockpiles. I committed it all to memory, every word. Even the tally of wheat the harvest had brought in, Lord Koa's assertion that his court's fruit bounty was enough to rival prior years in total, but especially troop movements. One regiment stationed here, another there. One at Duskwatch. Two near Lastwind. Half of one on the banks of the Esari river. That one was a medic unit. I committed the names of the encampments to memory even though I'd never heard of them in my life. I may have been from the mortal realm and extremely new to the life of royalty but even I knew what it meant when one country started moving their military around. My mother was preparing for war, this Court of Friends Lord was helping her, and, if their discussion was to be followed closely, it appeared the Queen of the Court of Light and Life was as well. That was one minor court and two major courts, at least, who would oppose Lark and the entirety of the Bone Court if it came to war between them. Did he know? Had he won any of the others to his side yet? Or were they all already agreed to help her?

Even as I memorized every fact and figure, my eyes planted firmly on my plate, I wondered why my mother was exposing so much of her court to me. I who had declared myself an enemy the moment I appeared in the center of her throne room. I who had fought her every move since the moment that elixir touched my lips. The fact that she allowed me to overhear any of this at all spoke to how certain she was that our vow could not be broken. And that distinct possibility made my very heart tremble with sorrow.

"May I be excused?" I queried, as a dutiful daughter would, once the meal had subsided and my mother and Lord Koa had moved on from valuable information to the regaling of past tales that I either had no interest in or did not find as amusing as them.

"Of course," my mother answered with a smile, though the way her eyes slid to mine indicated she was anything but pleased.

I didn't care. I took my dismissal in stride, pushing back from the table and leaving them all to their infernal conversation. I made my way down the hall to the room that had become something of my own, closing the door tightly behind me once I was within. I sent Tilda and Fern away, claiming that I was simply exhausted from the morning and wanted to lounge around for a bit until I was summoned again. They bowed their heads and left, though not without another of those irritating exchanged glances.

***

No one came to fetch me again for the rest of the day. I took that to mean that perhaps my mother's claim that she and Lord Koa were old friends was more genuine than I had thought. Maybe they really were just catching up after so long without seeing one another in person. Or maybe they were plotting the impending doom of the mortal realm. Either way, I wasn't welcome and I was quite certain I wouldn't be even if I attempted to join them.

So I busied myself with my note. I tried at the desk for hours. Standing with my eyes closed, my arms apart, folded, clasped. I tried rewording and rewriting the note, tried addressing it, tried signing it Ren or Seren, Dawn-paw or Belling. When I grew tired and frustrated, I sat on the edge of my bed and tried. Then I pushed back onto the cushions. My hope dwindled every time I thought of Lark's face, that orange apartment, even Gemini's dusty old home. I focused on the images of my friends burnt into my memory. Lark was my best bet, given our connection, but I tried the others when he didn't work. Cass with her high cheekbones and shining silver eyes. Rook with that scarred smile. Even Gemini with her gray, tangled hair and keen, sharp eyes.

It didn't work. I didn't feel even a thrum of magic in my veins, snaking out toward that note, reaching for it. And so I fell asleep with that hasty scrawl curled within my fingers.

I knew it was a dream because it couldn't have been real. And yet, I could smell the wood varnish wafting down from the high beams overhead, hear the scuffing of polished shoes against smooth, decorative tile, feel the tension in the walls, the challenge, the academic authority. Hadley. I was back at Hadley.

My feet moved of their own accord, whisking me away from the anthropology corridor and toward the stars, toward him. I hesitated outside of my own classroom, ran a finger along the imprint of my name carved just outside of it. But then I heard his voice and my gaze snapped to him.

He was coming out of his own classroom, head bent low over the book that a student was showing him, nodding along at whatever explanation he was listening to. My heart stopped beating. I stopped breathing. It was him.

It had been too long since I'd seen my uncle, really seen him, and I was quite certain that this hadn't been what he had looked like when I had. My mind was playing tricks on me. Unable to settle on a perfect vision of him, it settled for shifting views. He was both old and young, hair shaping and shifting from honey blonde to white, skin wrinkling and smoothing out again. His gait was labored one moment and springy the next. He was as I remembered him in continuity. Both the man of my youth and of my adulthood. Both my paternal figure and my friend, my colleague. I felt a twinge in my chest and then the tears on my cheeks a moment later.

When he finally looked up at me, that sharp gaze that remained keen no matter how old he got, my heart soared. I took a step forward, lips stretched into a joyous grin.

"Seren," he said, calling me by a name he never used, and my smile faltered, my outstretched arms fell to my side. Because that wasn't my uncle's voice. That voice belonged to the elixir.

Sorrow filled my soul as his lips set into a grim line and he drifted away, disappearing on some unseen wind. I fell to my knees, dropping my head into my hands.

Never again. I would never see him again.

Then there was rage. Hollow and unyielding and unforgiving. And it swept into me so wildly, so recklessly, that I lost my breath for a moment. I searched that feeling and found that it was not my own. My hand shot to my heart and then Hadley blinked away in an instant.

Beneath my knees were not the hallowed halls of one of the mortal realms most foremost universities. Instead, I knelt upon creaking mahogany. I rose slowly to my feet, gazing around at my surroundings in awe. The purple damask foyer. I would recognize it anywhere. My heart clenched and I sucked in a breath. No, not here. I didn't want to be here.

I looked to the door but found that it was not silver at all but a simple, solid brown with a window set high atop it. I whirled around to the stairs at my back. They were in the same place that they had been before but this time I could see light at the top of them, a landing leading into a long hallway with doors jutting off on either side. My brow furrowed in confusion and I turned back to the foyer, starting to take a step.

That anger slammed into me again, hard and fast.

I grit my teeth as I was thrown back into the world of consciousness. I sat bolt upright in my bed, sheets tangling around my legs, chest heaving, wild eyes darting around in the complete darkness. I took a moment to calm myself, to lie still despite that rage still roiling inside of me.

Lark.

I closed my eyes, sent him a feeling of calm as he would have for me.

The rage dimmed somewhat and then disappeared entirely. Too fast, like it had snapped away because it had been taken, not cooled. I sent him that comforting caress once more, then a curiosity, a question. He did not respond. I felt nothing through that connection.

Heart beating rapidly, I made to throw my legs off the side of the bed, unsure where I was even planning to go, but then I felt it. Now crumbled, still clutched in my hand. The note. I stared down at it for a moment, at the words I had written there for him.

Ursa is coming for Alban. My mother has your father's power. Don't trust Sophierial.

With a howl of fury that was entirely my own, I ripped it into a million pieces the good old fashioned way, with my hands.

Then I stormed from my room, still in my nightgown.

No one stopped me. Not the servants, not the soldiers, not anyone. They knew about the vow. I was sure of it. Why keep me from leaving if magic would do the trick itself? I didn't care. I just kept walking until I found a door. I needed to get out of this stuffy old castle. I needed air.

I threw open the door and ran right out into a storm.

I hadn't heard the rain pelting my windows or seen the lightening streaking across the sky. I hadn't felt the thunder rattling my bones. But I did now. I stopped a few meters from the door and turned my face upward. I let the rain fall on my skin, let it soak through my hair, my thin silk gown. I let it hide my tears and cool my rage. I felt the mud squelching between my toes, my hair sticking to my face, my neck, icy precipitation tracing long lines down my sodden back. And I stayed.

When my breathing finally evened out, when I could open my eyes and stare up at those dark and angry clouds, I saw the light. I turned my head slightly to see that someone was watching me from a window. I recognized him at once but Lord Koa only frowned before closing his curtain and extinguishing his light.

Still, I remained. I stood there until I was so thoroughly drenched I thought I might never be dry again, until the cold had taken up permanent residence in my very bones, until I couldn't feel that terror of Lark's pain, his fury, and then his silence through our connection. And until Tilda and Fern appeared, lifted me to my feet without a word, and helped me stumble back into my gilded prison, dripping rainwater on that shiny marble floor all the while.

Chapter Six

A Slight of Silver

"You certainly know how to make an impression."

I glanced up from the mountain of pillows I was currently draped over on top of a very plush mattress to find my father entering my room, door swinging shut behind him. I merely groaned, burying my face into the warm pillows as the morning sun shone in through my open curtains, bathing my body in golden beams of light.

"Your mother has been fielding questions from Lord Koa all morning regarding why her beloved daughter might have been kneeling in the mud for hours in the rain last night in a trance like state," he informed me, strolling toward the curtains and tossing them even wider.

I flinched, burying my head deeper into the darkness, willing it to take me somewhere far, far away from here. It, unfortunately, did not oblige.

"I'm sure she came up with a convincing lie," I murmured from beneath the pillows. "It's what she's good at."

"Seren."

The edge in his voice was enough to have me looking up, over my satin pillowcases, to find him standing in front of me, silhouetted by the light behind, his hands on his hips. He hadn't ever had much chance to be a father to me before but it seemed he had taken to the role well enough. Without being able to see his face against the harsh light of morning, I could tell it bore an expression of disappointment and, even worse, lingering expectation.

"I don't care," I told him with a sigh, finally sitting up despite the pounding in my head. "I don't care about Lord Koa or what he thinks or what any of them think of me or how that reflects on her. And I don't know why you do either."

"Like it or not, I am a man without magic in a land of powerful Fae. I wouldn't even make it to the border before they picked me apart."

"They're not as bad as you—"

"I'm Ariadne's whore. I'm the mortal she keeps by her side on a short leash, the man whose mind she held chained to her for years, the one she sired a daughter by and nearly started a civil war for. I'm hated, Seren. More than her. More than that other man from the Bone Court, the one who belongs to you."

My gaze snapped to his and he held it, as if challenging me to deny it. I didn't. I merely sighed, resisting the urge to throw myself back onto my pillows. I didn't want to have this conversation with him. I would rather sit through another macabre impersonation of a family dinner with Ariadne than speak to my father about the man who belongs to me. And I did not even want to broach the subject of his disturbing incarceration here or the fact that others apparently referred to him as my mother's whore. Even thinking those words and the truths they represented made me want to blast a hole through these walls so big that even magic couldn't fix it. But I held my temper in check and nodded to him in some poor consolation for compassion.

"So that's why you haven't left," I said, understanding. "Protection."

"And because I made vows of my own."

Our eyes met again and my jaw clenched.

"If you came here to drag me off to some breakfast, you can tell them I am unwell," I said, collapsing back onto my bed of pillows.

"Believable," he huffed. "Seeing as you were soaked to the bone by the time I sent the servants out to fetch you last night."

I turned away from him, fixing my gaze on the opposite windows and, through them, where the sun was making its daily journey over the horizon.

"Do you want to talk about it?" he asked a moment later, his voice quiet.

I didn't respond. I just kept my gaze pinned to the sunrise, holding back the tears as I sent yet another feeling down the connection that bound us. Again, no response. I breathed in a shaky breath and closed my eyes. Just let me know you're alive, dammit.

"Why haven't you left?" he asked and my eyes snapped open as I turned to him.

His head was cocked to the side in question, brows furrowed as if genuinely curious about my answer. I just stared at him for a moment, wondering if he had gone insane some time between last night and this morning, wondering if his memory had somehow been impacted by the elixir and the immortal life he'd had forced upon him.

"Excuse me?" I said a moment later when it became clear he wasn't going to explain himself without my asking.

"You haven't even tried. Why not?"

"The vow. I made a vow with her to save them. That she would let them go if I stayed."

"Ah, but she didn't let them go, did she?" he said, sitting back in an enormous coppery wing back chair that was placed beside the window. I just gaped at him, stunned. His lips pulled down and he sat up straighter in response to my surprise. "You didn't realize? Think about it, Seren. She vowed to let them go peacefully. But what did she do in those last moments after you shattered her amulet and set her father free?"

I thought back. I still remembered the look on my friends' faces when she brought them forward, shackled. I still remembered the way Cass' muffled sobs sounded in that echoing throne room, the tang of Lark's blood in the air around us. Every snap of bone, every twinge of guilt, of fear.

And then when I said my goodbyes, hugging them each in turn. When I made Gemini promise to get Alban out, and she had. When I shattered that amulet, and when...

"Rook," I breathed, in awe. "She told her guards to capture him."

"She did," my father agreed, nodding. "Thereby breaking her own vow."

I was on my feet the next instant, already padding toward the door in my golden silk nightgown.

"She knows she broke it," he called out after me and I hesitated, my hand already on the doorknob to leave. "She's doubled the guard at her gates. You have free rein of the grounds but if you tried to leave you would find it quite impossible. Not to mention the fact that your mind still seems to be completely vulnerable to her. The magic that held you to your vow is gone but the physical barriers remain. It would not be wise to attempt an escape before you have a way around them. I know you think of this room as your prison but trust me when I say it can get much, much worse."

I turned back to face him and saw the pain in his expression, the memories he must be reliving at the thought of my mother's invasions, at whatever cage she had designed to keep him here when all of the comforts of immortal life had failed to stem his desire to flee.

"Never forget who your mother is, Seren," he told me, his voice a whisper, "or what she's capable of."

My shoulders slumped as I let go of the doorknob.

"I could teach you," he said then and our eyes met again. "How to guard against her. I've had decades of practice after living with her inside my head for years. No one knows Ariadne Dawnpaw's tricks better than I do."

I crossed my arms, narrowing my gaze at him.

"What do you want in return?" I asked.

Something like hurt flashed across his features as he rose from that elegant chair and strode toward me. I did not balk. I did not turn away at his approach and, when he finally reached me, he put both hands on my shoulders and stared into my eyes with a look of intense sorrow reflected in his own.

"I am your father, Seren," he told me, quietly. "I know I haven't done a good job at showing you what that means. I know I wasn't able to be there for you before. But please, let me help you now."

My shoulders relaxed. I dropped my arms to my sides. And because my throat was too thick with the emotion choking me to properly respond, I nodded.

He leaned forward then, slowly, so slowly, and pressed a kiss to my forehead. He stroked my hair once and then was gone, pushing through the door behind me and out into the hallway beyond, leaving me staring at my empty room and, strangely, missing Xavier Belling more than ever before.

***

By the time Tilda and Fern came to dress me for some welcoming ball that my mother was apparently throwing in Lord Koa's honor, I was in a foul mood again. I had spent the majority of the day trying in vain to send that note. Lark still hadn't sent even a flicker of emotion down the connection between us therefore leaving me to wonder if he was alright. The man had been exiled, executed, captured, and tortured. He had never allowed himself to be taken from me without a fight. The fact that I didn't feel even the hint of one now unsettled me more than anything else. My nerves were frayed and I was on edge, more so than I would have ever admitted, by the time Fern placed that hideous crown atop my head.

"You look beautiful, princess," she breathed, her eyes wide in wonder at the sight of me.

My eyes snapped to the mirror and shot straight to that crown. It was dense and heavy atop my head, made of some ancient bronze that curled and looped in delicate vine-like patterns against my honey blonde hair.

"Take it off," I snarled.

"But princess—" Fern gasped, eyes wide with surprise.

Tilda's brows only furrowed as she met my gaze in the mirror.

"Your mother insisted you wear it," Tilda explained slowly, patiently, like someone instructing a small child. That only incensed me further.

"My mother does not command my body," I informed them, reaching up and plucking the crown from my head myself. "Just as she does not command my mind."

I tossed it onto the floor, the heavy clang of it like a warning bell ringing out to the whole court. Fern gasped again, her hands going to cover her mouth. Tilda just stared at the crown as it circled the marble tile again and again, finally settling.

"I am not a princess," I hissed, more to myself than to them. "I am not her doll to dress up and parade about as she wishes."

I reached down and grabbed a fistful of the skirts of the wretched chocolate chiffon they had dressed me in. I pushed my magic down into my fingertips and waited. It was entirely possible that nothing at all would happen and I would go trudging down those stairs and into that hall full of venomous enemies in the very gown my mother had sent for me. It wouldn't have surprised me, given the massive failures my magic had produced lately. But then I saw it. The color leeched away, the material smoothed and then shaped, as a ripple of my magic spread outward from my fingers.

I watched it curl around my waist and then up to my chest, transforming the dress as it moved. Tilda and Fern stepped away, both of them wide eyed. Fern seemed positively horrified. Because in every place my magic touched, that chocolate brown was gone and, in its place, a smooth, shiny silver that sparkled like the stars in the sky. Every time I moved, it shimmered, like tiny diamonds were woven so frequently into the fabric that they had become the fabric themselves. The poofy skirt vanished, replaced by a smooth column that hugged my hips before draping onto the floor in a pool of gleaming silver. The sleeves were gone entirely and in their place were two thin straps that exposed my shoulders and hung low to show my cleavage. Backless too, just how I liked it. In truth, I had subconsciously modeled it much after that dress which Cass had fashioned for me the first night in Sophierial's court. Only, I had foregone the slit and hitched up the bodice slightly. The color would stun them enough. I could, at least, have some modesty about me. This wasn't the Bone Court after all.

"Princess, you—" Fern started.

Whether she was about to tell me what statement this dress would be making if I wore it to my mother's court function or to say her piece about the crown once more, I would never know. Because Tilda pressed a finger to her lips to silence her before bowing her head slightly to me in acknowledgment. I nodded my head in return. A servant with a rebellious spirit. I would file that knowledge under could-come-in-handy for later.

"It's time," Tilda said then and she turned to open my washroom door.

Fern remained momentarily, blinking at me as if still stunned by my appearance. But she gathered herself quickly enough and, before I knew it, my servants were walking me down the hall to the throne room in which the ball was to be held.

I held my head high, steeling myself against the stares of the servants and soldiers that I was receiving on the way. I sent a feeling of anxiety down the connection, hoping to feel some soothing caress in response, but received nothing. So I gritted my teeth and straightened my shoulders as my servants stopped in front of the massive double doors to the throne room.

The soldiers standing there exchanged a glance and hesitated as if they were going to tell me that what I was doing was not acceptable. But then Tilda spoke with all the authority in the world to remind them of who I was. And they simply bowed and opened the doors.

I felt the silence on the other side the moment I was exposed to them. It was an effort not to shrink away and run back to my room. But the unprecedented rage spewing from my mother alone was worth the shock value dealt to the rest of the room. Even my father had frozen, the glass in his hand halfway to his lips. I nodded primly to him once as I passed, making my way around the now silent room, directly towards my mother.

I didn't recognize most of these people. I was sure they were nobles held in high esteem. They must have been to be classified as close enough to my mother to garnish an invitation to a welcoming ball for a Lord of a minor court. But all of them were wide eyed and whispering as I passed, head held high and smile upon my lips.

"Mother," I said in greeting, bowing low in a way that only she would know was mockery, letting my gaze flick from her to Lord Koa beside her while remaining as disinterested and aloof as I could. "A lovely ball, wouldn't you say, Lord Koa? After all, it is in your honor."

"Oh. Yes. Well, made all the lovelier by the presence of a fine young woman such as yourself," he replied, predictably, raising a glass in toast to my beauty.

I grinned back at him like a fool but sharpened my gaze into something wicked just the same.

"Lord Koa tells me he saw you in the garden last night," my mother finally spoke, every word clipped with fury. "Quite a tempest to be out looking at flowers in, wouldn't you say?"

"I find that beautiful things thrive most in the midst of a storm," I answered her, my glare narrowed to a point.

Her lip curled as she glared right back.

"Do enjoy your party, Lord Koa," I told him, turning my attention back to the Lord of the Court of Friends and away from my seething mother. "You've earned it."

Then I left them both fuming and stunned as I whirled on my feet to join the party beyond and finally felt that pull from somewhere far, far away. A little blossom of pride within the garden of my soul.

Chapter Seven

A Cousin Confidant

If he were here, I would have pinned him down with my magic and shouted at him until I made myself hoarse. I would have slapped him as hard as I could and then kissed the sting away. I would have taken him by the shoulders and shook him so violently he couldn't tell up from down and then I would pound his chest with my fists as I sobbed against him with relief. Unbearable relief.

But he wasn't here.

So I settled for pushing all of the rage I held within me at him. All of my fury with my mother, my anger toward Lord Koa, my sorrow for my father, and the lividness I had felt when she had tried to dress me like her prized possession, when she had attempted to make me into her princess.

I would never be her princess.

He reached back out with a caress but I snapped my magic away, severing the connection. For now.

He would find a way back to me, I knew he would. And I already knew that I would forgive him when he did. But for now I just wanted to be angry. I wanted to sit in silence and stew about the fact that he could have reached out to me at any time, could have let me know he was alive, at least. Because the not knowing had been killing me. Not knowing if he was alive or dead. Not knowing if he had been captured again, imprisoned somewhere I didn't even know of, somewhere I couldn't possibly get to. And knowing that I was here, playing princess and antagonizing my mother while he was out there somewhere. It was a fate worse than death.

I felt her then, poking and prodding her way into my mind. My hastily constructed walls were up in seconds but she hadn't been trying to read my thoughts. She was trying to deliver one.

I don't know what you think you're doing, she hissed into my mind and the accompanying sensation, like a high-pitched ringing in my ears, had me wincing and closing my eyes. But you've embarrassed us all in front of this court, our court. And if you think we won't be discussing this once the guests have gone, you're entirely wrong, girl.

I felt her absence like a gulp of fresh air in my lungs. She left me reeling so badly that I had to reach out and stabilize myself with a hand on the back of an ornate armchair which had been brought in for seating for the guests.

"Take a deep breath," someone was speaking quietly beside me and I felt my father's hand on the small of my back a moment later. "Let's get you some air. Come."

I went without argument, clinging to him as we made our way to the nearest door and stepped outside. It was a veranda, of course, a long outdoor hallway with benches and torches set into the walls at odd intervals. He led me to one of the former and motioned for me to sit down. But I didn't. Because this was the first time that I had actually gotten a real view of the Court of Peace and Pride outside of the palace.

The balcony of the throne room overlooked a wide valley between two lush, low mountain ranges. Rolling hills and plains as far as the eye could see. Green grasses interspersed with fertile farmland. A quaint little town was set into the mountainside only a mile or so away, lights on in every home, surrounded by an orchard of apple trees swaying gently in the evening breeze. Birds flew above our heads, soaring through the pink sky, toward the sun as it sank low on the horizon.

"Quite an outfit choice," my father said after a moment, having given me adequate time to take in the beautiful view of my mother's court, what could have been my court.

"I couldn't wear her colors," I told him. "I couldn't wear her crown."

"I know."

He took a sip of some amber liquid I didn't recognize and we both stared out at the sunset until the pinks and oranges turned to purples and then to a bluish black, until the moon rose high above us and the stars twinkled beside it.

"It's beautiful," I breathed once the world was asleep.

"It is," he agreed with a nod. "Despite everything."

I hesitated, allowed his words to sink in.

"How do I keep her out?" I asked.

He turned to me but I kept my eyes on the distant horizon, on that little town whose lights were still glowing in the distance.

"Your mind is yours and yours alone, Seren," he said, his voice lower so as not to be heard by the guests walking the length of the balcony behind us. "She can try to claim it but it's yours."

I took a breath.

"I try to build those walls but—" I started.

"For me, it's less of a wall. More like a lock and key. Simplistic, I suppose, for a mortal. Or a man who was..."

He faltered here, trailing off. I saw the pain in his expression for the memory of what he once was, what he could have been, and I reached out to squeeze his hand in my own. He looked down at the contact for a moment before speaking again.

"I don't have magic," he said, settling on another course of explanation. "I can't use that force to protect myself, to build anything up within me. If you have it, you should use it. But I can't teach you that. All I have are tricks. Ways to keep her out of your head entirely and, if those fail, a way to at least lock away what is most important to you, what you never want her to know."

"How do I keep her out entirely?"

"There are different ways. I find that distraction works best. And not making myself a target."

A pointed glance at my dress. I frowned.

"Create another person wholly different from who you really are and become that person whenever you're around her. She won't try to peek beneath the veil if there's nothing to entice her to do so."

"Be a good little princess then," I grumbled. "That's your advice."

"For now," he replied with a shrug. "I must be returning to the party. She will start to miss us both if we linger much longer."

I nodded, keeping my eyes on the darkening valley below as he turned and strode back towards the doors.

"Oh and Seren," he said after a moment. I turned back to find that we were the only ones on the balcony now. Everyone else must have gone back inside when it became dark. "She knows you have some special power. She wants to know what it is. Badly."

***

I was in a foul mood as I perched on one of those frilly little armchairs, third glass of wine in hand, surveying the preening peacocks of my mother's court as they danced and paraded about the elegant throne room. I stared at the russet marble floor below and tried in vain not to recall how Lark's blood had flowed upon it, how Cass had knelt here, sobbing, how desperately Rook had tried to slip his chains. A hard knot formed in my chest and I took another sip of wine to loosen it.

"Not a fan of parties, princess?" a male voice I didn't recognize queried from somewhere above me.

I turned, looking up into the smiling face behind me. He had a goblet of his own, held out away from him as if he feared spilling any on his exquisite copper suit. His hair was a spun gold, lighter than mine, brighter. And atop those high, angular cheekbones sat eyes of deepest almond, sparkling in the light of the chandelier. He cut a striking figure and would have been impressive had he been the first noble Fae male I'd ever met. But he wasn't. So I just scowled at him and stood.

"I'm out of wine," I announced with a growl and strode away to seek a refill.

Unfortunately, he seemed to feel inclined to come along and leaned on the bar next to me as I waited for the servant behind it to pour. To the rim, as I'd advised him.

"The alcohol will help now," he told me, eyes still scanning the crowd, still not looking my way though I knew he was speaking to me and me alone, "but you'll feel like hell in the morning."

"I've been to hell," I snapped, grabbing my glass and taking a deep sip for impact. "How much worse could it be?"

He snorted at that, finally turning to face me. He took his time setting his glass onto the bar while he looked me up and down. Once he had completed his appraisal, he lifted a hand, just as I was poised to take another sip, and covered the top of my glass with it, effectively stopping me.

"To keep your wits about you, then," he spoke softly, casting a glance over my shoulder.

I turned to see my mother was far behind me, near the stairs, greeting some courtiers that she hadn't gotten to yet. Understanding his warning at last, I lowered my glass to the bar next to his and turned back to face him.

"Who are you?" I asked, my eyes narrowed in a new sort of scrutiny.

"Family," he answered with a grin. When I furrowed my brow in confusion, he continued. "I'm your cousin, Irim. And you are Seren. It's a pleasure to meet you. I have to admit, I never thought I would."

"Cousin," I repeated, dumbfounded. "I-I didn't know."

"How could you? No one ever speaks of my mother, not anymore. The younger sister of a powerful Fae princess. The one who lost her mind to grief when the Bone Court killed her bonded."

My spine straightened. Bonded. I narrowed my gaze again. Did he know that I was bonded myself? Was that why he had brought up the mention of his mother's situation so casually? Lark had said that being bonded was incredibly rare and yet I found myself speaking to a man tied so closely to one. But he couldn't know. I hadn't even known myself until recently and I certainly hadn't told anyone of it. Still, it seemed frightfully coincidental that he should mention it to me now.

"Why?" I asked, still confused by the brutal honesty of this stranger's answer.

"Why do they not talk about her?" he asked, shrugging as if the matter was of no consequence. "Because people prefer to ignore that which makes them uncomfortable. It reminds them that they did nothing to help her in her time of need."

"No. I mean, why did the Bone Court kill him?"

His jaw clenched at that.

"Because he was a fool," he spat, turning away from me and preferring to watch the party while he answered this particular question. "My mother never admitted that to herself, that he might have had a share in the blame for his own death. And Ariadne, well she was looking for any reason to hate the Bone Court. She always is."

His eyes did not stray from the revelers around us but I could tell that last point was directed at me.

"I thought royal members of the Court of Peace and Pride were only allowed to have one heir," I said, recalling my father's mumbled utterance from a few days ago. "But Alban had two daughters?"

"That's a new rule," he said, covering his grin by taking another sip. "Can you think of why, possibly, our court's succession rites needed to be amended?"

I frowned. My mind was fuzzier than usual, due to the drink, but I could reason out what he was trying to say easily enough. The realization wasn't an easy one. My mother had lost me. I had been taken from her and presumed dead. Even if she didn't believe I had truly died, even if she had already begun trying to find me, the intention was clear. Ariadne Dawnpaw was unstable. Alban saw that with his own eyes and so passed a law that would keep her from conceiving another child with the intent to seize the throne. He had arranged it so that the succession would fall from my mother to... to this man before me. Irim. My cousin.

"Why are you telling me this?" I asked because I didn't know what else to say.

"You're new here," he told me with another shrug, finally turning back to face me again, "and I prefer to be the one who tells my story. I imagine Ariadne has every intention of turning us against each other with some claim that we're both fighting for the throne. I want you to know, from my own lips, that I bear you no ill will. We are family. That hasn't meant much around here for a long time but I intend to ensure it does again."

Something like respect passed through me at that.

"Besides, I saw how you entered in that dress. I saw the look on your face when you put your mother in her place," he said, his lips spreading into a wicked grin. "And I think you might be the only person in this whole infernal court whom I might actually get along with."

# Chapter Eight
An Unfitting Punishment

My father's lessons began in earnest the following morning. They had to be done somewhere far enough away from the palace that my mother could not sense them, somewhere it would take her longer than a few minutes to track us down once she realized we were both absent and, likely, scheming against her. He had chosen the stables as that location, claiming that Ariadne hated the stench and never ventured in here unless she had to. It was a good enough reason for me and I savored the smell of the horses more than before just for knowing how much she hated it.

"Focus, Seren," my father was saying, his voice low, firm.

I snapped out of my reverie and turned to face him.

"She attempts to remain unnoticed for as long as she can," he said. "That way she can rifle through your more baser instincts undetected. You'll need to learn the signs of her presence, a way to sense when she's there."

"I already can," I told him, shaking my head. "The moment she invades my mind, I know."

He blinked.

"How?" he asked, brow furrowed.

"Like... a magical alarm," I tried to explain, shrugging my shoulders. "I can just feel it. Is that... is that not normal?"

"I wouldn't know. But that's got lesson one skipped then. Alright. Shields."

I squared my shoulders. This was what I was waiting for.

For the next two hours, my father explained, in minute detail, what his shields looked like, how he built them, how he kept them in place, what he thought of while he did, everything. He even allowed me within him to sense them. They were mostly centered around his mind and mine was an emotional talent but I withdrew from him with a nod anyway, hoping he would believe that I could see them, hoping he would think I had inherited the same penchant for mind reading as my mother, and not question me any further on the subject. Because even though I trusted him as much as I could trust anyone in this place, I wasn't willing to expose that part of myself to him, to anyone. His last words to me from the night before still echoed in my head and had followed me throughout my dreams.

She knows you have some special power. She wants to know what it is. Badly.

She wouldn't. I wouldn't let her.

We trained until we were called away for lunch. Tilda came to deliver the news to us herself as I had requested. I still didn't fully trust the two servants who had been assigned to me but I trusted them more than any of the others. We left the stables one after another and entered the palace again through separate doors so that no one would wonder where we had been together. So that no one would know that we had been together.

My father made it to the dining hall first. I took a moment longer, pausing in the foyer long enough for Fern, who had been waiting by the door, to pull back any stray tendrils of my hair and ensure I was presentable enough that it appeared I had just left the confines of my room and not spent the morning in the stables. Some magic of hers had the stench wafting away from me as well. Not the case for my father, I realized, as I entered the dining hall and walked demurely to my seat, listening to the argument that had already begun between my parents.

"I wish you wouldn't spend so much time in those stables," my mother was saying, her nose wrinkled in disgust. "You positively reek of them."

"I like the horses," my father said simply, not bothering to look at her as he dug into his soup.

"Apologies for my tardiness, Lady," a familiar voice spoke and I looked up from where I had been adjusting my napkin on my lap to see that Irim had entered the dining hall and was striding forward toward my mother.

"It's fine, Irim," my mother replied, still glaring at my father in annoyance as my cousin leaned in and kissed her cheek before settling into the seat next to her.

His eyes flicked to mine and I let that cruel mask slip over my expression.

"Will Lord Koa be joining us?" Irim asked, spreading his own napkin across his lap as he turned back to my mother.

"Lord Koa has returned to the Court of Friends as of this morning," she answered, primly, finally looking away from my father and down to her soup which she began to sip delicately from a raised copper spoon.

"Didn't care for his party, did he?"

"Of course he did," she snapped, turning that glare onto Irim who held his hands up in surrender.

"I meant no offense, Aunt. Only that I saw Lord Koa leaving with his men this morning, heads bowed in conversation. He seemed to find the matter of his return quite urgent. I trust everything is taken care of within our friendly minor court?"

Irim raised a brow in challenge and my mother's lips snapped shut before curling upward into a snarl as she realized that my cousin had known all along about Lord Koa's departure but had wanted to see for himself what she had to say of it. Now that it was out in the open, he was making it clear how easily he could sow dissent within the court. The slip of a tongue, a well-placed rumor, and he could have the entirety of her nobility questioning just how loyal their only visible ally in this realm truly was. Maybe they would even remember the displacement of my grandfather, how odd it was for such an ancient and supremely powerful Fae to have fallen suddenly ill and been sequestered to a room where no one had seen him in months, perhaps even years. I wasn't quite sure how long ago she had locked him away.

My mother opened her mouth to bark some uninspired retort back at Irim but the sudden opening of the doors cut her off in a hiss.

"My Queen," one of the soldiers spoke, striding toward her.

I flinched at the title. She wasn't Queen, not yet. Not while my grandfather lived and breathed. Not if I could help it.

"You have a visitor," he told her once he had approached, quietly but not so quietly that we couldn't hear him.

My eyes slid to my father to find that he hadn't so much as glanced up from his soup. Whoever this was, he had been expecting it or, perhaps, he didn't care. Irim met my gaze as I turned back to the doors and gave me the tiniest shake of the head, lips falling from their ever present smile. My brow furrowed in question just as the doors swung open and Ursa appeared in the threshold.

She hadn't come of her own accord this time. That was clear from the way the guard behind her pushed her forward into the room. She hissed, turning a wicked glare onto him, as she stumbled forward and then took a few steps of her own.

"Where is my father?" Ariadne called out coolly.

"I—I didn't—he isn't here," Ursa answered. She raised her hands and then lowered them.

My gaze snapped to her wrists where angry red whelps ringed around them, stark against the paleness of her skin.

"What happened?" my mother asked, her voice had gone cold as ice as she narrowed her eyes into a glare.

"I found them," Ursa spoke and my heart hammered against my chest as I tried, in vain, not to appear too interested in her tale. "They were in some dingy apartment in the Court of Wanderers. It's Lark's place. He's kept it for hundreds of years. Not many people know about it. They were there, with him, with Alban. I watched them for days, waiting for the right opportunity. Finally, my brother left, that hulking shadow of his in tow. It was just my sister and your father in the apartment. I knew she wouldn't hurt me. Cassiopeia isn't capable of hurting one of us, one of her own."

I was making a conscious effort to breathe. I felt Irim's eyes on me but ignored them as I forced that cruel mask to remain in place.

"I walked right in the front door," Ursa recalled with a scoff. "It wasn't even guarded. The arrogance. She was sitting with him in the bedroom. The moment I looked at her I knew she wasn't surprised to see me. I told her that I was only there for him but she put herself in between us. And then I—"

She broke off here, closing her eyes and taking a breath.

"I forgot my sister's... talent," she said and all the breath went out of me at that. "She so rarely uses it. I should have known but I didn't realize it was a trap until the two males shadow stepped right into the bedroom with us. Then Casseiopia, she took your father and shadow stepped away while Canis... unleashed his rage."

She tucked those blistered wrists behind her, hanging her head in shame. She had failed. And had exposed her treachery to her family in the process. Though it seemed they had already known if Cass' premonition was the reason they had anticipated the betrayal.

"When was this?" my mother spoke then. Her voice chilled the very air around us, every word clipped, filled with rage. It flowed from her, enveloping us all in a red haze of fury. I gripped my spoon a little tighter in weathering the storm.

"Two nights ago."

I froze. Two nights ago. That feeling of undiluted rage I had felt flowing through our connection. I closed my eyes. Oh, Lark. I sent him a feeling of understanding, of soothing comfort. His answering gratitude was a caress against my soul.

"Where are they now?" my mother asked and my eyes snapped back open.

"I—I don't know. They shadow stepped away as soon as they were… when they were done with me. They already had a plan. Cass knew where she was taking your father. I assume Canis and Rook followed afterward," Ursa said and, in response to my mother's growing agitation, rushed on. "I've been following them, tracking them. The trace on my brother's power was severed once he, well, with his execution. But Rook—"

"Weak magic means a weak trace," Ariadne snapped. "It will do you no good if the trace isn't on your brother or your sister."

Weak magic? I distinctly remembered Rook's unimaginable speed as he slashed the throats of a dozen soldiers on a winter-capped mountain not so long ago.

"Besides, I highly doubt you will have access to their traces much longer if they are housed within the Bone Court and you've just revealed your hand," my mother drawled, crossing her arms and allowing her displeasure to seep into her tone.

Ursa's eyes grew wide, frantic, as the soldiers on either side of the room stepped back to close and lock the doors. Irim tensed. I clenched my fists in my lap. My father just kept eating his damned soup.

"You'll find them," Ariadne snapped. "And this time, when you do, you won't go in by yourself."

Ursa was nodding vigorously by the time my mother finished giving her orders, wide eyes glancing toward the locked doors and back to my mother like a bear caught in a trap.

"In the meantime, your failure must not go unpunished," my mother said and then turned to the soldiers on either end of the room. "Seize her."

The six of them lurched forward in an instant. Ursa's daggers were circling her wrists the next. She winced at the pain of using her arms even as she did, even as she sent the first obsidian knife whirling through the air towards the first guard. He evaded it narrowly, the blade embedding in the mahogany door behind him. Another reached for her arm but those daggers moved of their own accord and he was on the ground, spurting blood from the stump where his hand had been a moment later.

Ursa whirled, dancing on her toes as she brought down each guard in turn with exact, precise movements. Hurling knives as distractions or dealing grave blows with them, defending against the soldiers' own blades with the swirling mass of her own, ducking and dodging, rolling and sprinting. When only two opponents remained, she flipped into the air and shot all of her knives outward at once. One flew just inches from my nose. I jerked back just in time to avoid it. Ursa noticed at the same moment my mother did, how close I had come to joining the guards bleeding out on the ground around us at my mother's orders. Ursa's eyes widened as my mother's narrowed.

"Enough," Ariadne bellowed, rising to her feet, her power rumbling through the marble floor where it met Ursa, still standing, across from the table.

Ursa fell to her knees with a grunt, teeth gritted against the power binding her there.

My mother didn't move a finger. She just kept her vengeful gaze on the princess of the Court of Blood and Bone as the marble beneath our feet liquified and rushed toward her. I watched in horror as that marble twined upward, twisting around Ursa's legs, her arms, her waist. I knew what it was to be shackled by such an impenetrable substance. I knew the fear in her eyes more intimately than I cared to admit, to remember.

Panicked, she twisted in an effort to escape. That's when my mother held her mind. Paralyzation by thought. That's what she had called it, said it was one of her neat tricks. I cringed, looking down at my bowl to avoid watching what was coming. I felt Irim's eyes burning into me and looked up at him.

"Watch," he said, his voice so low that no one else could have heard it. I knew what he meant. Witness the atrocity that my mother was about to commit, see the monster that lurks beneath the pretty surface, remember who she truly is, and understand what she is capable of. It would be invaluable information when I finally managed to escape. Any inkling of information I could gain regarding my mother's newfound capabilities in the uncharted territory of those amulets would be vital to her opposition.

So I looked.

My mother had already rounded the table and was approaching her prey. The soldiers still standing were bent over and panting, one of them bleeding soundly from a wide gash in his right leg, the other with hands covered in blood that seemed to belong to his companions, not him. But the hatred in his eyes was a visceral thing as he stood by and watched what his Queen would do with her captive.

I kept my eyes on Ursa as my mother approached. Tears were streaming down her cheeks, wide panicked eyes stared up at my mother, up at her fate. It was all so familiar, too familiar. An heir of the Bone Court, bound before my mother, bleeding, terrified, crying. I saw Cass, I saw Rook, I saw Lark. But I did not look away. I forced myself to watch as Irim had commanded. I forced myself to commit every one of my mothers heinous acts to memory. I would make her pay for each and every one of them later.

The crack of bone split the air around us and I twitched. My father's hand found mine under the table but he did not look up, did not watch. Irim's gaze had hardened, his lips set in a firm, grim line.

Another crack of bone had Ursa crying out in pain. I was shaking now but I kept my eyes open, kept watching.

The third crack was the loudest and it was the last. Not because my mother had decided to stop but because Ursa had fallen unconscious as a result of it, slumping face forward onto the ground, her cropped hair splitting out around her. I wondered if she had ever felt her father's power used against her before. She had seen it, of course, from both Perseus and Lark. She knew it better than most, I imagined, given its hereditary link with her family. But had she ever felt it? Had she ever expected to? It seemed an additional cruelty dealt by my mother, using her enemy's power against one of their own.

"Take her to the healer," my mother snapped to the two remaining guards who rushed forward to do her bidding, again. "But tell Mivian to take her time with this one."

The soldiers nodded once before dragging Ursa away, those heavy doors shutting loudly behind them in the otherwise complete silence of the dining room.

My mother's heels echoed through the hall as she strode back to the table and took her place again, simply clearing her throat and diving back into her soup. My father continued eating his, having never even looked up from it in the first place. Even Irim turned back to the meal, though it appeared as though his appetite had completely abandoned him. They all went back to eating as if this were a normal family dinner that hadn't just been interrupted by the brutal torture of a member of an opposing court's royalty. It was almost as disgusting as what we had just witnessed.

"Tomorrow, I thought we might—" my mother started.

I couldn't take it any more. I pushed back from the table, my chair scraping loudly against that accursed marble, as I stood and strode from the hall without another word.

I kept my head held high until I was on the other side of those doors. Then I leaned forward and hurled what little I had managed to put into my stomach onto the marble floor below.

Chapter Nine

A Sudden Departure

I spent the next week spending as much time away from my mother as I could. Luckily, my father and my cousin both seemed to recognize the attempt for what it was and assisted me in making it happen.

I spent each morning training with my father in the stables, working to strengthen my mind. I was more determined to succeed than ever after witnessing the paralyzation of thought once again. I refused to allow that to happen to me, to let my mind fall prey to my mother's ministrations. I vowed that when she tired of trying to win my favor and resorted to her more favorite tactics instead, I would be ready. When she came for my mind, I would be ready to defend it. And that was precisely what I had been practicing to do with my father every day for the last week. The process had been more grueling than I had anticipated. It demanded my full focus and attention. Because of how immersed I had become in my tasks, I'd avoided thinking of what had occurred in the week since we had watched Ursa be broken in the very dining hall where we sat for family meals.

I hadn't asked about her, where she had gone, but I had overheard some of the soldiers saying she limped out of the palace before the healer was even done fixing her, likely on her way to fulfill her next mission.

I had tried to warn Lark, kept trying to send that note to him, to Cass, to Rook, Gemini, anyone who I could trust. Anyone who might be able to pass it along to him if I failed to deliver it to him personally. But I failed every time. And now I had given myself less time to spend trying.

Because mornings were spent with my father but my afternoons had become Irim's. He'd shown me the enormous library of the Court of Peace and Pride when it became apparent that I was in dire need of a distraction. When I'd raised a brow and asked why he brought me to a trove of dusty old books, he had laughed and said I could stay down here all day reading scandalous romances or I could venture toward the more academic tomes, whatever I wished. Just that phrase alone had a drastic effect on my mood.

Whatever I wished.

It had been so long since I had been given free range of whole room full of books, so long since my time had been my own, to read and explore and meander through these shelves however I saw fit. It was a small freedom but one no one else had bothered to offer me. But Irim seemed to understand the feeling of being trapped. I never mentioned it though, never asked why he seemed to understand my situation so well, and he had spent every day since trying to help me find that little bit of happiness I had drawn from academia before. He brought me a select few books and I'd found that academic curiosity I thought I had lost rekindled in the dim light of that forgotten old library. He handed me books on the origin of magic, the history of the courts, family lineages and their known specialties. We sift-ed through ancient writings on experimental magic, treatises on practical magic, hidden mentions of dark magic. We skimmed sections regarding the nature of time, the expanse of space, the force of magic itself, the feeling of it. We even read through religious texts that were older than the court itself, molding leather bound books from before the Divide which hailed a pantheon of gods and attributed the might of the royal families to them.

A week into our exhaustive search of the library, I ran a finger along an ancient scroll mentioning the feeling of magic. It was the first mention I'd found, in everything we had read in the last week, of any sort of emotional connection to magic. And it was fascinating. The writer, some Fae from the fourth century by the name of Lichen Cloudlight, was hypothesizing that magic might not just be a force of nature we were capable of bending to our will. It might be a living, breathing thing, with thought of its own, emotion of its own, and that's why Fae who specialized in those fields, mind and soul, might be more powerful than others.

"Find something?" Irim asked in the silence that descended upon us whenever we both became engrossed in whatever it was we were reading.

My eyes snapped up to him as I removed my finger from the page.

"Oh, um, just something that I thought was intriguing," I told him.

He watched me for a moment longer before going back to his own reading. I hesitated before resuming mine. He hadn't asked me about my power, not once. Whether it was because he assumed it was the same as everyone else in our family or because he didn't want to ask, I wasn't sure. Maybe he didn't want to pry. Maybe he just didn't care. It was hard to tell with Irim. One minute he was the devoted, thoughtful scholar scanning every line of ancient text and teasing out meanings held between them. The next minute he was the thoughtless noble sycophant, more interested in the latest court gossip than anything meaningful, looking for some mischievous, wicked delight to entertain him. I wasn't sure which of those personas was the true Irim but I hadn't decided to trust either one of them yet, not fully. I had, however, decided I liked him.

He had seen how greatly I struggled to come up with a good enough excuse to miss lunch, to skip out on dinner, those first few days after what happened with Ursa so he had brought me here so that I would have one. He was tasked with his own assignment, he told me. Something about a drought on the eastern side of this court, a problem that Ariadne had given him to fix. But weather magic was old and droughts were uncommon so, when they occurred, he had to retire to the library to refresh his memory on how to perform it.

He had claimed, that first day that I'd managed to stomach making it to breakfast, that the process of finding that mention of proper weather magic in a room full of books, would be made easier with some assistance. I had offered my services the moment his eyes met mine and my mother had waved a hand without looking at either one of us, obviously not seeing how a room full of dusty old books could make a difference in my imprisonment here.

But they had.

Because Irim was teaching me about magic without teaching me anything at all. He let me read anything and everything I could get my hands on. He found for me anything that I requested. And he didn't ask any questions about why I wanted it in the first place. He knew he couldn't teach me, not without Ariadne sensing something was amiss, so he was content to lead me here and to let the scholars of previous centuries teach me themselves. I was eternally grateful for the gift he had given me, even if I wouldn't be foolish enough to trust him. Not yet.

"You're going to have to come to dinner, eventually," he told me, eyes flicking up from where he had been reading in silence a moment earlier.

I met his gaze and frowned.

"I know," I replied, turning back to my own reading.

But the sharp shutting of his book called my attention back to him and I settled back into the faded armchair, readying myself for whatever argument was coming.

"I'm leaving tomorrow," he said instead and my lips parted in surprise. "I've found what I needed and the drought won't fade without it."

He held up the book in question and I clenched my jaw, nodding. I knew he would leave eventually, knew this haphazard peace we had slapped together wouldn't last forever. But tomorrow...

"I can come up with another reason for Ariadne to allow you to use this library," he told me. "If you wish."

I shook my head, setting the scroll down and leaning back away from it.

"I'll come here when I want," I replied. "I won't need an excuse as long as I don't miss meals."

He frowned, watching me closely. The question was not asked but I could see it in his eyes all the same; *and you think you can stomach those? I couldn't.* But I didn't have a choice.

"That book of practical magic," I said instead, ignoring the unasked and unanswered question between us for the time being. "It made no mention of communication. I know there-well, I saw someone once vanish a letter to its recipient. How—"

"Dangerous territory, Seren," Irim interrupted, shaking his head with a frown. "Trying to get me to help you smuggle information out to your friends."

"I'm not—" I started, cheeks burning.

"I want to help you, Seren, I do. But you have to trust me when I say that teaching you how to do that would not be helping you. Your practical magic is chaotic as it is. And that form of magic, your mother will have set up wards to watch for it. Any attempt at communication with the outside, she's sure to know about. And when she comes to interrogate you... I don't think even your lessons with the mortal will save you."

The mortal. He meant my father. He still called him that. A lot of people in the court did. It grated on me for some reason. That he would always be the mortal to them. Even as he survived for centuries without aging a day. They would call him the mortal. Not for what he was, but for what he had been, to her.

But I saw through my haze of annoyance to the truth that Irim was setting before me. My mother would be watching for attempted communication. She would have guarded against it, set up wards to alert her if I should succeed in sending that note. Maybe those wards were what was keeping me from sending that note at all. I gritted my teeth, clenching my fists in rage. How had I not thought of that?

"My route to the eastern territory passes through the Bone Court's land. No one knows where Canis is but if you have a message you're comfortable with sending through Perseus—" Irim started, pity in his gaze.

"No," I cut him off with a shake of my head. "Thank you."

He nodded and stood, setting the book aside and approaching me.

"It was my absolute pleasure to meet you, cousin," he told me, sticking out a hand.

I eyed it for a moment before I took it in my own and shook.

"Until we meet again," he said with a wink and then strolled from the library and into the hall beyond.

I watched him go, mind racing with all that I had just learned, before turning back to the scroll I had set aside.

***

"Don't strain so hard," my father was saying three days later as we stood a few feet apart in the vast stables. "It shouldn't be so much effort. It's your mind, Seren. Remember that. She is the unwanted visitor. Not you."

I relaxed my muscles, focusing on that wall I had built up around my mind. It was much better than before, much stronger. I'd crafted it of obsidian, the memories of Ursa's gleaming blades cutting into me time and time again during the first training of my power I'd ever been given swirling in my mind until I'd formed them into something impenetrable, something mine. It shifted and moved like a shimmering onyx liquid, encompassing some thoughts and leaving others open, then flowing back to cover those, ever shifting, ever changing, so that it was harder to find a point of entry, a spot of weakness. She could probe my mind and my wall would respond, reshaping and reforming to cover any thoughts I wished to divert her attention from. And if she did manage to break through and step inside those walls, she would be in the long shadow of darkness cast by them, shrouded in the night, as she prodded blindly through my consciousness.

"Now, add magic."

This was the latest phase of my training, the part that my father couldn't really help me with. The part that I had figured out on my own. Thanks to that scroll I'd found in the library that Irim had granted my access to. Magic wasn't a force. Magic was a being. You didn't harness it. You begged its permission. And sometimes it granted it to you.

I took a deep breath and called out to the void in question. It answered, power thrumming through my veins far stronger than it had ever been before. That was what I had learned as well. When you invited it in rather than stealing it for yourself, when it came to you willingly, readily, it was more powerful, more pliable. I shaped it now, molded it around my walls, enforced it with feeling. I used my anger as my front lines, the rage I felt for all that she had ever done to me, for all that she had done to others around me. My sorrow was my archers on my wall, raining down sadness and pity on a field soaked with my tears. My joy huddled in the center, protected and unbound. My fear stalked the night lands of my mind, riding shadowed horses in a cavalry that bent to my will.

My mind created the darkness, the obsidian walls and shifting shadows. The magic brought it to life. And all of it was an homage to my love, to that small shard of Lark locked safely away in an iron box buried beneath that fortress of my soul. And to the court he belonged to. The court that took me in when I had nothing and no one to call my own.

I couldn't feel him when I was like this, when I protected him by keeping him so far away from my conscious thought. But it was worth it if it could protect that which lied between us, if it could protect him and the others.

"Good," my father told me though there was no way for him to really know outside of my body language. He had told me that I always heaved a great sigh of relief when my mental state was finally crafted to right where I wanted it. "Now try—"

"What is the meaning of this?"

My eyes snapped open, those shadow warriors misting away in the breeze of the door to the stables as my mother slammed it open and stormed inside.

Chapter Ten

An Insidious Invasion

"**A**riadne," my father said simply, evenly. He was calm, so calm. How did he do that?

I made an attempt to appear the same, banishing all thoughts of what we had been doing, locking them away in the vault within my mind, as I faced my mother, my cruel mask slipping back into place.

"I was just showing Seren the horses," he told her, not a hint of the truth of our treachery in his tone. "Would you care to join us for a morning ride?"

She stared at him, eyes narrowed in a way that told me she was searching his mind now, or trying to. When she had apparently found nothing, she turned to me.

I felt it.

That prodding sensation at the edges of my subconscious. I pulled up that obsidian wall and waited, my soldiers at the ready, my magic humming in my blood. Her power swept over the lines, right over my soldiers of rage and to the archers on the wall, making it as far as the cavalry of fear. Then she pulled out of me and it was an effort to remain standing upright as she whirled on my father.

"You've been training her," she spat, venom dripping from every word she hissed at him. "How dare you."

"She is our daughter, Ariadne," my father said, his voice still frighteningly even as he held his ground against this powerful self-proclaimed Fae Queen. "And she fears you."

Ariadne's jaw clenched.

"You claim that you want us all to be a family. You claim that you want her to feel comfortable here, that she can call this place her home, but you treat her as though she is a prisoner."

"She is a princess," my mother hissed. "She is a representative of this court, of my court. As much as I would love the play the doting mother, there are certain responsibilities—"

"None of which you have to invade her mind to complete."

"She wore a silver dress to Lord Koa's ball. She may as well have slapped me in the face."

"Ariadne," my father said, his calm tone turned soothing as he approached her. He laid a hand on her shoulder and met her gaze with one of his own that appeared so full of love that I nearly stumbled back a step. "This is our family. This is our daughter. You cannot force everyone—"

"Do not," my mother growled through gritted teeth and my father winced as he found himself being forcibly lowered to his knees on the hard dirt ground of the stables, "presume to tell me what I can and cannot do."

Eyes widening, I gasped, and stepped forward to help him.

"And you," she hissed, gaze snapping up to me.

I could no longer move. That paralyzation of thought that I had been training to guard against, that feeling that I had promised myself I would never experience, took hold of me now, rooting my feet to the spot so that I could not move. My heart beat rapidly in my chest, panic rising within me as I remembered the last time I had seen someone held this way. The sound of Ursa's bones cracking beneath the weight of that marble and my mother's heavy gaze. The fear in her eyes. The sorrow in my cousin's. The cold calm in my father's. I let out an involuntary whimper as she turned back to my father who was held in a similar state on his knees before her.

She reached out a manicured hand and brushed his cheek with it.

"I know you believe this is an intrusion," she said to him, gaze softening as she caressed his face. "I know you think it's wrong. I know you're still clinging to that mortal morality even now that you're one of us. But I have always done and will always do what is best for our family. And if that means this, then I will do it. Gladly."

A shiver went through my spine as phantom shakes surged through my immovable hands.

"I've gone to great lengths to assure the two of you remain by my side for an eternity," she told us, raising her gaze from my father's to meet mine. "You don't appreciate it, neither one of you, the sacrifices I made for your immortality. The deals I had to strike with that self-righteous fool in the Court of Life. You haven't thanked me. Not once. So do it. Thank me."

The words were tumbling from my lips before I could stop them, before I could even think of them.

"Thank you," I said at the same time as my father.

As the horror of what had just happened washed over me, Ariadne turned toward the door, taking a few steps away from us.

"I tend to hold grudges," she said over her shoulder. "But since you're my family," a pointed glance in my father's direction, "I will forgive this particular betrayal. But this pathetic training stops now. Not that it was working anyway."

Then she left the stables, slamming the door shut behind her.

The moment she was gone, my father and I were released from our invisible bonds. We both bent over, heaving in great gulps of air as though we hadn't been able to breathe enough of it in while she had held us, suspended in our own minds. My hands went to my lips, where those words had tumbled out, where my own voice had betrayed me, done her bidding.

I looked up to my father, our eyes meeting in strained horror.

He was wrong. He had been so very wrong.

My mind or not, she had more control over it than I did.

***

I was on edge for the rest of the day. My father and I did not speak another word to each other as we filed out of the stables and headed to our own rooms, our own methods of coping. Tilda and Fern helped me bathe in silence, dressed me without a word, and still did not ask about what had happened as they pulled my hair up into the preferred updo of the Court of Peace and Pride and dabbed some rouge onto my cheeks. I assumed they already knew. They had known of my lessons with my father, had been the only ones I'd trusted enough to tell so that someone could fetch us if we were needed, if our absence had been noted. Even now, I was certain that they hadn't been the ones who had told her.

I wasn't even surprised she had found us. I had assumed she would, eventually. After all, she was aware, herself, of how important we were to her, how much she gave of herself to have us by her side. She was bound to notice the hours at a time in which neither of us could be found at the palace. She was bound to figure out that we were together. She was bound to come searching for us herself, hurt that we would do anything without her, anything outside of the full family unit.

Family. I scoffed at the word. This wasn't a family.

Blood did not make a family.

A knock at my door made even Tilda jump as Fern hurried away to greet my visitor. I didn't even look, certain it was my mother come to remind me of the hold she had over me.

I nearly sighed in relief at the voice speaking from the doorway instead.

"Is she here?" Irim was asking.

I rose from the stool I had been sitting on and strode from the washroom even as Tilda ran after me, proclaiming that my hair was still half unbound.

I met him in the threshold, throwing my arms around him in a much warmer embrace than he expected. He froze, every muscle in his body going rigid, as I pulled away and dragged him inside, ordering Fern to close the door behind him.

"What happened?" he asked, taking in my half done hair and pretty makeup so in contrast to my haunted eyes and hollowed out cheeks. "You've lost even more weight. You look like you've seen a ghost. Seren—"

"She did it," I breathed, hardly believing the words as I said them while simultaneously feeling foolish for the doubt. "The paralyzation."

Irim's gaze narrowed and then he looked up to the servants waiting nearby, comb and pouf still in hand.

"Leave us," he commanded and his normally light, happy tone was firmer than I'd ever heard it.

Tilda and Fern, wisely, did not argue. They exchanged that infernal glance only once before bustling off to do as they were told. The door was open and shut behind them before I could blink.

Irim held my gaze, jaw tense.

"When?" he asked.

"This morning," I told him. "In the stables."

He muttered a curse, running a hand through his blonde hair as he paced away from me.

"She-she made me speak," I said, shivering at the memory. "She made me thank her."

He huffed.

"Her narcissism knows no bounds," he muttered.

"I didn't know she could do that."

"It's that damn amulet around her neck."

I tensed.

"You don't think I recognize the amulet of Altair when I see it?" he asked, raising a brow as he met my gaze. "But how do you know it?"

"I spent a few weeks with Perseus," I told him and he nodded in understanding. That was, after all, the King of the Bone Court's power held within that glowing blue amulet. "So you can't do that? Make someone say something?"

He shook his head.

"I can't control anyone," he told me. "I can't paralyze them or make them speak or anything that she can do. I'm not even sure she could before the amulet. It's hard to know with Ariadne. She was always powerful but this..."

He waved a hand around him as if to gesture at everything that had occurred since she'd acquired the amulet.

"I had hoped she could be reasoned with," he muttered then and I got the feeling that he was speaking more to himself than to me. "I came here hoping we could avoid a war. She's gotten what she wanted. You and the mortal. She's got her family. She's got her throne. She's got the whole court bowing to her, doing her bidding. And yet it isn't enough. Such lofty goals paired with such unchecked power... you have to get out of here."

His gaze snapped up to mine and I was surprised by the intensity of it.

"I-I can't," I started.

"Seren, you don't understand. If she can control your mind, your voice, maybe she can control your power," he said.

I froze, my lips parting in surprise. I hadn't thought of that, hadn't even considered it as an option. And he didn't know. Irim didn't even know what my power was but he had sensed it or at least something about it, something that he didn't want my mother to have access to. And he was right. At least, his instincts were. My power accessed the soul, hers accessed the mind. If she gained the ability to control both...

"How?" I asked, lowering my voice to a whisper despite the fact that we were alone. "She has her wards, her guards. I'm practically untrained. She tore into my mind this morning despite my walls, despite my magic."

"The library," he said, already strolling toward the door. I followed him, my feet moving of their own accord at even the barest hint of a possible escape. "You can't just walk out of here but maybe we can find something to cloak you against her wards, to hide you just long enough to get past them and beyond."

We were walking swiftly, side by side in the abandoned hall. I watched Irim's rigid posture as he strode toward the library, gaze sharp and keen, focus complete. His shoulders were tense, his arms stiff at his sides, every muscle on high alert. Then a thought came into my mind that I hadn't considered before. When had he returned? How had he gotten back so quickly?

But then we reached the library and the doubt vanished from my mind. The doors, however, were locked. It took me a moment to process that fact as I had never known them to be locked before. Irim pulled on the doorknob once and then again. The third time, he hissed in pain, gazing down at his hand as he snapped it away.

"You wasted no time at all, did you, Irim?"

That voice, the cold, cruel malice of it, had me turning slowly to face her.

My mother stood only a few feet away, arms crossed and brows raised in suspicion. But this time, she wasn't alone.

Chapter Eleven

A Last Resort

The guards filled the space around us a moment later without even having been ordered to do so. Irim and I backed against each other, bracing ourselves for a fight we would surely lose. We might be royal fae, a member of this powerful woman's own line, but we were outnumbered ten to one and she had that softly glowing amulet hung around her neck. My cousin was quiet, contemplative, as he focused on the nearest guard. When I realized what he was doing, I narrowed my focus to the one closest to me and felt his ire, his utter contempt for me, for this task. I pulled myself out of him and faced my mother.

"We aren't permitted to read now, mother?" I questioned her lazily, letting the words roll off my tongue in that cold unruffled way I had learned from Lark.

"Access to the library is a privilege, Seren," she answered with a matronly tsk of disappointment, clasping her hands behind her back while she circled us like a vulture. "You've proven yourself unworthy of it. And you."

She turned to Irim.

"Did you really think I wouldn't find out about what you did in Falhone?" she asked.

Falhone. I committed the town's name to memory even as I recalled Irim mentioning it as the location of the drought, the place he was being sent to fix.

"You mean how I brought the first rainfall to your people there in months?" he inquired easily, tilting his head to the side as if he truly couldn't understand her displeasure with him.

My mother's jaw clenched and I readied myself for the blow. But it did not come. Her focus, instead, remained on Irim and he narrowed his gaze right back. I wondered what it was like when two Fae, gifted with the specialty of thought, engaged in mental battle. I wondered what she was seeing in his mind, or trying to see, and what he was sensing in hers.

"Cloaking," she said a moment later.

I knew we were done the moment she spoke the word but the way Irim deflated at my back reinforced that belief even further.

She knew. She knew why we had come to the library, what we were trying to do, what we were trying to avoid. She knew that he had come to help me escape, that we were already putting a plan into motion. She knew that I was aware I wasn't magically bonded to her, to this place, not anymore. Just that I was held here by her physical guards and magical wards. I had lost my advantage, all of them, in those few brief seconds that she had been inside my cousin's mind.

"It wouldn't help you," she told us, waving a hand in dismissal even as she bit back the anger threatening to overtake her. "My wards are set to sense her thought, not her body. The moment her consciousness leaves my home, I will know. She wouldn't have even made it to the gates."

Irim deflated even more.

"I knew you didn't like me, nephew. But this is unforgivable."

Ariadne lifted a finger and Irim rose from where he stood, floating toward her on an invisible wind. I reached for him but her power shot into me, binding my arm to my side, imprisoning me within a paralyzation of my own mind for the second time today.

"I weary of dealing out punishments to those who disappoint me," she crooned, dropping him onto his knees before her as she did. "So Seren will do this one."

Her eyes snapped to mine and my heart bottomed out.

But then I was moving, walking forward, toward Irim. She turned him so that he was facing me, still down on his knees, arms pinned to his sides. I fought the movement, tried to turn and run, tried to break free of her hold. But my feet kept moving forward, kept stepping toward my cousin, even as tears streamed down my cheeks as well as his own.

"It's okay," he murmured when I had drawn close enough to hear him. "It's okay. I know it's not you."

"Silence," Ariadne hissed and then raised her arm.

Mine raised as well.

"No," I sobbed, begging now. "No, please. Don't."

I dropped my arm or, rather, she dropped it. And a lash of wind cleaved the room in two. My preferred physical strike, the easiest one I had found to wield. It barreled into him, striking him right in the chest, leaving him doubled over and gasping for air, choking on the wind that had been knocked out of him as he sputtered on his knees.

"Interesting," she said simply.

"D-don't," I stuttered, tears flowing freely down my cheeks as Irim gathered his breath and rose once more.

Another slash. I cried out with him when it struck home and sent him sprawling onto the ground behind him. He crawled forward on shaking arms. She had released him from his paralysis so that she could strengthen mine. I could barely speak, could hardly lift my chin in some pitiful act of defiance as she began to raise my arm again. I fought it. I fought against her control as hard as I could. I put everything I had into fighting it. Willing my arm downward, screaming at the magic within me to stop, to fade away, to die and wither into nothing so that it might not hurt anyone ever again. I asked it to leave, begged it as I wept. But it did not answer to me. Not anymore.

Because it only answered her.

She dropped my arm and an internal wind left my body in a whoosh.

The soldiers cursed and scrambled away as a column of wind blew through my chest, arcing over that marble floor, and battering Irim against it.

He howled in agony.

Tears were flowing freely now. I wept as she held my mind, as Irim screamed against the physical bonds that held him now, that russet marble which the entire palace was made of and seemed to only respond to my mother's commands. It wrapped around his arms, his legs, his torso, holding so tightly I knew it hurt. Perhaps even moreso than my wind which slammed him against the hard marble, trying to fling him out of it but only succeeding in battering him against it.

Panicking, Irim tried to slip his bonds. He wriggled, screaming blindly, pulling arms and legs in an attempt to break free. In response, my mother curled her fist and the marble constricted even tighter. His eyes widened a fraction at the sudden squeezing sensation and then he slumped forward, unconscious.

My mother released me in the same moment and I fell to the floor. I crawled toward him, sobbing, begging, weeping.

"I'm sorry," I choked, reaching for him. "I'm so sorry."

I thought it was over. My mother had dealt her punishment and it had been severe. I would promise not to leave. I would promise not to try to escape again if she would end this suffering. If she would only let Irim go, let him run far, far away from this horrid court. I would make the vow again. She knew that. She had to know that.

Then I felt the prodding. Like a tingling sensation on the edge of my consciousness, an alarm ringing out in my mind to inform me that the space was no longer my own, that there was an intruder within. I didn't have the strength nor the desire to build my walls. She had taken them from me, had extinguished any rebellious spirit that had risen within me these last few weeks and destroyed it entirely. How could one resist this power? How could anyone ever defeat her?

She rifled through me, searching. I knew what she was looking for and knew she would find it. It was only a matter of time. I didn't have the strength to fight her. I never had. My only chance was to give it to her. Maybe, if I did, she would stop searching. Maybe only my surrender of this part of my soul could keep the others safe. If she found this, maybe she wouldn't find them.

So, shaking, I gave it to her.

"Very interesting," my mother crooned.

"Irim," I sobbed, reaching for him. "Irim."

But he was turned away from me and he did not move when I called him.

She drew it out of me, the power, my own power. She held it, caressed it, examined it. In that moment, we were connected. I could feel her excitement, her eagerness, her ambition. And I could feel her power as well, immense and blinding but hidden somehow beyond a thin veil which kept our two souls separated despite being entwined emotionally and mentally. It was an invasion of the worst sort.

Then she was pulling away but so was I, as though she had grasped that power and was pulling it out of me. A sharp cry escaped my throat but then Irim was moving as well and my attention was drawn to him. He jerked suddenly, twitching against the cold marble, and I felt my power moving towards him, slithering against the smooth russet in his direction.

No. I tried to stop it, tried to cut it off before it could reach him, tried to push my mother away and regain control but it was too late. No, please. That's enough. No more. Please.

But either my mother couldn't hear me or she didn't care to listen. Because that power, my power, kept moving toward my cousin. And then it enveloped him. I blinked and the court was gone.

I stood in a blooming field full of wildflowers whose leaves tickled my legs. A vibrant sea of pink and blue and green spread before me as far as I could see. In the midst of them was a home, not just a house but a home. I could tell the difference though I didn't know how. Smoke curled from the chimney of the small stone house. The door was wide open, welcoming, beckoning. I took a step forward without meaning to and looked down.

This wasn't my body. This wasn't my mind.

Irim.

My cousin's young legs ran forward through the flowers. His then and my now merging as we both giggled over our shoulder at the boys who fell behind. Other kids from the town, out to race in the wildflowers like they, like we did every day. Mother was calling from the house, appearing in the doorway with a warm smile and bright, sparkling eyes. Blonde hair, bright eyes, a slender frame. She wore an apron and a patchy dress, not the sparkling gowns and crowns that a princess should wear. Father was coming in from the forest, axe slung over his shoulder, sweating through his light linen shirt. He'd torn another hole at the bicep. Mother would have to mend that one as well. She stood onto her tiptoes when he reached her and planted a kiss against his lips, both of them murmuring to one another.

My home. My family. My life.

Irim.

I thought I heard my cousin call back. Not the child whose memories I was living but the present Irim, the adult. He answered me but it was muffled somehow as though he had been locked away in his own mind.

I felt my mother as well, a looming presence observing all of this but not directly involved. How was she doing this? Or... was I doing this? I'd never done anything like this before.

The cabin flashed and then vanished and suddenly I stood in the rain. My body was larger, longer. I could tell without looking. The field of wildflowers was gone to smoldering ash. Something had burned them, all of them.

Lightening flashed above me and wet, blonde hair stuck to my face. I was running as I had been before, still the same distance away from the house which was still there, I saw now, but only barely visible in the flashing light and darkness of this storm. No one was chasing me now. This wasn't a race against boys from town. This was a race against death itself.

I sprinted, anxiety clawing up my throat to strangle me with blind panic. I both knew and did not know why I needed to get to that house. Just that I did. Nothing else mattered but this.

Save them.

That voice was not my own.

Irim? I asked.

Save them, he repeated and said nothing more.

Save who?

I blinked rainwater from my eyes, still running, but I wasn't getting any closer to the house. No matter how hard or how fast I ran, I remained in this field of burned wildflowers, lightening flashing around me, rain falling down on me, never getting where I knew I needed to go, never making any progress.

And then I saw Father. His head was bowed and his clothes were soaked through with rain as two guards in bronze armor led him out of the house. Mother stood in the doorway, held back by another guard of the same armor, screaming. Her shrill cry pierced the storm and reached into me, gripping my soul so tightly I knew it would never let go. I would hear that tortured scream for as long as I lived. I would never forget.

A cry tore from my own throat as well and I threw myself against the tempest, running harder, faster. It didn't matter. I wasn't going anywhere at all.

They led Father away from the house, pushed him onto his knees in the mud, and leveled a sword at his neck.

It was done in an instant. One blink and a life ended. The soldier pulled his hands back and swung. One blow and it was done. Father's head rolled through the mud as his body slumped, lifeless, to a puddle below. Mother fell to her knees, wailing in agony. The soldier no longer bothered to hold her up. He shoved her away from him instead, sidestepping the once princess and leaving her there, sobbing, weeping, crawling toward her beloved through the mud and muck. I screamed and ran and screamed and ran but never reached her, never comforted her, never wept with her.

Couldn't save them… couldn't save them…

Irim's voice echoed in my mind, real and broken.

Irim, I tried but that endless cycle did not halt.

Couldn't save them… couldn't save them… couldn't save them…

Another flash and I saw the home again, years later. Mother was there, sitting in the sunlight, staring out at a field of wildflowers that had begun to regrow. She wore a dress that was tattered and torn, not mended. She hadn't bothered to mend anything in a long time. A book was on her lap but it was closed, she didn't read it. She never read them. I kept bringing them but she never even opened them. She didn't paint either or sew or sing. None of the things she used to love. None of the things she taught me to love. She just sat and stared and never uttered another word. Not since that night.

People whispered she was crazy, that her sister had broken her mind as well as her heart, that she would never be the same again. But I maintained hope because I had to. Because I couldn't lose them both.

Couldn't save them... couldn't save them... couldn't save them...

Irim, I called to him. Irim, please. Listen to me. It wasn't your fault. None of this was your fault. Irim!

But he didn't hear me or he didn't believe me. He just kept repeating that mantra over and over within our shared mind.

Couldn't save them... couldn't save them... couldn't save them...

I wondered what she had done to him in making him relive these most painful memories. I wondered if she had broken him as thoroughly as she had broken his mother. Because she had been the one to order those soldiers to kill his father. I was sure of it. I wasn't sure how I knew, only that I did. It had been her.

Then I was yanked out of Irim's subconscious and tossed back into the world of reality, back into my own mind and body. It was so sudden that it left me gasping. Hands pressed to the floor, I bent over to catch my breath, stunned like one who'd had a bucket of icy water tossed over her head. My senses returned slowly. The feel of the cool marble beneath my palms, the taste of iron in my mouth as blood from my bitten lip filled it, and the sight of Irim twitching beside me, my mother looming over us both with a satisfied smile on her lips.

"Take him to the healer," my mother barked to anyone who was still listening. "And take my daughter to her room."

"No," I muttered, reaching out for my cousin, tears soaking my cheeks as I choked out again, "No, please."

But firm hands gripped my arms and hauled me upward. Then they were pulling me back down the hall from which I had come only moments ago, striding alongside my cousin as he searched for a way for me to make my escape. They dragged me down that hall and I let them. I hung limp in their arms, too numb to kick or scream or fight my way out of their grip. Too afraid to run back to Irim, to see what I had done, to face my mother again and risk that loss of control, that horrible paralyzation.

My guards did not speak as they deposited me in my bed chamber and slammed the door shut behind me. I did not try to leave. I knew it would be locked or, at the very least, they would be waiting on the other side, ready to drag me back within.

If this place hadn't been a prison before, it was now.

And I was a prisoner.

Chapter Twelve

A Shadow Unbound

I wasn't sure how long I sat at the base of that door, knees pulled up into my chest, sobbing. But darkness had fallen a long time ago and only thin slivers of moonlight illuminated my room. I had refused every attempt at entry, every visitor who had come to my door. I'd turned away my maids when they had come offering food. I'd turned away my father when he had whispered through the wood to ask if I needed someone to talk to. And after my tears were all cried, after my sorrow was spent, I remained sitting against that door, numb.

I stared into the room before me, the gilded cage that had become my prison, a place I was beginning to believe I would never escape. I looked down at my shaking hands and thought about what they had done. Wind, I'd known. It was my chosen force of nature, the physical manifestation of my clumsy magic. It could hurt, it could harm. I'd known that. But I had never used it to do so before. Not like that. And emotions, I could sense, always. But the memories. Where had that come from? Was that even something I had done? Or was that a capacity of my mother's and she had simply brought me along to torture me further?

I was shaking, I realized, my fingers trembling as I raised them to my cheeks and wiped away my tears. Irim's screams were still echoing in my mind combined with his mother's agonized wailing. I knew I would never forget either one of them. I knew I would never forgive myself for the part I played in hurting my cousin this day, no matter whether I had intended to or not. Something within me broke at that realization.

I couldn't do it. I couldn't let her use my power like that, wield it like that. I couldn't let her hurt people through me. I couldn't let her use me.

My eyes flicked to the razors, the ones that Tilda and Fern had left behind in their haste to clear the room at Irim's command. They were sitting on the edge of the copper tub, the one they had bathed me in, the one that they shaved me in. I crossed my room in a few short strides and stood before that tub.

One life. One to save hundreds, thousands. One given to keep this power from an evil Queen's hands. That's what Gemini had said, that's what she had told me, all those weeks ago. Had she known then? Had she suspected what I might come here, eventually, to do? My mother had gotten a taste of what I was capable of. What might she do if she discovered the true nature of my power?

I reached for the blades, sliding them between my fingers, feeling how small they were, how light.

I could do it. I could take this away from her at least. I could remove one weapon from her arsenal. I could weaken her so that someone, anyone, might survive just a bit longer, fight just a bit harder. I ran the blade over my thumb, letting it bleed, and stared down at the blood.

The Court of Blood and Bone. My home. My real home.

I closed my eyes and tore down those walls that I had so carefully crafted with my father. I banished the soldiers, threw down the archers, sent my cavalry riding away. They had never defended me well anyway. I pushed that joy down deep, deeper than I had hidden it before. I walked through those shadows until they swallowed me whole. Until I didn't know where they ended and I began in that swirling vortex of darkness. I let them contort around me, brushing against me, their presence like a caress against my skin. I let them pierce me, flow into me, seek out that shard of me so connected to their master. I felt them whisper his name against my breath, filling my lungs with their darkness. Lark. Lark.

Lark.

I opened my eyes when I realized the blades were gone. I looked down at my hands to find they were covered in blood. I had been gripping those razors too tightly. I stared at the sticky red substance coating my fingers and rose to my feet, blinking in awe. I hadn't even felt it.

"Ren?"

My gaze snapped up at the sound of the name, my preferred name, the one that no one had called me since—

"Cass?"

I stared at her and she stared right back at me. I lowered my hands, feeling the blood fall from the gashes in them, trail down my fingers, and drip onto the floor. The mahogany floor. And behind Cass, purple damask walls.

I shuddered, whipping my head around, taking in my surroundings. The same stairs, the door in front of me, even the same artwork. That little statue of a goldfinch peered at me from where it perched on the side table pushed against the opposite wall. My bloody hands shook as I took a step back, away from her.

"You-are you real?" I croaked, tears forming in my eyes as I fought against the hope blossoming in my chest. It couldn't be. It wasn't possible.

"Are you okay, Ren?" she asked, stepping toward me, concern clear in her expression, and not a trace of that wicked gleam in her eye, that otherworldly imitative presence.

I lunged forward and grasped onto her arm but she did not vanish. I barked out a laugh, bitter and yet sweet, and sank to the floor at her feet. It was her. It was really her.

"Rook!" she shouted, turning her wide eyes toward the hallway beyond as she gripped my bloody hands in confused terror. "Rook! Come now!"

HOME

Chapter Thirteen
A Promise

Cass went to fetch bandages while Rook carried me through the open archway into the room on the other side, a sitting room. I couldn't help but stare at the vibrant artistic decoration as he settled me into a love seat in front of a roaring fire. He stepped away without a word, moving so that Cass could take my hands in her own, could wrap those bright white bandages around my wounds, her own stained with the blood I'd bled onto her while I held them in my excitement.

"Hold still," she fussed over me like a veteran nurse and I almost smiled from the sheer delirious joy of it. Almost. "The cuts are deep. I won't be able to bandage them properly if you don't hold still."

"Who cut you?" Rook asked then, his deep, gravelly voice like a dagger in the night.

My gaze snapped to him even as Cass shot him a warning glare over her shoulder.

"I did," I said.

Cass' working hands halted only briefly before resuming their work. Rook's frown deepened as shadows darkened in his eyes.

"We can talk about it later," Cass intervened before he could say anything more now. Her voice was light, too light, and it wavered. She was putting on a brave face, smiling warmly to keep me calm, to keep me stable. She looked up into my eyes and breathed, her own widening in wonder. "How did you get here?"

"I-I don't know," I confessed. "One minute I was in my room back at the Court of Peace and Pride and the next... the next..."

I glanced behind her at the foyer. At that door which was no longer silver, had never been silver. And I couldn't help but remember the elixir's words from a time that was not so long ago but already felt like eons had passed since, spoken through an imitation of my uncle.

Home. Wherever you believe your true home to be.

My chest clenched and I turned to Cass and Rook, already trying to stand from where I had been lain on the couch.

"Where is he?" I asked as I faltered and fell back onto the cushions.

My head was spinning, my very limbs numb and shaking. Whatever I had done to get here, it had thoroughly exhausted every part of me and, of course, the blood loss wasn't helping. I felt the fatigue now, seeping into my very bones, and wondered how I hadn't noticed it before. Cass had. Rook had when he had lifted me and carried me to a couch only ten paces away from where I'd appeared.

"He..." Cass hesitated, glancing at Rook once, holding his gaze.

"Where is he?" I repeated, more forcefully despite the fact that I was in no position to threaten anyone.

"He's out," Rook told me and that seemed to be the definitive end of our conversation.

"That's it?" I asked, glaring back at him. This wasn't shaping up to be quite the welcome I had anticipated upon my return. "After everything that's happened, after all this time apart, that's all you have to say to me? He's out?"

"Ren—" Cass tried, reaching out a hand in a soothing gesture.

"Where's my grandfather?" I snapped, cutting her off.

They looked at one another again and my patience snapped in two.

"So help me God—" I started.

"Come with me," Cass said before I could go any farther, standing and offering a hand.

I reached out and took it, this time taking my time to get my feet underneath me. As tired as I was, as spent from whatever magic I had utilized to get here and from however much I had been drained by my mother's own control of my magic as well, I needed to see him, needed to know for myself that Ursa hadn't gotten to him. Not yet.

Cass took me up the stairs, taking them slowly and one at a time to allow me to keep pace. Every muscle in my body screamed in protest but I hauled myself up those steps anyway and into the first room on the right.

She stood by the door while I approached the sleeping form of my grandfather.

Alban Dawnpaw must have been quite handsome in his youth, if youth was something that existed for Fae. His face was thin and angular with the quintessential high cheekbones and perfect skin attributed to all Fae. But his golden hair was luxurious, even now. His nose was perfectly straight and exceptionally sized. His lips were puckered and full. Even his wrinkles were distinguished. And sleeping like this, even unconscious, he radiated power. I felt slightly more alive for just being in his presence, my magic calling out to him, reaching for the familiar.

"He hasn't woken up," Cass told me from the threshold, her voice low as if she feared she might wake a sleeping beast. "He was asleep when Gemini grabbed him and he's been asleep since. Some of his color has returned. He doesn't look as... cadaverous as he did when he first arrived. Gemini says that's a good sign. She thinks his power is returning to him slowly, whatever will return that is. We had a healer in, one that we can trust, obviously. She said he will live but, in what manner, that's yet to be determined."

Cass was doing that thing she did whenever she was nervous where she just kept talking even when she didn't really have anything to say. I could tell, from the way she was shifting back and forth on her feet in the doorway, that she was practically bursting with questions, practically imploding at not being able to embrace me. So I turned to her and opened my arms.

She was in them in a moment, squeezing me tightly as I felt the tears soaking into my shirt.

"I thought we'd lost you," she whispered against my hair. "I thought-when you made that vow, we all thought we'd never see you again. And that you sacrificed yourself for us, for him."

She cast a glance over to my grandfather but I knew that wasn't who she meant.

"I'd do it again," I told her and I meant it. Every bit of it.

Despite what I had seen, what I had felt, my mother do. Despite how she had used me, tortured me, broken me, I was here with Cass and Rook. Lark, Gemini, and my grandfather were safe because of the vow I'd made. And even if my mother hadn't broken it, even if I were still bound by it, even if I were bound to her for an eternity, I would have done it. If only to save them, my friends.

"We don't deserve you," she whispered. "We've never deserved you."

"Yes, you do."

I pulled away, looking into her eyes, shining with tears, and knew mine looked the same. She smiled tentatively, the corners of her lips lifting up in the ghost of that radiant expression I had so loved, so missed.

"How did you find us?" she asked, her voice barely a breath.

"I really don't know," I confessed because I knew what she was worried about. If I had found her, others could too. "I don't even know how I did it. I-I'm learning just how much I don't know about my own magic, Cass. About what I'm capable of."

She must have seen the pain in my expression because she threw her arm around me and steered me out of the room, leaving my sleeping grandfather behind as we descended the stairs again to the foyer below.

"Let's get you something to eat," she said then, her voice bright and cheery like it used to be. "You look like you haven't had a good meal since you left."

I would have laughed. Week ago, I would have looked into Cass' smiling face and chuckled at the joke. But I couldn't muster even a snort. Not now. Not broken as I was. Cass noticed and that light in her eyes dimmed ever so slightly as she pushed me down into a seat at the table and waved her hand.

Meat and cheese and fruits of all variety appeared before me.

"Take your pick," she said with a wink.

I froze. That wink, it reminded me of Irim, of the way he had winked at me just before he left for Falhone.

Until we meet again...

Couldn't save them... couldn't save them... couldn't save them...

I pushed the pile of cheese in front of me away, suddenly nauseated.

"I'm not hungry," I told her. "If I—"

"Where is she?"

An angry snarl sounded from the direction of the foyer. I recognized his voice in an instant, was on my feet before I had even consciously made the decision to stand. My heart was pounding against my chest like a drum, my shaking bandaged hands dropped low at my sides, my legs trembling from the effort of holding myself up despite my exhaustion.

It was him. He was here.

I sent a feeling along our connection. A fraction of my joy, the happiness I felt at hearing his voice again. He must have followed it because he came storming into the room without a word of direction from Rook who followed after him.

"You're here," he breathed, his whole body going slack with awe.

"She just popped into the foyer. We-oh," Rook started, stopping because I ran for Lark, barreling into him as hard as I could.

He did not even falter back a step as I wrapped my arms around him, tears streaming down my cheeks, hair flown into my face. He wrapped his arms around me without a second of hesitation, smoothing my hair back, looking down at me with an awed grin that seemed to mean he couldn't believe this was happening. I echoed the sentiment and opened my soul to him as he opened his to me.

The others wisely found somewhere else to be, backing out of the dining room and back down the hall into that foyer. I heard Cass hissing at Rook to give us our space before even her whispers faded away to the distance and we were utterly alone.

I felt his joy first, strong and overwhelming as it bloomed in my own soul, filling my heart so full I thought it might burst. But then I found traces of the other emotions as well, hidden just below the surface. Fear, sadness, anger, helplessness, confusion. I pulled back from him, keeping my arms wound around him as I looked up into those dark eyes. He drank me in, adoring gaze sliding from my eyes to my nose to my lips. He lifted a hand and ran it through my hair, letting it stray between his fingers, holding me there as if we could stay like this forever. I inhaled him, his scent. Wood smoke and leather. I closed my eyes and felt his arms against me, firm and strong. I sighed and opened my eyes again, staring up into his own as they flashed silver.

"Never again," he vowed.

I didn't have to ask him what he meant. I didn't want to. So I leaned in close to him again, resting my head on his chest and breathing him in once more.

"Never again," I agreed in a whisper.

Chapter Fourteen

A Confession of the Bonded

I had so much to tell them. I tried to. As soon as Lark managed to let go of me and pull me, by the hand, back to the sitting room where the others sat, I tried to warn them of everything that was coming, of everything my mother was planning. But I had gotten as far as Ursa before Lark announced that I looked exhausted. I cut him a glare, ready to defend myself, ready to make some quip about it being impolite to tell a woman she looked tired. But he just lifted me off of my feet and carried me up the stairs and I found such comfort in his arms that the words died on my lips as the exhaustion resurfaced.

So I let him walk me to a bedroom toward the end of the long hall at the top of the stairs. I let him tuck me into a bed of plum and charcoal, let him lean down and softly kiss the top of my head before closing the curtains, turning off the lights, and leaving me to sleep in peace. And I did.

For a long, long time.

I had been correct in my assumption that whatever magic had brought me here had drained me entirely. It was truly a wonder I had been able to stand at all when I appeared in the foyer of this house, much less climb the stairs to see my grandfather and descend them once again for a meal that I hadn't eaten. And that was what, ultimately, pulled me from my slumber. Still groggy, still exhausted despite knowing inherently that I had slept longer than ever before in my life, I awoke to a grumbling stomach and deep, tormenting hunger clawing at my gut.

Pushing myself up off of the bed, I swung my legs around to find that I was still wearing the chocolate gown of my mother's court. I winced at the fabric clinging to my body as my feet touched the warm wooden floor. I took a deep breath, reentering myself, remembering where I was. This wasn't the Court of Peace and Pride. Not anymore. I wasn't with her now. I was with him, with my friends. I was safe. I was home.

I looked up to find that Cass had sneaked some clothes into my room at some point. I assessed the array of options and smiled to myself. Cass was nothing if not excessive. Three outfits to choose from and she'd managed to plan for any possible mood I might find myself in. All of them gray or some variation of the color. One was a dress, simple yet elegant with long sleeves and skirts that flowed, unbroken, to the floor at my feet. One was basic. Gray leggings and a gray racer back tank with an optional sweater, reminiscent of what I had worn before with them when we had climbed down the edges of the cliffs near the Court of Light and Life. And the last were a pair of gray corduroys and a cotton tee shirt.

In the end, I decided to mix and match. The leggings and the tee shirt, making her simple outfit even simpler. Then I went to the mirror. Staring at myself in the new clothes, I saw how different I looked. Since they had last seen me, I had gone through that immortal transition and it had changed me in every way I had felt it change me. My face was my own but different somehow, made to more closely resemble their kind. My body was slimmer, even more so for all the weight I had lost skipping meals to avoid my mother in her court, and more toned though I had lost much of that without physical training as well. I looked emaciated. Immortal, yes. Ethereal and beautiful, yes. But sad, malnourished, and decaying. I heaved a shaky breath and pulled my hair into a ponytail. Without servants to attend me, this would have to do. I preferred it anyway.

Then I squared my shoulders and strode toward the door, pulling it open in one hard wrench, and nearly yanked it straight off the hinges. I balked, staring down at my hands as I realized I'd hardly opened a door for myself since I'd been turned into one of them. It seemed I didn't even know my own strength.

"Easy, tiger," someone's amused voice drifted over to me from further down the hall. I looked up to find Rook watching me, leaning against the banister of the stairs at his back with a smile curling his lips. "Cass will rip you a new one if you damage her precious house."

"Her house?" I asked, furrowing my brow as I stepped into the hall, closing the door behind me painfully gently.

Rook snorted.

"Who else would drape it top to bottom in this tacky purple?" he asked with a grin.

"Why purple?" I asked, still confused, as I met him at the stairs. "I thought the Bone Court's colors were black. Just black. Why—"

"All will be explained," he promised, placing a gentle hand on my back as he guided me toward the steps, leading me downstairs. "But first, breakfast. Or, I suppose, lunch."

I frowned, looking at the clock in the foyer as we descended into it. It was, indeed, well past midday. As if on cue, my stomach growled and Rook led me on with another gentle push in the direction of the dining room.

Lark and Cass were already there, gathered around the table as if they'd been waiting for us. I was ashamed to say, however, that my attention went immediately to the mountain of sandwiches sat on a plate in front of Cass, and did not waver.

"Sit," Rook whispered kindly into my ear and I took the place he motioned toward, the end of the table where I had sat the night before, where Cass had pushed me down onto a seat and summoned a spread of food that my mouth now watered in memory of.

Lark waved a hand and three sandwiches appeared on my plate as Rook took his seat next to Cass.

"Eat," Lark told me with a frown and I didn't miss the way his eyes swept over my thin frame, lingering on the sharp jutting of my collarbone over the neck of my tee shirt.

I didn't need to be told twice. I reached for the first sandwich just as they all politely averted their gaze. No one asked me to tell my story. No one begged me to tell them what happened, to clarify what I had meant the night before when I said I had things to warn them about, but after the first sandwich, I launched into my tale all the same.

They all listened in relative silence. Lark was quietest of all. Rook muttered a curse from time to time. Cass gasped at moments and roared in shock and outrage at others. I held their gazes, even when it was difficult to do so, because I hoped it could show them just how important what I was telling them was, just how much all that I had learned about my mother truly mattered. But when I reached the end and there was only a little bit left to tell, I stopped. I hadn't mentioned Irim, not at all. I hadn't told them of how we'd met, how he'd sauntered right up to me at Lord Koa's ball and introduced himself, claiming to be a friend. I hadn't told them how he'd taken me to the library all those times, earned my friendship but not my trust, slowly without trying, without making any demands or asking anything of me in return. And I didn't tell them about my last moments with him, about what I'd done, what she had made me do. I could barely stomach the memory myself and talking about him, after what I'd done to him, felt cruel in a way.

I didn't tell them about the blades either. And Cass and Rook did not mention them when I left it out of my story, how I had arrived in the foyer bleeding from deep gashes in my hands that I had told them were self inflicted. They exchanged a glance at my omission but did not correct me, did not intervene so that Lark would know what I had done. Or what I might have done if some magic I still couldn't name had brought me here.

But he had an answer for that.

"You shadow stepped," he said when I was done as if the matter were of no consequence, as if it was no surprise that I had managed such a feat of incredible magic on my own without any training.

Cass' eyes widened. Rook's lips parted in surprise. They turned to me.

"How-but is that possible?" Cass asked, looking between us in wonder.

"I felt it," Lark said, holding my gaze even as the others' darted around the table. "When you did it, I felt it. Like you tugged on me to pull you here."

It was silent for a moment as his words sank in and I realized how true they were. He had been my anchor. When I was sailing through that darkness, alone and afraid, I had reached out for him and he had tugged me back to shore. He had pulled me home.

"Wait," Cass said then, eyes narrowing in shrewd examination as she turned her attention back to her brother. "You felt it?"

The corner of Lark's lips quirked up in a smirk. I hadn't seen that smirk in so long that my heart felt heavy at the very sight of it.

"We haven't been entirely forthcoming with you," Lark told our friends. He looked to me, questioning. I gave him a slight nod and felt him relax through our connection as he delivered the news he knew would change everything. "We are bonded."

Cass' gaze shot to me. Her eyes were wide, her jaw dropped in shock. But the sound of a scraping chair pulled my attention away from her and to Rook who was now kneeling in front of me, his hand on his chest.

"If you are bonded to my prince, I am bonded to you," Rook explained, expression completely serious as he made his vow. "Moon of my heart. I will follow you into darkness. I will stand beside you in the light. My sword is yours. As is my life. My Lady."

He bowed his head as the magic which bound the vow sizzled in the air between us. I blinked at him, glancing up at Lark who simply sat, hands clasped beneath his chin, amused grin in his lips.

"He's been waiting a long time for me to be bonded," he said as if in explanation.

Rook rose then, sheathing the sword he had laid on the ground beneath me, and resumed his seat, much more solemn-faced then before.

"If you're done," Cass intoned, raising a brow as the warrior scowled at her. She ignored him, turning to her brother again. "I'd like to know more."

"Such as?" Lark drawled, spreading his hands wide as if to indicate the topic were open for discussion.

"When?"

"You'll recall that male in the Court of Rivals that made the unfortunate mistake of laying his hands on dear Seren? Then."

Cass cringed at the memory.

"Strictly speaking, I didn't have to hurt him as bad as I did," Lark said, frowning slightly himself as he considered it. "I found I was quite unable to control myself."

Rook gaped at him. Cass shook her head, turning to me.

"And you?" she asked.

"I—" I started, wide eyes gazing at him.

"That's a very... intimate question, Casseiopia," Lark spoke in low warning and Cass understood. If not for the tone than for the fact that he addressed her by her full name.

"Can you talk to each other?" Rook asked, almost eagerly, the solemn mood of his vow having apparently worn off. "Mind to mind, I mean?"

Lark and I exchanged a glance.

"Where did you hear that nonsense?" Cass spat.

"An old friend of mine. I met him in the Court of Rivals. He said his parents were bonded, said they could communicate via their minds without ever saying a word out loud to one another," Rook answered, defensively.

"This friend," Lark started. "He didn't happen to be from the Pride Court, did he?"

"He-oh," Rook said, his face falling. "That's why. Because they already had that as their specialty."

"Who was he?" I asked, surprising myself at the question as they all turned to me. But I couldn't help it.

Irim had told me his parents were bonded, I had seen them for myself in his memories, and they were the only other ones I knew. He'd also claimed his mother had gone crazy after her soul bonded lover had passed away. I had seen that as well. A woman, somehow seeming aged despite her eternal youth, staring out into a sunlit field forever. My gaze flicked to Lark to find that he was already watching me, that intense gaze back and just as potent as ever. I fought the chill inching up my spine. Oh, how I'd missed his examinations.

"Irim," Rook recalled easily. "Irim Tuliproot. Can't believe I forgot about him. He was a fun guy, always lost a whole day's wages every time he sat down to cards."

Rook snorted at the memory. I froze, heart beating faster at the mention of his name. Irim, my cousin Irim, was an old friend of Rook's? His last name was Tuliproot? There was still so much I didn't know about the man who had tried to help me escape. Despite seeing his memories, the best and the worst of them, despite feeling his pain for myself, I didn't know him. Not truly. But Rook had. And maybe Lark and Cass had as well. And yet, none of them knew what he'd done, how he had helped me, how I had hurt him.

My hands began to tremble and I hid them under the table. Luckily, no one seemed to notice as they dug into the sandwiches, chatting amongst themselves, laughing over memories of days spent in the red court. But Lark saw. He always saw. And he shot me a look through raised brows that indicated we would be discussing this Irim business later.

I simply stuffed another sandwich into my mouth, once he had pushed it gently toward me, and didn't look up at him again for the rest of lunch.

Chapter Fifteen

A Future with Friends

Lark had an errand to run after lunch that he claimed couldn't be avoided. He took Rook with him and promised they would return in a couple of hours. He squeezed my shoulder on the way out, gaze lingering on mine as if assessing me, looking for any cracks in my expression, any hint of the turmoil churning inside. I hid it well with a smile and a wave good-bye. Then I strolled into the sitting room where Cass was already waiting, lounging on the love seat by the fire, eyebrow raised my way expectantly.

"If you think we're not about to have the girl talk of your life about this soul bonded thing, you're out of your mind," she informed me, patting the sofa next to her love seat swiftly.

I joined her, lounging on my own couch as she laid upon hers. For a moment, neither one of us spoke. We just laid in silence, staring at the crackling flames and the way they danced on the artwork she had hung and framed all around us.

"Are we in the Court of Dreams?" I asked after a time.

"Yes," she answered. "What gave it away?"

"The purple," I said, waving my hand, and she snorted. "The art. You guys really stick to a theme, don't you?"

"When in Rome."

"Why here? Rook said this was your house."

"I came here a long time ago because someone told me that there was someone here who could help me understand my gift."

I hesitated. I knew I was treading on dangerous ground. It was common knowledge that Cass preferred not to speak of her premonition, not to even use it unless she absolutely had to. I'd seen it only three times since I'd known her. Once, to defend her brother from Medusa. Once, when she looked into all of our futures and saw our capture. And once, to save my grandfather from her treacherous sister. I didn't dare ask her about that second occurrence. I didn't have the nerve and I was sure, laying here beside her in the firelight, that she was just as disinclined to remember that day as I was. I wouldn't push it.

"Did they?" I asked instead. A simple question. One which left her room to expand upon her answer or to cut off the conversation at the knees.

"Yes and no," she replied, noncommittal. "But I fell in love with this place regardless. I think I would have chosen it if I had been born to another court. I have the heart of an artist. I'm only missing the talent."

I smiled at that.

"How long did you live here?" I asked.

"Fifty years," she replied but her voice had gone near-silent.

I didn't press the issue any further but it seemed she wanted to talk about it all the same.

"I came here shortly after Lark got banished," she explained. "There were... things that happened, choices he had to make because of unforeseen circumstances. I knew I might have foreseen them, might have even stopped them, if I had used my gift. But I'd kept it buried for centuries, using my magic to stifle it rather than release it. I thought maybe, if I had known how to use it, if I hadn't been spending so much energy on hiding it rather than learning it, weaponizing it, maybe Lark wouldn't have had to make the choices he did. Maybe he wouldn't have been banished."

I remained as still as one of her various statues, waiting.

"So I came here and I tried. For fifty years," she told me. "And it gave me the gift of knowing when Ursa was going after our brothers, of being able to warn them. But it showed me other things too. Horrible things. Once you know the future, Ren, you cannot unknow it."

I swore she shuddered even in the warmth of the room. I watched her shadow on the wall as she drew her arms around herself.

"There are some gifts that aren't meant to exist," she whispered. "Mine is one. Your mother's is another."

I did not speak again for some time, considering all that she had told me. I could see how knowing the future might be more of a curse than a gift. But at the same time, by her own admission, it had allowed her to save her brothers, had helped her save Lark and my grandfather. Still, I knew what it was like to look back at the results of your magic and wonder if it was worth it, to even fear what you might be capable of because of it.

"You haven't been here since Ursa went after Taurus and Lark?" I asked.

"Before that," she answered, shaking her head. "Ursa was all over the realm for a while. She was unsettled, wasn't satisfied with staying in one place for too long. I left here the day I heard she had returned home. I was hoping to find that she had broadened her horizons in her travels, that she might be open to setting aside this ridiculous blood rite succession nonsense, to agree with me not to fight. Instead, I think I reminded her of it. She became obsessed with her training, going so far as to bring Gemini into it. I stayed at the Bone Court with her because I thought that if I did, my presence would at least be a constant reminder that she didn't have to fight at all, that she could choose peace, that we could all live."

Cass sighed, staring into the fire.

"Gemini didn't tell me when she left," Cass said. "We were supposed to have lunch together. I was always making her lunch and taking it to her training rooms, making sure she was eating, making sure I tried to convince her at least once every day. I showed up at Aunt Gem's and she just wasn't there. I yelled at Gemini, slammed her door on my way into the street so I could shadowstep to Taurus. I knew she would go for him first. That was the last time I saw Gemini until she popped into our living room back in the Court of Wanderers apartment with you and Lark. He knew we hadn't left things well. He tried to mediate things between us but then we all got captured and I guess all was forgiven once we'd made our escape. Thanks to you."

My eyes were burning but I wasn't quite sure why.

"Are you really immortal now?"

The question hung between us, suspended in the thick air of the warm sitting room. I breathed in and out, letting my chest rise and fall.

"Yes," I answered, my voice quiet in the still, silent room.

"You look different," she told me but there wasn't a hint of judgment in her tone. Just a simple statement of fact.

"I feel different."

"Did it hurt?"

"More than any pain I've experienced in my life. And afterwards... well, that girl I was, I'm not her. And I don't think I can ever be her again."

Cass was quiet at that.

"I'm afraid—" I started and then stopped myself. I paused, so long that Cass rolled up onto her elbows and peered at me from her love seat. I heaved a breath and kept my eyes on the ceiling so I didn't have to look at her while I made the confession I had been thinking since I took that elixir, thinking but far too afraid to ever say aloud. "I'm afraid he won't see me the same way. Not like before."

She frowned.

"You can't possibly mean that," she said, brows furrowed in confusion or surprise or both.

"The girl he was bonded to, the one he grew close to, I-she's gone, Cass. Forever. I'm... this now," I told her, gesturing down at, not only my changed body but the hardened heart inside. "The bond is the bond but I don't know if he can love someone so wholly different."

"Are you?" she asked then, sitting up and peering over at me. "That different? You're still Ren. Still the same girl who's so damned stubborn she can't just pick one of the outfits I painstakingly curate for her. No, she has to combine them to make something of her own."

She gestured at my gray tee shirt and leggings and I snorted.

"You still have that goofy snort, that dimpled smile. Your eyes still shine the same way when you're happy, when you're laughing. Your table manners have taken a hit, I'll give you that—"

"I was starving," I cried defensively.

"That happens when you sleep for sixteen hours straight," she countered argumentatively but she was grinning from ear to ear all the while.

I shook my head, rolling my eyes.

"And that," she said, pointing. "The famous Ren Belling eye roll."

I snatched a pillow from the couch and threw it at her head. She dodged and we both came up laughing.

"You're still you, Ren," she told me, her tone turning serious, though still as light as the brightness of her eyes, as our laughter subsided. "Still the same lovable pain in the ass as before. You just get to be a pain in our ass forever now."

I smiled at her, grateful for the attempt, but remained not completely convinced.

"Without too many details that might scar me for life given that they're about my brother, tell me everything," she said then, leaning forward, elbows propped up on a pillow, chin in her hands, and eyes sparkling with the possibility of gossip. I grinned back at her. Girl talk, indeed.

"There isn't much to tell," I confessed with a shrug. "We sort of got... separated before too much happened between us. He told me we were bonded, explained what a bond was, said I could take my time sorting through it, and I kissed him. You guys showed up then and the rest is history."

"Future," she told me, her dark eyes sparkling. "The rest is future."

I turned away to hide the crimson flush of my cheeks but couldn't help but smile at the implication. That I had a future here. Not just with Lark and whatever was between us. Not just because of this bond and how it had caused Rook to pledge his life to me, a fact I was still marveling over. But because of this, with Cass and I, sitting here by the fire laughing and chatting about boys and love and feelings. Because of friendship.

"Whatever happens," I said then, casting my gaze back to the fire as the flames grew higher and the sun outside the curtained windows began to set, "I'm glad I met you, Casseiopia."

"And I you, Seren."

Chapter Sixteen

A Dangerous Plan

Lark and Rook returned in time for dinner to find that Cass and I had taken it upon ourselves to make it all from scratch. The kitchen, admittedly, had seen better days but our friendship had not. My apron bore splotches of the tangy, citrusy sauce we had made, Cass' was sopping wet from a spill of the water we'd used to boil the pasta, and we were both covered head to toe in flour and little bits of goey dough that had escaped the final rolling and cutting procedures. But we were laughing, happy and smiling as the two males strode in, sniffing the air like wolves on the hunt.

"Just in time," Cass sang out as she strained the last of the pasta and set the steaming bowl aside.

"You cooked?" Rook asked with a snort as he reached for a noodle only to have his hand smacked away. I chuckled and bent to retrieve the garlic bread from the oven while Cass began her berating of the fae warrior and his table manners once again.

"It smells delicious," a low, warm voice spoke from beside me as I stood up, setting the bread on the stove top and turning.

Lark was right next to me, leaning against the counter directly behind him which put him only a foot away from where I stood at the stove.

"It's the sauce," I replied, stupidly.

He smirked, the corners of his lips dragging upward tantalizingly slowly.

"Want a taste?" I asked, my own mouth going dry at the look he was giving me.

I had forgotten what it was like to be so near to him, what it was like to have his full attention on me, his eyes pinning me down where I stood. He raised a brow and I dipped the spoon into the sauce before lifting it to his lips. He opened them, leaning forward and letting the spoon dip into his mouth. I put all of my focus into keeping my hands from shaking and spilling it all over him. He gave a gentle suck and then released, leaning backwards, palms braced against the counter top behind him.

"Mmm," he moaned and my knees nearly buckled beneath me. He met my gaze and gave me a wink. "Delicious."

I stopped breathing.

"Can we eat, you two?" Rook called out from where he stood at the counter. I turned to see that they were both watching us, smiles on their faces and eyes shining with knowing. "Or is Ren going to burn the other loaf of bread because she can't stop staring into your eyes?"

I muttered a curse and wrenched open the door of the oven, reaching in for the second loaf of garlic bread as Rook guffawed and made his way toward the table. Cass just bit her lip and turned back to the noodles. Lark smiled, giving my arm a squeeze, and leaving me to my work, undistracted.

Five minutes later, Cass and I had plated our meal and were bringing it to the table to Rook's loud complaints regarding how hungry he was and how could we possibly expect him to sit around in a house that smelled like this without being able to partake in the bounty. Cass just slapped him on the back of the head as she dealt him his share and then took her seat on the opposite side. I settled into my own chair and waited for Cass' cue.

"Oh, go ahead you brutes," she muttered a moment later, rolling her eyes.

Rook grinned like a fiend as he dug in. Lark was far more refined, taking normal, polite bites.

"It's incredible," Lark said after a moment, casting a glance at his sister and then at me. "You two have outdone yourselves. Truly."

"Enough for seconds?" Rook asked through a mouthful of noodles, holding up his plate as he nodded his agreement.

Cass sighed before slamming another helping onto it.

"Should we take some to... my grandfather?" I asked then and the table fell silent. "I mean, can he-how have you—"

"The healer is coming shortly," Lark told me. "She comes twice a day. You missed her this morning but you can meet her this evening. She will take care of it."

I nodded, sitting back in my chair as the others resumed eating, wondering if I was supposed to meet her, if I needed to, if he was my responsibility just because we shared the same blood. I was grateful for all that they were doing for him, for keeping him safe from my mother while he recovered, but I didn't even know the man. I wouldn't know what he needed, what he might have wanted, and she would ask. Healers always did.

I caught Lark watching me and smiled. He returned the gesture but remained unconvinced.

"Where were you?" Cass asked a moment later to the tune of forks scraping against plates and quiet chewing.

Rook looked up at her and then turned to Lark.

"Sending correspondences," Lark answered, waving his hand so that more of that amber liquid appeared in his glass. "Breaking traces. You know, errands."

"Breaking traces?" I asked, stunned as I turned to Rook, remembering what Ursa had claimed about him, how the Bone Court had his trace, how she could use that to find him. "I didn't know that was possible."

"If you know the right people, anything is possible," Lark answered with an easy smile but I saw the way Cass gripped her fork tighter.

"You went to Nyx," Cass was practically growling.

I stared at her, caught off guard by her tone.

"He's the best in the business," Lark replied with a shrug.

"He's dangerous, Lark," she snapped, her teeth gritted in rage.

"So is our sister," he answered, pointedly, smile faltering ever so slightly to show he would not be questioned on this. Cass relented but only slightly.

"You should have told me."

"Probably. But you would have tried to stop me. And any deal I would have had to make with Nyx was far less of a problem then what would happen if Ursa discovered this place, your place."

Cass relented even more, her jaw slackening.

"I don't want him here," she said simply.

"He won't come within ten blocks," he promised.

"But he can do it?" I asked, tension clear in the bite of my voice. "He can break the trace?"

Lark exchanged a glance with Rook.

"He can do it," Rook said, tone far more solemn than it had been before.

Cass was already shaking her head by the time she turned back to her food. I imagine she would have been muttering unhappily to herself as well if we hadn't all been there.

Toward the end of our meal, someone knocked on the door and Lark stood but Cass beat him to it, snapping at him that this was "her own damn house" and she could get "her own damn door". No one stopped her then. But as she left the room, she barked out my name for me to follow.

I set my napkin on the table and strode after her into the foyer where she was already opening the door with a smile on her face, completely different from the fury she had just unleashed in the dining room.

"Floura, hello," Cass said in greeting. "Please come in."

Cass moved aside to admit a small woman who looked no older than I was. She wore a bright yellow dress that completely washed out her sallow skin and mousy brown hair. She smiled timidly at me as Cass made the introductions.

"This is Seren," Cass told me. "His granddaughter."

She nodded as though she had already known and smiled politely as Cass pointed her in the direction she'd undoubtedly ventured many times before. I hesitated in the foyer, unsure if I should follow after her or remain here. She didn't seem the sort to ask many questions, if she could even speak at all. Somehow, I got the impression that the only sound which might come from her would be something more akin to a squeak.

"Are you sure it's safe to let her in like this?" I whispered to Cass once Floura had disappeared up the stairs. "If she told anyone where we were, if word got back to my mother about where I—"

"Healers from the Court of Blessings are sworn to secrecy. Patient confidentiality. She's bound by magic. She couldn't tell anyone who her patient was or where he lived even if she wanted to," Cass explained and my eyes widened in stunned surprise.

"Oh, that's—"

"Convenient?"

She smiled.

"We're drinking, right?" Rook asked then, already tossing a bottle of liquor back and forth in his hands as he passed through the foyer. "I think Ren could use some of the hard stuff after what she's been through."

I stilled.

"Don't be an ass," Cass hissed as the warrior walked by us and into the sitting room. Cass turned back to me, apologetic. "Rook doesn't mean half of what he says. It's just how he copes. Getting drunk and making jokes. But if it gets to you—"

"I'm fine," I assured her, gripping her arm and offering a smile.

She nodded before turning and joining the warrior, already scolding him about venturing too close to one of her priceless works of art.

"He's alright, isn't he?" I asked, peering up the stairs when I felt a familiar presence behind me. "Should I be up there with them?"

"Do you want to be?" Lark asked, his voice low, close.

"No."

"Then stay here."

I nodded, turning to face him, and let him lead me into the sitting room with his friends. Cass was already draped over the love seat like before. She reached for me the moment I entered and I crossed the room and took her hand, letting her pull me down so that we were both curled up, laying down on the cushions together. Rook stood by the decanter behind us. Lark settled into the couch I had occupied before when it had just been Cass and I alone in this room.

"Tell us about Sophierial," Rook said then, pouring himself a glass, and the room fell into a silence much more tense than it had been before.

"Asshole," Cass murmured.

"She said she was trying to write us a note to warn us about her plans," Rook cried out defensively, holding up his hands. "So I'm asking about the plans."

"I don't know them," I confessed, shaking my head. "Only that she's involved. Whatever my mother and Lord Koa are planning, Sophierial has a hand in it. I just thought that, since you had been trying to form some sort of alliance with her when we were there before, maybe you should know that she'd already chosen her side."

The room fell silent again but nobody looked at one another, nobody exchanged a glance.

"That's two major courts," Rook spoke into the silence, voicing aloud the concern we were all feeling in our gut, raising his glass to his lips with a grim frown. "And one minor."

"So we'll have to convince the rest," Lark said and we all turned to him.

"Lark—" Cass started.

"I've already spoken to Lady Wispa Amberberry of the Court of Wanderers. She has some... concerns but I think she will agree to ally with us as long as we can get the others and my father's permission, of course," Lark said and we all stared back at him, wide eyed.

"So that's where you went all those days you left the apartment," Cass breathed in fascination. "And here I thought you just wanted to leave me with the old vegetable."

Rook snorted.

"Ally five of the minor courts against one of their own and two of the major courts," Rook repeated, practically in disbelief. "They'll never agree."

"We have to find a way to make them," Lark said, his voice far firmer than it had been before. "Or Ariadne rips open the divide and walks straight into the mortal plane. I think you all can guess what will happen then."

The room fell silent once more. I wasn't sure what the others were thinking but I couldn't help but remember the way it felt when she had held my mind so thoroughly, so completely. When I had lost myself entirely to her power, her control. The way I had been imprisoned in my own body, forced to watch my own actions but helpless to stop myself. The paralyzation by thought, the words spoken in my own voice that I had never intended to say. I closed my eyes and felt Cass pull me closer, wrapping her arms more tightly around me.

"I'm guessing you've been working on the royalty here?" Rook asked, raising a brow at Lark in question.

"I've been... preoccupied," Lark answered.

His gaze flicked to me and I saw the pain in that expression, felt it through our connection. He had been trying to find a way back to me, searching for a way to bring me back, to bring me home. Maybe that had been why he had engaged this nefarious Nyx's services in the first place. Maybe he had been that desperate, to enlist the help of someone that elicited such a strong emotional response from his sister, someone she didn't trust, didn't even want within ten blocks of her house, someone she called dangerous.

My heart felt heavy as I watched Lark and felt it as clearly as if it had come from within me. He would have done anything, sacrificed everything, to get me back.

It was lucky that I'd found a way to return before either one of us could do something we would regret.

Chapter Seventeen
An Explanation

I couldn't sleep that night.

Once Rook had stretched his arms and claimed he was heading to bed, Cass had announced that she was tired and Lark had taken one look at me before asking his sister to see me to my own room as well. He'd been right, of course. Despite having slept for sixteen hours straight after collapsing the night before, my body was utterly exhausted from the day I had spent using more magic than I'd ever even known I was capable of. I wanted to linger, wanted to stay behind and finally have some time alone with him. To talk, just the two of us, to tell him what I had gone through, who I had become. But the dark flicker in his eyes as he watched the flames lick higher in the grate, the way his jaw set as he clenched his glass tighter in his fist, told me that it wasn't the time, it wasn't the night. And I was too tired to have that conversation anyway. Not yet.

But even though I could barely keep my eyes open in front of that fire with my friends, the moment I was alone in my own bedroom, I couldn't close them again. I kicked off my sheets and stood, alone in the dark. I crossed the room and threw open the curtains, letting the light of the moon shine into the room. I looked down at the black silk sleep set that Cass had loaned me. Black shorts and a button up short sleeve shirt. It felt smooth and cool against my skin. I reached down, running a finger along the hem, feeling the material. Black because it was Cass'. Black because it belonged to the princess of the Bone Court, to the sister of my bonded. I breathed in, turning my gaze through the clear window and to the stars above.

Maybe we needed to have that talk after all.

Before I could change my mind, I crossed the room in a few quick strides, opening the door and stepping silently into the hall. Lark's door was only a few paces away from mine, closed against this dark and empty hall like all the others. I padded forward on bare feet, being as quiet as I could. I hesitated just outside of his door, looking down at my nightclothes and wondering if he might get the wrong idea. What was the wrong idea? I reached out to knock but froze when I heard voices speaking lowly from within.

"You're going to have to ask Karma for help," Rook was saying. "You know that, don't you?"

"I know," Lark replied with a sigh, more exhausted than I'd ever heard him. That alone made me want to turn back for my room and leave he and the warrior to whatever scheming they were up to so that they might both get some rest afterwards. But the name they spoke and the familiar way they mentioned it had me hesitating. I hated myself for it but I inched closer to the door, pressing my ear to the wood. Who was Karma?

"I can go. I can talk to her if you don't want to."

"No. She will want to hear it from me. And she'll want to torment me while she does."

There was a moment of silence before someone spoke again.

"What about Ren?" Rook asked slowly, carefully. "If Karma knows—"

"Ren stays by my side unless she decides not to. I won't hide her away because of some ancient bitterness."

Another pause.

"Karma might take offense—" Rook started.

"Karma is not the only member of the Dream Court royal family," Lark snapped. "I will go to her first because she is owed that due to our... history. But I will not allow her to cost us this war because of petty jealousy."

A silence that was nearly louder than Lark's outburst followed. My first instinct was to shrink away from the word war. Silence from within the room told me that Rook was experiencing a similar reaction. That was it, then. That was what Lark expected to naturally follow my mother's actions. She was gathering allies, making plans to disrupt every law and structure this realm had in place. Of course it would mean war to stop her. I hadn't wanted to believe it but there it was. There would be a war. And we were on the other side of it. That meant we needed allies and soon.

My lips parted and I stepped slightly away. The mention of war should have been what bothered me the most but something else scratched relentlessly at my brain. I still didn't know exactly who this Karma was but I knew enough to guess and the idea of it had me clenching my fists so tightly that my nails dug into my palms. I was so distracted by my thoughts that I didn't hear it when the near-silent Rook crossed the floor of Lark's bedroom and flung the door open. His jaw slackened when he saw me standing on the other side. I could do nothing but smile at him even as my cheeks flushed red with humiliation.

"I-sorry. I'm here to—" I started but Rook cut me off with a snort, his surprise vanishing in favor of amusement.

"I know what you're here to do," he said, raising a brow to Lark as he strode past me and into the hallway.

My cheeks burned as he gave me a wink before turning away and heading for his room. I bit the inside of my cheek until he was gone and then turned back to Lark.

"Is he always so insufferable?" I asked.

"Always," he answered with a grin, standing up straight and crossing his arms. "I thought you were asleep."

I couldn't help my examination as my eyes drifted over his room. All black, unsurprisingly, but tastefully decorated all the same. A door leading to the right and one to the left, likely a closet and a washroom. A desk on the left wall topped with piles of letters and various papers, a black jacket slung carelessly over the dark velvet armchair set near a towering bookcase, an enormous bed topped with luxurious sheets and a thick, black fur blanket. He raised a brow, noting my gaze toward the bed, and I shook my head and spoke.

"I couldn't sleep," I told him.

He nodded slowly, watching me as I strolled toward the bookshelf, lifting a heavy silver statue and setting it back down.

"And you thought I might help with that?" he asked, brow raised in flirtatious challenge.

I glanced at him over my shoulder and rolled my eyes.

"We need to talk," I said finally, taking a deep breath as I turned to face him fully for the first time.

He stood in the middle of his room, hair disheveled, top two buttons on his black shirt undone. I tried in vain not to stare at the top of his muscled chest peeking out above them. His dark eyes drank me in, watching me slowly, carefully.

"Okay," he answered finally.

Neither of us spoke for a minute and then I realized I should be the one to begin the discussion since I'd been the one to claim it was necessary in the first place.

"I-things have changed. I'm not the same person I was when we-when you—" I started, stumbling over the words.

"I know," he answered, softly, and I felt that comforting caress against my soul, calming me, encouraging me, as it had for all the time I'd spent in my mother's court. I heaved a shaky breath and met his gaze.

"A lot has happened and I just don't know where we stand."

He cocked his head to the side, watching me.

"Magical bond or no, Ren Belling, I am yours," he replied.

My breath hitched at the simplicity of that statement and the sincerity in his eyes as he spoke it.

"Why?" I breathed a moment later before I could think better of it and felt instantly foolish in the glow of the warm smile he offered me in return.

"Why does the sun rise each day?" he asked with a shrug.

"Actually, it doesn't. The sun stays in the same position. It's the earth rotating around it that..." I trailed off when I noticed his smirk.

"I was trying to be poetic," he drawled and I smiled sheepishly as he took a few steps until he was standing in front of me. "The truth is, Ren, I knew you were the one for me the moment you waltzed into that office of yours and put me in my place. Then later, when the bond clicked into place, I knew it because it felt right. I felt... whole."

He took my hands in his, staring down at them as he readied himself to say whatever was coming next.

"I didn't tell you because that's a very... intense thing to tell someone. Specifically, someone you've just met. Especially for mortals. I didn't want to scare you. But it's been there for me, Ren, all along. And if you're worried that this change in you makes me want you any less, let me put those fears to bed right now."

He ran his hands from my own, up my arms, squeezing my shoulders as he drew me in. I closed my eyes when his lips met mine. He pulled me closer, one hand tangled in my hair, the other around my waist. I allowed myself to melt into him, allowed my body to meld with his own, and sank into the feeling of the kiss until my only thoughts were of his lips, his tongue, his roving hands. He pulled away too soon, his dark eyes flaring silver as he met my gaze, likely as heated as his own.

"Tell me you want this, Ren, and I will promise to spend every day of my immortal life trying to deserve you."

I raised my hand to cup his cheek, staring into his eyes as they shined with something deeper than desire, something closer to adoration. My heart skipped a beat.

"You already do," I whispered.

He grabbed my hand where it rested upon his cheek and kissed my palm, keeping his eyes on mine.

"How much did it hurt?" he asked and every muscle in my body tensed. I dropped my hand and he let me go, drifting further away from him at the change in conversation. I looked away, shuddered a breath.

"Why, Lark?" I replied, my voice low. "Why ask about that? Why now?"

"I need to know exactly how much pain to inflict upon her when we meet again."

His eyes flashed again but with something else entirely now.

"Every bone in my body broke, reshaped me into something new, into... this," I gestured at my new, immortal form as his jaw clenched. "I went... somewhere else. I can't explain it. The elixir gave me a choice. To live or die. I almost didn't—" my voice cracked, tears came unbidden to my eyes, "I heard you there. You... you brought me back. When nothing else would have. And then when I..."

I trailed off again, looking down to my hands where Cass had removed the bandages earlier today. The gashes in my palms were still there but only slightly, not nearly as deep as they had been before, thanks to the quick healing of immortality. My hands shook as I held them up to him.

"She used me, Lark," I whispered, barely able to voice it aloud. "She held my mind and she used my power to-to hurt someone. Badly. I couldn't stop. I just had to watch while she-she—"

He gripped my hands, pulling me toward him into a comforting embrace.

"She made me her weapon," I sobbed into his chest. "And I vowed that I would never be her weapon again."

"I understand, Ren," he whispered soothingly as he stroked my hair and I knew he did. Knew it from the words of comfort he whispered against my ear, knew it from the rigidness of his stance as he fought to hold his fury at bay, to keep it directed at the one who most deserved it. I knew he understood from the way he held me, like something he had almost lost.

We stayed like that for a long time, him just holding me, just smoothing my hair and rubbing my back, whispering to me. And I let him comfort me because it had been a long time since anyone truly had and because I needed it. At some point, we laid down in his bed. He covered me in the fur blanket and held me close until my eyes finally fluttered closed and I cried no more.

Chapter Eighteen
A Bold Choice

I underestimated how easy it would be to sneak out of Lark's room and back to my own.

The first part was easy enough. Slipping out from underneath his arms as he dozed away in the morning sun proved simple. Tiptoeing over the squeaky wooden floors of the hallway, however, far more difficult.

"Morning, Ren," a male voice spoke from down the hall just as I reached my door. I could hear the amusement in his tone before I even turned.

I whirled to find Rook leaning against the side of his own door, directly beside mine, grinning like a madman. He raised a brow so I growled in response before wrenching open my door and slamming it closed behind me loud enough to wake the whole house I had just taken great pains not to disturb. Though, if my slamming door hadn't done it, Rook's resulting howling laughter must have.

I found another three outfit choices sitting on my dresser and closed my eyes, pinching the bridge of my nose with a sigh. Cass had been here again.

But this time, when she had sneaked in to my room to leave these for me, she had undoubtedly seen that I wasn't here. I took a breath, looking over my choices. All gray, all similar to the last options she had given me. I reached out to touch the soft fabric of the gray leggings and hesitated, remembering Lark's words from last night, ones he had spoken before holding me all night, wiping away my tears, healing my broken heart, my broken soul, one piece at a time.

Magical bond or no, Ren Belling, I am yours.

Mine. He was mine. So I could do something to show him I was his.

I selected the leggings and racer back tank, the soft sweater that went over them. I dressed slowly, taking my time. I pulled my hair up into a ponytail, dabbed on a bit of the cosmetics that Cass had left here for me at some point, and then I stood in front of the full length mirror by the door. I stared at my reflection, noting the bags beneath my eyes, and then gripped the edge of my sweater. I closed my eyes, feeling for the magic, calling out to it. A moment later, I felt it thrumming through my veins. I whispered my request, lips parting as I breathed in the force all around me, and opened my eyes to find the gray leggings, tank, and sweater had all turned a deepest, darkest black.

Winded from just that small use of magic, I turned on my heel and pulled open my door.

I could hear them all downstairs, the clatter of dishes emanating from the dining room letting me know they were all sitting down for breakfast. I strode toward the stairs, hesitating at my grandfather's room, peering through the open door to find him still slumbering away in his bed. Then I turned away, worried that he would awaken to find me staring at him if I lingered too long despite how irrational that was, and made my way down the stairs to the foyer below.

I could hear Rook and Cass laughing as my feet hit the cherry wood floor beneath me. I heard Lark mutter something low and they all burst out laughing again. I couldn't help my smile as I rounded the corner and stepped into the room with them.

They all turned my way simultaneously, laughter ceasing as they took in my outfit of choice. Rook's eyes bulged in surprise. Cass' lips parted, still moving, as if she were saying something but no one could hear her. Lark smiled, his lips stretching wider than I had ever seen them, and shot me a wink.

"You look good in black," he said, simply.

I grinned back at him as Rook beamed, turning back to his conversation with Lark from before. Cass gave me a knowing glance as I approached my chair and took a seat. Then she leaned across the table to me.

"I have so many more outfit choices for you now," she squealed, practically giddy, as she reached out and gave my hand a friendly squeeze.

I looked up to find Rook watching me as well, knowing grin on his lips. I just rolled my eyes and tore into my croissant.

"What's on the agenda today?" Cass asked, settling back into her seat.

Lark looked up, eyes meeting mine briefly before turning to his sister.

"We try for an alliance with the Court of Dreams," he said.

The room fell silent. Cass stared back at her brother. Rook even stopped eating.

"You mean, meet with Karma," Cass spoke slowly.

"She's our best chance at making this work," he answered, carefully.

I schooled my face into an expression of blissful ignorance, pretending I had never heard the name before in my life, and slid a bite of eggs into my mouth before peering around at all of them as innocently as I could.

"Who's Karma?" I asked.

This time, no one looked my way. They seemed to be making a concerted effort not to do so.

"I, um, I think that second round of sausage is just about done," Cass said suddenly, wiping her mouth with a napkin as she stood from her chair and practically ran to the kitchen.

"Need some help with that?" Rook cried out, sprinting after her.

I watched them go and then turned back to Lark, brow raised, to find him nearly as uncomfortable as the others. He shifted in his chair, clearing his throat.

"Karma is the Lord of the Court of Dreams' daughter," he explained. I waited, knowing that wasn't all there was to it. He cleared his throat again, practically a full on coughing fit, before he continued. "She's, um, she's my ex."

"I see," I said simply, turning back to my breakfast.

Lark waited the entire time I cut into my sausage before speaking again.

"You... see," he repeated, treading carefully.

"Yes, I see," I replied, looking back at him. "I do know what an ex is, Lark. You used to date her."

I waved the knife in front of me as if to drive home the point that I completely understood and utterly didn't care.

"It must have ended well," I continued, reaching for my tea and taking a sip, "if you think she will be open to negotiating an alliance with you on behalf of her court."

He blinked at me.

"It, um," he tried, rubbing the back of his neck with one hand. I had never seen him so out of sorts and it had me gripping my fork much harder than intended to know that some other woman managed to affect him in such a way. "Well, no. Not really. She likely won't be very pleased to see me."

"But going to her is better than going to her father?" I guessed with quite a bit of help from the conversation I had overheard the night before.

"Karma has a soft spot for mortals," he told me. "And as much as she might hate me now, she knows I'm usually right about these things. She will posture, she will try to get under my skin, but she will agree."

I watched him, letting my fork dangle over my plate as I stared at him across the table.

"And we're all going?" I asked, raising a brow.

"I would like you to come," he replied, clearing his throat again. "I'd like to show you this Court. It's full of beauty if you know where to look. I think you would like it."

"And Karma?"

"I'm not sure if you'll like her. I'm not sure that it matters. Just know that we need her."

"Like we needed Sophierial."

I raised a brow in challenge. But he didn't take the bait. Instead, he smirked back at me, that gaze turning heated.

"So you were jealous," he said with a knowing grin.

"Please," I replied with a roll of my eyes, "you said it yourself. You're mine. So what do I have to worry about?"

His dark eyes flared silver and I felt his desire permeating the room around us.

"Careful what you say, dear Ren," he drawled, his voice low in warning, "or you will find out what it means to be mine."

"All bark but no bite," I mused.

His eyes flared silver again and my thighs clenched against my chair.

"Either take her on the table or go to your room," Cass snapped as she reentered the room, bearing a new platter of sausages. "The eggs are getting cold."

Rook snorted, entering behind Cass, taking his seat again and reaching for the fresh sausage as she placed it onto the table.

"Cowards," Lark muttered, scowling at them, clearly annoyed at having been interrupted.

I just smiled to myself and resumed eating my breakfast. Making the Bone Court prince squirm was a past time I could get used to.

But as my friends fell into a discussion of the best way in which to approach the heir to the Court of Dreams, my smile disappeared more and more. These were matters of diplomacy, of politics. I'd never much cared for politics in the mortal realm. I imagined they were only more complicated here. And now that I was bonded to this Karma's ex boyfriend, I couldn't see a way in which this went well for us. And if it didn't, if the Bone Court remained the only ones willing to stand against my mother when she sought to destroy the Divide, the separation would fall and the mortal realm with it. So I would work with Lark's ex. I would work with anyone I had to in order to win this war and save the mortal realm which I could never return to again.

"When do we leave?" I asked once they had all finished their meals and were locked in a discussion of court politics regarding the Court of Blessings.

"There's a party tonight," Rook explained, exchanging a glance with Lark.

So that had been why he had broached the subject last night. A party would be the perfect time to approach her. Enough witnesses that she wouldn't feel bombarded by all of us and a location on her terms where she felt comfortable.

"At Karma's?" Cass asked, her lips slanting to a frown.

Rook nodded, holding her gaze. After a moment, she straightened.

"Then I suppose I should find something stunning for Ren and I to wear tonight," she said, grinning my way like a fiend. "There's this incredible little dress shop over by—"

"Actually," Lark interrupted, "I had hoped to claim Ren's company for myself this afternoon. She has never seen the Court of Dreams. I was planning on walking her through some of the artists quarters. If she's interested, that is."

I beamed at him.

"Yes, I—" I started and then turned to Cass. "Although, I should help—"

"That's alright," she assured me with a smile. "I'm an expert when it comes to shopping. I'll make sure to get you something amazing."

"Oh, I can wear the one you left in my room this morning. It's really no trouble."

"Absolutely not. That's a common day dress. This is a party, Ren. You're going to look absolutely fabulous," she promised before turning to her brother. "Have her back by six."

"It's going to take you four hours to get ready?" Rook asked, raising a brow.

"It will take as long as it takes," Cass answered, cutting him a glare. "You males are always so impatient despite how thoroughly you always end up enjoying the results."

"I swear to have her back by six," Lark promised, standing up and striding toward me, holding out a hand.

I took it, letting him pull me to my feet and sweep me out of that house and into the morning sun beyond.

Chapter Nineteen

A Walk of Dreams

I wasn't sure what I had been expecting the Court of Dreams to look like but it wasn't this.

My first thought, when Lark and I exited Cass' house, leaving it nestled against lines of others in similar fashion behind us, was that we had stepped right back into the mortal plane, right into the bustling city I'd been raised in, spent most of my life in.

Modern skyscrapers towered overhead several streets away and, where we were, a busy street was strewn with restaurants and cafes and shops, all with outdoor seating, racks practically in the street. The intoxicating aroma of freshly baked bread wafted over to me on a breeze from the nearest cafe where fae of all varieties lounged on outdoor couches or at umbrella-covered tables, sipping coffee and tea and partaking in pastries and bagels. Females chattered as they sifted through the displays of brightly colored clothing on the racks outside of the shops, venturing inside for more. Murals, bright and vibrant, covered every available wall. On the sides of the cafe, on the fronts of the shops, curling up and around restaurant entryways. Each a commissioned piece, Lark told me, all to support local artists, all to remind the fae living here what this place is really about.

It was beautiful. Every mural a new emotion, every scent, every sight a new work of art. It was difficult not to stare, not to stop on every street corner and gawk at the beauty of it all. Most of the murals were coated in vibrant color, a living rainbow of paint come to life against otherwise lifeless brick. Some were darker, finding meaning in pain and shadow rather than light and life. All of them were meaningful, all of them were beautiful, and I couldn't help the way my eyes shone with tears as we turned the corner and I beheld a whole new street of them, a whole new row of different murals, different art to admire. It was overwhelming but in a good way.

"I thought you would like this," Lark said softly, nudging my shoulder with his own. I looked up into his eyes to find him smiling at me. I couldn't contain the grin I offered him in response.

"It's beautiful," I breathed.

"It's the best of us," he whispered back. "No matter how dark things get, no matter how troubled the times become, this art remains. These artists who create beauty from their fingertips have a safe haven here and, in return, they have turned the city itself into its own work of art, a culmination and collaboration of them as its meant to be. Their thoughts, their ideas, their very souls mark the walls of every establishment in this city. There is no where to hide from the truths they paint. They are everywhere, all around you. A reminder."

My lips stretched wider and he reached for my hand, lacing his fingers through mine.

"Come on," he said, giving me a gentle tug as he stepped forward, onto the street. "There's something I want to show you."

I followed him down the street, around a corner, and down another. I tried not to halt, tried not to pull him back as I lingered whenever a mural caught my eye, but I couldn't help myself and, the third time I stopped, he fell in beside me, letting me look for a long while before letting out a low chuckle.

"If we continue at this rate, I'll never have you back in time for Cass," he mused without a trace of annoyance in his tone.

I looked up at him and noticed the gentle smile on his lips, the way he squeezed my hand. I turned back to the mural I had been staring at.

"I can't help it," I confessed. "There's so many of them."

"We can spend the whole day looking at them if you want," he promised me. "And another day after that."

I met his gaze and knew he meant it. He would. For me.

"We have a party to get to," I said, squeezing his hand and smiling before stepping away from the mural so that he knew he could lead me on again. I left the rest unsaid. And a war to fight... I shuddered.

"Don't remind me," he groaned but he pulled me along all the same.

I didn't stop again, didn't pull him back to wait as I stared at another beautiful work of art, despite how many times I wanted to. His pace quickened as he led me onto one of the busier streets and then a sharp turn down an alley. We emerged on the other side, standing in front of a bar called The Evening Starr. My gaze snapped to his.

"Owned by a friend from back home," Lark explained with a shrug as if that explained the second Evening Starr location here in the Court of Dreams, a sister to the one back in the Bone Court, back by Gemini's home.

Then my gaze fell to the facade and my heart clenched in my chest. I stopped breathing as I stared at the mural which encompassed the entire facade of the bar. Pure, undiluted night. A black as thick and real as Ursa's obsidian knives. And amidst that void, constellations. Painted delicately with some material that seemed to glow, sparkling like the very stars themselves. Beneath them and woven throughout, galaxies, entire universes, a multiverse of planes overlapping and synchronizing in beautiful harmony. I picked them out quickly, the ones standing out, sharper than the others, the major constellations of the mortal plane. Taurus, Ursa, Canis, Cassiopeia. So real, so ethereal. I felt like I could stretch out a hand and find it shrouded in the cold darkness of space.

"Cass had it commissioned," he told me. "Shortly after she got here. She never told me why but I got the feeling that it means just as much to her as it does to me. And in this place... I think she just needed her own slice of home. Even here. Even after everything that had happened."

Home.

I swallowed, fighting the tears threatening to make their appearance.

"Thank you," I whispered. For showing me this, for bringing me here, for knowing how much I would love it. I didn't have to specify. Lark knew. He nodded once in recognition and fell quiet, both of us staring at the galaxy painted before us in wonder.

Some time later, when we had both broken from our reveries and turned back down the street to walk more casually now, without destination, just enjoying the sights and sounds of the city, Lark turned to me.

"You don't have to let Cass dress you up, you know," he told me, a bit uncomfortably. "I mean, if you'd rather choose your own dress for this evening, I know of a few dress shops nearby. I doubt they're as extravagant as the ones Cass has her eye on but—"

"I don't have any money."

My cheeks heated with the shame of the admission but it was true. I had nothing here, wasn't even sure what the currency system of the fae was. I knew Cass had dropped a few coins into my hands every time I went to the market but I hadn't learned much past how many of them sufficed for an apple. A dress would likely be a sum I hadn't ever encountered before. And I hadn't the slightest idea how to earn the money to pay him back.

Drawn out of my thoughts, I stopped, turning back to realize that he had halted some time ago. Lark stood in the middle of the street, watching me, his head cocked to the side as it always was when he couldn't quite puzzle me out.

"Money," he repeated, blowing a breath out. He ran a hand through his hair and shook his head. "You've been added to my accounts, Ren. You didn't know? Anywhere you wish to go in this city, anything you wish to purchase, it's yours. On me."

"I-you didn't have to—" my blush was deepening furiously. He grinned at it.

"The concept of money isn't quite the same here as the mortal realm, Ren," he told me, gently. Teaching. "It's more... fluid. Less meaningful. I think you'll find that a lot of shops here won't even charge you at all but if they do you give them my name."

"That's it?" I asked, blinking at him, stunned.

"My stunning generosity is widely known."

He shot me a wink and I snorted.

"I don't doubt it," I said.

"So the dress," he repeated.

"Whatever Cass selects will be fine. I'm sure she will be better at finding something than me anyway."

"Then lets spend the rest of the time we have showing you this city," he offered his arm and I took it, grinning broadly as we stepped back into the thoroughfare, making our way to another street full of murals.

***

I should have taken Lark up on his offer.

In a way, I had been right. Cass had picked out a beautiful dress, one of the most exquisite gowns I'd ever seen. But she had selected something that was pure Bone Court fashion which seemed to comprise of showing quite a bit of skin beneath very little material.

It was two pieces. The top was a sort of cropped black jacket made of a velvety material that shone like the night itself, tapered tightly to fall just inches below my breast, revealing much of my midriff. It was trimmed in real gold, the ends dangling gently against my skin. The long sleeves ended in thick golden cuffs that sharpened to a point at the base of my palm. The neckline was low cut, extremely so, so that only two inches of material connected between where the bodice dipped and where the top ended altogether. The neckline was trimmed with a thick ribbon of gold that plunged with my cleavage on both sides and connected at the top in a collar that rose up my neck. My breasts were large enough to stretch the hole exposing my chest so that nearly half of each breast was revealed.

The bottom was a simple skirt of that black as night fabric, trailing all the way past my ankles to spool on the floor below. The top began just above my navel and was cut into a v shape that seemed to point directly toward my sex. It covered my entire behind, mercifully, but sliced into two slits that went all the way to my thigh, leaving one too thin piece of black fabric in the front, just enough to cover my more sensitive areas while still revealing the entirety of my legs and the beginnings of my hips. And the shoes she had left for me, simple black stilettos with a strap above the ankle. Dangling gold earrings and a glittering circlet of gold that looked so much like I crown that I left it there entirely.

I was just putting in the earrings when a soft knock came at my door and I turned toward it.

"I'm going to kill you, Cass," I called out and heard her laughing on the other side.

"Let me see you first, at least," she replied.

Rolling my eyes, I crossed the room and pulled open the door.

Cass stood on the other side, dazzling in a scandalous gown of her own. Hers was short, no pretense of a skirt to add slits too. It was one full piece, the same black and gold as my own, clearly made by the same seamstress. She had a collar as well, hers made of the black material that crisscrossed in two thick straps, clasped together by a golden broach in the shape of a pointed rhombus. Her shoulders were exposed as those straps crossed over her chest and flowed down into a tight bodice that her breasts were practically bursting to escape. Her waist was cinched with a thick and elegant golden belt, carved into such intricate designs that I couldn't focus on a single one of them as they melded into one whole. A black chain slunk around her waist beneath the belt and below that, the dress flowed only slightly outward before vanishing entirely just past her hips, the tops of the skirt grazing her upper thighs as she walked into my room, the heels of the stilettos with gilded straps that crisscrossed all the way up her legs to stop just over her knee tapping against the wood as she did.

The most beautiful part of her outfit, however, was not the dress at all but the shawl she wore around her arms. Almost as though the gown's creator had saved all of the fabric on this dress for that stunning piece, what Cass' skirt lacked in fabric, the sweeping shawl made up for. It began in two thick bands of gold around her arms, decorated in the same way as that belt around her waist. Like sleeves made separately, the black as night fabric flowed from those bands and downward until sweeping outward in flares of wide sleeves, trimmed in gold and decorated with whirls and swirls of the same fabric. It caught the light and shimmered as she did a little twirl and gestured about.

"You look incredible," I told her and meant it.

"So do you," she told me, raising a brow. "Good enough to eat."

I snorted.

"You should have come for lunch with us," I said.

"I was busy giving my dressmaker exact specifications. She's used to my measurements. I think it threw her off to have a whole new set of them."

She eyed my legs that were longer and thinner than hers, my breasts that were bigger. I just turned back to my mirror and resumed putting in my earrings.

"Do you want help with your hair?" she asked and I nodded.

Cass was moving before I could say another word, pulling out the pins I'd already managed to secure, albeit poorly, and doing it herself. I'd never had this before, the feminine assistance, the preening and prepping with someone who actually cared about how I looked, how I felt about my own appearance. I'd grown up with an academic man in a dusty old university. I'd never really had a female friend before, had never really learned much about doing my hair or my makeup, had certainly never worn such stunning dresses or attended such lavish parties. It was nice, in part, to have her here. But something about it made me nervous as well. As though I wasn't meant to be wearing these dresses, to be looking like her. Beautiful, ethereal, like a goddess. A golden goddess of the night.

But when she was done, when she pulled away from me, having done both my hair and makeup in the fashion of her court, I couldn't help but smile at my reflection in the mirror. She grinned over my shoulders, giving them a squeeze before heading toward the door.

"I'm sure the guys are waiting, whenever you're ready," she said, already opening the door and stepping into the hall. "Try not to kill my brother when you come down those stairs, Ren."

"No promises," I told her and she blurted a laugh, warm and rich. Then she gave me a wink and left me alone in my room.

Chapter Twenty
A Party for the Ages

I heard Cass and Rook's laughter from the top of the stairs as I began my descent. I couldn't help the smile on my lips at the sound. My friends, in the place that I would someday consider to be my home, laughing with one another, all dressed up for a party, a night on the town. It was almost possible to forget, just for a moment, that it was Lark's ex's party and that we were going there to secure an important alliance in an upcoming war. Almost.

"There you are!" Rook cried out when I became visible halfway down the stairs. "You guys weren't kidding about the four hours thing, were you?"

Cass punched his shoulder and muttered something about it being impolite to point out how long it had taken a woman to get ready. But my eyes found Lark's and I didn't hear another word the others said.

His lips were parted slightly, his dark eyes set firmly on me, lowering slowly from my face, down my dress, to my heels tapping on the stairs as I descended them. That silver shine flashed in his eyes and I felt a rush of emotion pressing into me. I stilled on the last step, nearly overcome. He had lowered that wall, just a fraction, had allowed me to peek behind the veil enough to feel his adoration. It wasn't enough for him to tell me I was beautiful, he wanted me to feel how he did when he looked at me. My breath hitched and I stared at him in wonder.

"Like rippling night," he whispered when I finally approached, reaching out an arm for me to take. I did. As Cass took Rook's arm and led the way out the door, Lark lowered his voice as he leaned in and said, against the shell of my ear, "you have no idea what the sight of you in black does to me."

"Show me later," I answered with a wink.

A low chuckle rumbled in his throat as I pulled him forward and out into the night beyond.

The streets of the Court of Dreams were even busier than they'd been during the day. The cafes from breakfast had turned into venues for poetry readings, live music, karaoke. The shops had lit neon signs and were livelier than ever. Long lines stood outside of every bar. The very air here was electric, alive. It was a city, a true city, with a vibrant, beating heart. And I couldn't help but stare at it in awe yet again as my friends led me through the narrow streets and onto a much larger thoroughfare.

I kept expecting the buildings to become smaller, more spread out. I kept expecting to look up and find myself on the edge of the city, near the suburbs where large sprawling country homes would rest for the nobility. But instead, my friends led me into the heart of the city, right up to the door of a towering skyscraper. I couldn't stop myself from craning my neck toward the top as we stopped.

"Keep low profiles," Lark whispered in warning and my gaze snapped to him as he extricated his arm from mine and stepped away.

"Where are you going?" I asked, blinking at him.

"I'm dead, remember?"

I gaped at him.

"You aren't coming?" I asked.

"The dead don't attend parties where they might be recognized, I'm afraid. But I leave you in good hands. Your date for the evening," he announced, sliding sideways so that Rook could slide in, pumping his brows. I rolled my eyes.

"We're going to have a hell of a night, Ren," Rook promised with a mischievous grin, placing a hand on my lower back to guide me toward the door.

But I saw the way Lark's eyes snapped to the point of contact a moment before Rook realized what he'd done. He pulled away as if I'd bitten him just as Lark growled, "Touch her below the waist and I'll gut you."

"Loud and clear, boss," Rook said, eyes widening as he removed his hands from me entirely and, obviously unsure of what to do with them at all, folded them in front of him.

Cass looked over her shoulder at us, amused smile on her lips. But Lark was gone, vanished into the night like a shadow.

I looked ahead, at the enormous, elaborately decorated lobby that we were making our way into. There weren't many people milling about on the sofas that littered the space. They were either heading outside for some air or riding the elevator up the many stories to the top where Karma's party was being held. Or so I learned from Rook in hushed tones on our way up to the penthouse. I didn't say a word in response, just let my eyes scan the crowd, the decor, the art, taking it all in.

Not everyone here wore purple. Every color of the rainbow was visible both on the street and in the penthouse above. Reds, oranges, and purples were the most common but I saw blue, green, and yellow sprinkled throughout. No black though. No, that was just us.

A fae male in a crimson suit eyed me the moment the elevator doors opened and took a few steps as if taking the duty of welcoming us upon himself. But the moment he was within range, Rook wrapped his arm around my bare waist and pulled me close, leaning down to whisper against the shell of my ear.

"Stay close," he said in low warning.

Then he nipped my earlobe, grazing it suddenly with his teeth. My muscles went into shock, my posture turning rigid as he pulled away and smiled down at me. I just blinked up at him but noted that the male in the crimson suit had faded back into the crowd at the sight of his affection.

"Claiming me," I remarked with a scoff, blowing out a breath. "How very patriarchal of you."

"I lay no claim," he answered, grinning all the while. "Just doing my job."

I rolled my eyes.

"Call it a benefit," he murmured and I punched him playfully in the shoulder.

He laughed, holding up his hands in mock surrender.

"Bar," Cass said simply and all of our eyes shot to the bar on the other side of the room. It was surrounded by party goers in every color of the rainbow but only one of them wore purple. She sipped delicately on a straw sticking out of her fruity drink. Her dark hair fell over one shoulder as she sighed and frowned at the men on the opposite side of the bar, pushing each other around near what appeared to be a one of a kind vase.

"Karma?" I asked.

"Kismet. Her sister," Rook answered with a shake of his head and I might have imagined it but he seemed to be pulling me further into the crowd in the opposite direction.

"We'll split up," Cass said, tearing her eyes away from Kismet. "I'll check upstairs. You two scope it out down here."

I nodded. Cass turned and was up the flight of glass stairs before I could say another word.

"Want a drink?" Rook asked, spinning toward a servant passing by with a tray of drinks in his hand.

"Aren't we supposed to be looking for Karma?" I asked, raising a brow as he held a glass out to me, some unknown pink liquid sloshing around within it.

He shrugged.

"Nothing says we can't look and enjoy," he told me with a wink.

I just snorted, shaking my head, and turned back to where Kismet still sat forlornly at the bar.

"Shouldn't we ask her?" I cried over the increasingly loud music. "I mean, she's her sister, right? And this is her sister's party? Wouldn't she have a better idea than anyone where she might be?"

He followed my gaze to Kismet again and frowned.

"Be my guest," he replied but something had darkened his tone. "But you'll be asking her alone. I'm not going over there."

"What? Why not?" I asked, brow furrowed in confusion as I took a sip of the horribly fruity cocktail in my hands.

"Trust me when I say do not go there, Ren."

He took my hand and began to lead me through the party.

"What do you mean?" I hissed through my teeth as the bodies pressed in around me.

"Suffice it to say that Kismet is an interesting individual and I'd rather not go over there unless I have to."

"But why—"

"Rook!" someone cried out excitedly and I looked up to find that we had stumbled into a wall of men dressed in red and they seemed to know my date. "If it hasn't been nearly a century. Crazy running into you here. Where have you been?"

"In exile, remember?" another man in red pointed out with a grin.

"That's right, that's right, with that little dark prince of yours. Tell me, where is he tonight? He's always a lot of fun, that one."

Rook stared at them. So did I. They didn't know?

The song blasting from somewhere I couldn't fathom changed and suddenly the writhing bodies around us pulsed and shifted and I was separated from my date. I lunged, reaching for him, but it was too late and I was swept away with the crowd as Rook answered them with words I couldn't hear. I called out to him but it was pointless. So I let myself move with the rhythm of the crowd until I could escape it. Once I did, I found myself standing off to the side, near the bottom of the stairs where a long hallway led back to what appeared to be washrooms. I stood there for a moment, craning my neck over the crowd to see if I could spot even one of my friends.

"I love your dress," a melodic, feminine voice spoke firmly from my side. I turned to find an incredibly beautiful woman in a long, silk purple gown, slit at the thigh and plunging neckline, standing beside me. It glittered silver, shining in the light of the chandeliers as if made to do so. She held a glass of dark red liquid in her delicate hands and raised it to take a sip as she looked me over from head to toe. "They say purple is the new black but nothing can beat the original, eh?"

She raised a brow at my dress and my lips parted.

"Who are you here with?" she asked, curiously, cocking her head to the side.

"I-who?" I asked, uncertain if I'd heard her correctly.

Her soft pink lips turned upward in a smirk as she arched one perfectly manicured brow again and shifted so that her dark ringlet curls tumbled off of her shoulder and down her back.

"I have friends in the Bone Court," she cooed, clearly amused by my ineptitude. "Which of them brought you here tonight?"

"Rook," I blurted, remembering that he was my date.

That smile faltered immediately. Her posture straightened and she lowered her glass to her side.

"Where is he?" she spat. "That brute. I told him he wasn't permitted to attend another one of my parties for the next millennia!"

I blinked, caught off guard by her statement.

"There you are, Ren," Rook said from my side and I turned to find him standing next to me. I wasn't even sure when he had arrived. But he narrowed his glare at the woman beside me and snarled a greeting. "Karma."

"Rook," she snapped. "I thought I told you never to return to my court. In fact, I distinctly remembering your own king telling you never to return to any court."

"As it so happens, my exile seems to be over."

"Is it? Why are you here, though? Let me guess. Casseiopia?"

"Right here," Cass said from the steps behind us and Karma peered up to her.

When their eyes met, however, there was nothing but pure venom between them and when Cass spoke again, there was not a single trace of that radiant friendliness she had always spoken to me with.

"We need to talk, Karma."

Chapter Twenty-One

An Epitome of Strength

We followed Karma up the stairs and down the hall without a word. My companions seemed to know where we were going already, barely looking ahead as they passed door after door. She paused outside of the last door, pulled a key from a pocket in her elegant gown, and placed it into the lock. With a click, she was pushing through into a library on the other side.

It was, without a doubt, the most beautiful room I had ever seen. Built-in bookshelves made of a weathered white wood with gold inlay flowed from floor to high ceiling. Every available wall space was covered with an ornate painting or a delicate porcelain bust. The ceiling was open to the night sky and windows beyond the art revealed the shining lights of the city that stretched out far beneath them. It was breathtaking but not so much as the man sitting upon the lilac couch in the center of the room, one leg propped onto the other, smirk on his lips. Karma froze when she saw him as my friends and I filed in around her.

"Lark," she said, her voice completely devoid of emotion.

"Hello, Karma," Lark drawled as Cass draped herself over the armchair beside him and Rook settled in front of the window, arms crossed as he stared out at the city.

"I should have known you wouldn't stay dead."

His grin broadened as Rook snorted.

"You cried over him, admit it," Rook teased.

"I wouldn't waste the hydration," Karma spat and my muscles tensed, on edge.

Lark must have noticed because his eyes slid to me and he patted the cushion next to him softly, gently. I strode forward, holding my head high as I settled in next to him on the sofa. He pulled me closer, against the side of his body, sending a clear message. Claiming me, I thought, remembering what I had accused Rook of earlier that night. I refrained from rolling my eyes at the territorial act.

Karma's eyebrow arched as her gaze slid from Lark to me.

"What do you want?" she asked, crossing her arms and waiting.

"Why must I want something to come and say hello?" Lark queried, holding his hands up, innocently.

"Don't insult me. You wouldn't come back from the dead just for a social call. So what is it? What's happened?"

Her eyes raked over me once again as she settled herself on the other sofa, directly across from ours. She leaned back, crossing her legs and waiting.

"Ariadne is trying to start a war," he answered, his eyes cold, unforgiving.

Karma rolled her eyes and blew out a breath.

"Not this again," she muttered. "What is it with you and this woman? You cannot leave her alone. Tell me, how did going up against Ariadne Dawnpaw work out for you last time, Lark?"

"Fairly well, I'd say."

He dropped a hand to my knee then, running it up toward my bare thigh and Karma's eyes flew to me again as my breath hitched.

"No," she gasped. "Seren?"

I blinked, swallowing.

"This is unbelievable," she huffed. "You've got to have the worst Stockholm Syndrome of all time."

"Enough, Karma," Rook warned from where he stood. I looked to him. I'd hardly ever heard Rook lower his voice like that.

Karma just shook her head and sat back, crossing her arms again.

"Ren is here because she chooses to be," Lark assured her. "Because she escaped her mother's mind control after she managed to use it to control her magic and force her to use it against someone."

Karma's lips fell into a frown.

"Ariadne's mind control can control someone's magic too?" she asked, finally concerned.

"So you finally believe she can control minds?" Cass snapped from her spot on the arm chair. She was glaring at our hostess, tangible hatred piercing her gaze. "Because you were so very certain the last time we came to you that such a thing was impossible."

"I've come around," Karma answered breezily as if nothing that Cass said was of any importance. The dismissal only made my friend sink even further into her chair.

"Ren," Lark said my name encouragingly and I turned my gaze to Karma.

"She paralyzed me by taking over my brain, made me watch while she threatened people, hurt them, and then she held my mind and forced my power outward, directed at one of the only people in her court who had been kind to me," I told her, my voice clear, strong. "She made me hurt him. Badly."

Lark gave my knee a squeeze in encouragement and I found that it bolstered me somewhat.

"Where is Alban?" Karma asked, ignoring me, my pain, and turning back to Lark.

"Safe," Lark told her. "Hidden away from Ariadne who tried to steal his power for her own."

"I had heard someone claim he was sick. I didn't believe it."

"She nearly drained the very life from him trying to harness his magic."

"Is that how she's been doing it? The rifts?"

"You're aware of more than you let on, Karma."

"These parties aren't just an excuse to get drunk and dance until the sun comes up, Lark."

I looked between them, at the easy conversation, the familiar rhythm of banter, and got a sinking feeling in my gut.

"What does any of this have to do with me?" she asked then.

"She turned her daughter immortal," Lark said and Karma's lips parted in surprise for the first time at that. "Courtesy of some elixir Sophierial had been holding onto. The Court of Friends tried to abduct Ren in the middle of Bone Court territory. She ripped a hole in the Divide open right in the center of the Court of Wanderers, exposing our plane to the mortals on the other side. She launched an attack on my father, she's weaponized my sister. Any one of these could be considered an act of war. She's committed them all. And that's not to mention the crimes she committed before, the ones we're still ignoring today."

"You need allies."

"I need to send Ariadne a message."

"And what is that?"

"The Divide stands. The mortals stay mortal. She does not intervene, she does not lead, she does not enslave, mentally or otherwise."

"Slavery, you think that's what she's planning? To take the mortal realm for her own?"

"I think Ariadne Dawnpaw has a penchant for controlling mortals that I don't particularly care for."

"And for that, you want to start a war?"

"I'm not making a declaration. I'm merely making it clear that should she decide to start a war, truly start a war, she will expect the Court of Blood and Bone to stand with its minor court brethren against her."

"Her and the Court of Friends and the Court of Light and Life."

"Sophierial will not go to war. Her people have never fought. They enjoy their utopia. They won't risk it."

Karma hesitated here. Her lips parted as if she intended to say something then snapped closed again. She was obviously warring with herself about something. Eventually, she relented. She sighed and lowered her head.

"I didn't know Sophierial would ever actually use the elixir," Karma muttered, so quietly it was hard to hear. But, of course, fae hearing was spectacular. Lark leaned forward in an instant.

"You know something about the elixir?" he asked, surprise leaking through even his carefully crafted mask of indifference.

"Ariadne requested Sophierial's help in researching a way to make that mortal of hers stick around forever. Court of Life and all that. Sophierial had a theory but needed a healer to actually do the experimentation. No one in the Court of Blessings would ever agree to attempt such a thing so..."

"Kismet," Lark breathed, falling back beside me. "Kismet helped Sophierial create the elixir."

"It was only supposed to be used once! Then it was supposed to be locked away and forgotten forever."

"That isn't how discoveries like that work, Karma," Lark spat, annoyed. "No one was ever going to forget such a powerful tool. This makes so much more sense. Ariadne claimed the elixir was ancient, that it had been locked away in the Court of Life for a millennia. There was no way something like that would have remained secret so long. The possibilities alone—"

"I know," she snapped back. "I know that now. Looking back, it seems obvious but at the time it seemed a reasonable enough request and Kismet is always so sad, moping about the house. You should have seen how excited she was to be working on something of such magnitude. I thought it would help her."

"And now it has started a war."

"You don't know that. Two major courts and a minor. Even if you managed to convince we who remain–"

"All I'm asking, Karma, is that you take everything I've said to your father. Tell him what we know, what you know, about Ariadne. Give him the opportunity to do the right thing."

"The right thing as you see it."

She kept her arms crossed, her gaze narrowed.

"You're afraid," someone said and I was stunned when all eyes shifted to me and I found that I was the one who had spoken. Karma's glare narrowed to a point as if she wasn't sure whether or not looks could kill but she was willing to try it. It was too late, however. I'd already seen, already felt her fear. I already knew the true meaning behind her hesitation, her arguments. "You've kept this beautiful city functioning, unmarred by the cruelties of war or the harshness of broken politics, for centuries and the thought of risking it or the beauty you've helped thrive here, scares you. It's the only thing that scares you."

Her jaw slackened, her crossed arms falling only a fraction but it was enough. I'd gotten to her. I shifted forward, aware that the movement caused the black fabric of my dress to fall between my legs so that my leg beside Lark was revealed all the way to the bare skin of my hips. He noticed, gaze darting straight there, burning like a brand against my skin.

I felt the desire, mine and his, but pushed it aside and focused on the fear, on Karma's feelings, as they poured out of her without her knowledge.

"You would fight," I said, using the sensations of her emotions to predict her actions. "You would stand beside us and the others, would face down my mother and the destruction she threatens to bring, would risk your life to save this place, to preserve these people, this beauty. You would set aside yourself but not your court. Never your court."

Karma flinched, withdrawing within herself, or trying to. She stared at me as if trying to discern how I was doing this, where I was picking up the pieces of her fragmented heart and reading them as clearly as if they were etched into the wood between us.

"You are not weak, Karma," I said softly, pulling on that thread of her biggest doubt, her worst fear. Her lips parted in awe, eyes widening as I continued, gently. "Caring about something, loving something, is not weakness. Fighting for it with every breath in your lungs is the epitome of strength."

The room fell silent as I finished. Even Lark did not speak, his fingers now tracing lazy circles above my knee. He watched me for a moment longer before turning his gaze to Karma who was staring at me openly, wildly, her lips opening and closing as if trying to speak but unable to.

"We will protect this court with every weapon in our arsenal," Lark vowed in the silence, his firm tone so striking in the stunned quiet. "Join us and we will stand by your side as you stand by ours. And if this city falls to ruin, it will only be because the rest of them already have."

It appeared to take a great effort for Karma to pull her gaze from mine. When she finally did, it settled on Lark, on the promise he had made and the sincerity in the words still reverberating in the confined space.

"It won't be like it was before," she said then, her voice much softer, gentler, but still warning, still firm. "You'll tell me. The sacrifices you choose to make, the risks you take, you won't keep me in the dark."

"Any decision that impacts you or this court, I swear to you, will be revealed long before it is made."

She considered for a moment longer, a heartbeat, and then nodded.

It was done. I found it suddenly far easier to breathe as Lark stood and extended a hand, taking mine in his and pulling me up beside him. My skirt fell to cover my legs again and I smoothed out my sleeves as Rook and Cass joined us.

"Come to us when it's done," Lark told her, meaning the impending conversation between Karma and her father. "You know where to find us."

Karma's eyes slid to Cass but the latter just disappeared without a word, taking Rook's hand and dragging him along with her, obviously eager to be out of this female's home the moment she was able. Karma frowned but nodded her agreement.

"Goodbye, Lark," she said simply and turned back for the door which led out of the study and back to the penthouse where the party was in full swing.

The moment she was gone, the lock clicked back into place behind her, Lark turned to me. When his eyes met mine, they burned with a familiar silver fire.

"You did incredible," he breathed against my lips, already leaning toward me. "You were made for this."

Then he kissed me, raw and warm and real. And as his lips pressed against mine, his warmth leeching into me, caressing me, wrapping me in their warm cocoon, I allowed myself to melt into him. I placed a hand on his chest and leaned in, my body brushing his. A perfect fit. I sighed pleasantly into his mouth and his arms tightened around me.

Home. This was home.

And then the darkness closed in and we were spinning away through light and color and sweet, sinister shadows.

Chapter Twenty-Two
A Word Between Friends

"Checkmate."

Rook cursed, slamming a fist down on the chessboard between us so that the pieces went scattering. I raised a brow, already picking up the fallen pieces and returning them to their proper spaces.

"You said you played this growing up," I reminded him, my tone light, teasing. "How are you still so bad at this?"

"Easy," Cass said from where she lounged on the love seat in the sitting room, book open in her hands. "He's stupid."

Rook turned to glare at her, snarling.

"Again," he spat and I busied myself with placing the chess pieces back in their starting positions as Cass and Rook stuck their tongues out at one another.

Lark had left early that morning, before I had even awakened, because he had been summoned away to meet with Karma and her father. Apparently, the heiress of the Court of Dreams had wasted no time in speaking with her father, as we had requested, and he had wanted to talk to Lark himself. I hadn't seen him since he shadow stepped us right back into the foyer of this house. We had all been exhausted and all retired to our individual rooms for the evening. I thought, perhaps, Lark might have had other ideas but it was clear that Cass had some things she wanted to say to him in private, likely about Karma and whatever bad blood there clearly was between them. So Lark had watched me walk up those stairs, my bare legs on display through the slits of my gown, his dark eyes thick with desire before he was forced to turn away and speak lowly to his sister.

I wondered what might have happened if Cass hadn't intervened and felt equal parts grateful and frustrated. Whatever it was between Lark and I had grown too great to be ignored. I felt it. He felt it. We'd spoken of it. We'd made the decision to act upon it. But organizing a war, assessing and creating alliances, preparing for the moves of our opponents took up more of our time than we anticipated and I was beginning to wonder if this bond and these feelings might have to wait until the war was over, until we had time for ourselves, for each other.

So I'd been jealous when Cass had informed me this morning that Lark had made time in his busy schedule for his ex girlfriend. That wasn't fair of me. He wasn't seeing her for his own personal interests. She was the heiress of the Court of Dreams, she was the link to our best chance of an alliance. And I was being petty. So I'd found Rook as soon as he awakened and brought the chess board out from where Cass had placed it in storage, returning to old distractions, old games. If Rook had known why I'd suddenly wanted to play having only heard him mention it once in passing, he hadn't led on, and had graciously sat with me through three games now.

Though that was starting to be more because of his determination to finally beat me than it was about the game itself.

We were halfway through the fourth game, after three straight losses for Rook, when the door opened and closed in the foyer and I was temporarily distracted as Rook considered his next move.

"Not the knight," I said, pulling my attention back to the game as Rook reached for the aforementioned piece. "Why would you move the knight? My bishop is right there."

"Maybe if I had some quiet I could think," Rook hissed in response.

"Sure, that's what's stopping you," Cass huffed and I smiled.

Rook gave a low growl as footsteps sounded on the cherry wood floor. Lark appeared in the threshold of the sitting room, smiling down to where Rook and I sat at the chess board.

"This again?" he asked with a grin.

"I will beat this female," Rook hissed his vow and Lark snorted.

"Likely not."

"I'll have you know—"

But it turned out we wouldn't know. Because at that exact moment, someone knocked on the door.

Every gaze in the room snapped to the foyer.

"Gemini?" Rook asked, turning from the foyer to Lark.

"She's the only other one who knows we're here," Lark answered.

"Ursa—" Cass started, sitting up on the couch in alarm.

"Ursa wouldn't knock," Lark replied and then whirled toward the foyer again.

We all rose in unison and followed after him. The foyer filled with the sounds of footsteps as we all padded across the wood and toward the front door. Before I could get a step past the stairs, Rook positioned himself protectively in front of Cass and I and our steps faltered. Lark had reached the door. He turned back once more to look at all of us before flinging it open.

My jaw dropped at the sight that awaited us.

Irim, pale and thin and shaking, was half collapsed in the doorway. He reached out and gripped Lark's lapel to keep from falling fully and Rook surged forward.

"Stop!" I cried before he could properly punish my cousin for touching his prince.

Rook hesitated briefly but it was enough. I pushed through the protective wall he had made himself into and knelt before my cousin, pulling his hands from Lark's jacket and into my own. He sank to his knees in front of me, tears streaming down his cheeks. We gazed into one another's eyes for a moment, so many words left unsaid. My apologies, his forgiveness. Then he wrapped his arms around me and tucked his face into my hair.

"Ren," Lark spoke gently and I looked up to him, tears falling from my own eyes as well.

"Don't hurt him," I choked out.

Lark watched me for a moment, thoughtful, then turned to Rook and nodded. The fae warrior stepped away. Enough for me to help Irim to his feet and lead him inside, into the foyer.

"He's Pride Court, Ren," Lark reminded me, still gently, but with an undertone of warning.

I looked back at him over my shoulder as I led Irim forward into a chair that Cass had summoned from the sitting room.

"He saved me, Lark," I told him.

Lark blinked, looking from me to my cousin and assessing the situation. For a brief, terrifying moment, I thought he might send my cousin right back out on the street. Or worse. But Cass intervened.

"My house," she said, stepping between us. "My rules."

She held Lark's glare, raising her brow in challenge, and then stepped forward when he finally relented, backing up a step to give us space.

"I'm sorry," I told Irim, taking his face in my hands and pulling his gaze to mine. My hands were shaking. I wondered when that had started. "I'm so, so sorry."

Without a word, tears still falling freely down his cheeks, with trembling fingers of his own, he gripped my hand in his and turned it, pressing my palm against his cheek. It was the forgiveness I needed, the exoneration I hadn't known would mean so much to me.

"What happened?" I asked softly.

"How did you find us?" Lark added, far more firmer than I.

Irim's gaze swept up to the Bone Court prince. His lips pulled down into a frown.

"Gemini," he said simply. His voice was rough and his eyes darkened as he stared back at my bonded.

Lark shook his head, muscle in his jaw twitching, and turned his gaze to Cass. He didn't need to say a word. She just gave a brief nod and disappeared, undoubtedly to fetch her aunt who would likely be getting the scolding of her life from her nephew.

"You went to Gemini?" I asked my cousin, stunned that he would think to do such a thing. He glanced up at Lark again and they both sat there, glaring at one another for a minute. I sighed, standing and wiping the tears from my eyes with the back of my hand. "Is anyone going to explain what all this bad blood between the two of you is?"

"He's Pride Court," Lark repeated himself as if that was explanation enough.

"No," I said, shaking my head. "That's not it. It isn't like you to despise someone so much just because of the court they belong to. I know something happened between you. What was it?"

They stood there quietly for another moment, still glaring at one another.

"They killed my father," Irim said finally, his voice so low I nearly missed it. My gaze shot to him. That couldn't be right.

"No," I said, shaking my head. "I saw your father die, Irim. It was Pride Court soldiers that did it, not—"

"Your father threatened a king," Lark reminded him with a tone of formality, interrupting me in my confusion.

"He was angry," Irim snapped. "It wasn't a real threat. He never would have gone through with it. Your father did not have to report his actions to Ariadne. Perseus knew what she would do."

"My father made the decision he thought best. Your father was a citizen of the Pride Court at the time. My father had no jurisdiction over him and could not offer what he demanded."

Irim snarled, actually snarled, at Lark. He leaned forward in his seat so that I had to raise a hand and place it on his chest to keep him seated. At the hatred on my cousins face and my nearness to him, Rook stepped tactically forward, his fingers drumming against the blade at his side.

"Don't allow history to repeat itself, Irim," Lark warned, his voice nearly a growl as his eyes shot to my hand pressed against Irim's chest. "My bonded seems to have developed a fondness for you."

His words had the desired effect. Irim pulled away from me as if I'd burned him, eyes widening more than I'd ever seen before. He looked from me to Lark and back again as I stood, heaving a sigh and rolling my eyes.

"So territorial," I chided Lark but he only gave me a wolfish grin as I took a step toward him.

"You-you're bonded," Irim repeated in shock. "With him?"

"I am," I told him with a nod.

"That's why you wanted to return so badly. That's why you were so... it all makes sense now. That separation, being so far apart from him, it must have been—"

"Agonizing," Lark finished and I couldn't help but go to him, let him wrap his arm around my waist and pull me close, at the truth he had just exposed.

"I'm so sorry, Seren," Irim said then and I thought he might be telling the truth. "I didn't know."

"How could you?" I replied with a shrug. "We don't make a habit of advertising it."

Irim nodded slowly but I could see that he was still trying to understand, still trying to put the pieces together.

"Why are you here, Irim?" I asked then, making my tone as gentle as I could. It was clear that he had gone straight to Gemini from my mother's court in order to find us. I wanted to know why.

"I want to help," he said then and his snarl turned feral. "Whatever you're doing to her, whatever you're planning, I want to help."

I knew what he was remembering. How it felt to have your mind invaded, to find yourself on your knees and unable to rise, to watch as a dozen soldiers did not intervene while your friend was turned into a weapon to use against you, to be stripped bare, the worst events of your life playing over in your head while you were forced to watch them from somewhere far away. I had to close my eyes at the memory myself.

"Why?" Lark asked. "Why should we believe you would turn against your court when you never have before?"

Irim's gaze slid to me and I forced myself to meet it.

"You didn't tell them?" he asked, lips parted in surprise.

"Not the details," I confessed. "I was... coming to terms with it myself."

Jaw set in grim determination, Irim turned his attention to Lark and Rook.

"She found us going to the library together. And for that crime and whatever idiocy she'd cooked up in that certifiably insane paranoid mind of hers, she accused us of treachery, of scheming against her. So she held our minds. She forced me to my knees and used Seren against me. First her wind, then her.... other capabilities. I couldn't fight back and she knew I wouldn't, even if I could. I wouldn't hurt you."

He was looking at me now and I felt the tears forming again.

"I saw the tears streaming down your face," he said then, his voice going quiet. "I tried to tell you I understood, that I knew it wasn't you, but I couldn't."

I nodded because I couldn't say anything more. When I looked at Rook, that strong, protective fae warrior, I saw the shock and disgust plain on his face. Lark was a burning mass of simmering rage beside me. I just took a deep breath and stepped forward. I placed a hand on Irim's shoulders and we stood like that for a minute before I leaned in and embraced him.

"What a nice little family reunion," a familiar voice intoned and I stepped back to see that Cass had returned, Gemini Morningstar in tow. The older fae was watching Irim and I with a catlike grin on her lips.

"Aunt," Lark growled. "A word."

Then that dark fae prince stormed from the room, leaving his ancient aunt with no choice but to follow after him.

Chapter Twenty-Three
A Second Chance

Cass and I got Irim settled into his room on the second level, pretending all the while that we couldn't hear Lark angrily lecturing his aunt about all that she had risked in exposing our location to an heir of the Court of Peace and Pride from below. We also took great pains to ignore the silent, hulking presence of Rook as he took up his position in the threshold, refusing to leave Cass and I alone with the rival male for even a moment. His lips were set in a grim frown as his shrewd eyes kept watch from the doorway, arms folded across his chest, and legs bent casually as if he were just another fixture of the house itself. The only noise he made was a single grunt once when Cass nearly pushed him over trying to get past him in the threshold with a massive comforter set. She grumbled an order to get out of her way and then tossed me one side of the blankets so that I could assist in making the bed.

Irim was quiet, for his part, while Cass went through the list of rules that she claimed every guest in her home was expected to follow. I didn't mention that it was the first I was hearing of them.

"He's here, isn't he?" Irim asked from where he was leaning against the dresser across the room just as Cass got done explaining the meal schedules. "Alban."

Cass and I faltered in our bed making, exchanging a glance.

"Can I see him?" Irim asked, taking a breath as he stood to his feet.

"I don't think that—" Cass started.

"He's my grandfather."

Cass' gaze flicked to me.

"I'll take you to him," I said then, turning and taking Irim gently by the arm. I gave him a warm smile, hoping to put him at ease. He had hardly relaxed a single muscle since he had stepped into this home and been surrounded by his former enemy.

We stepped out into the hall, bypassing a glowering Rook on the way. The warrior took a step forward to follow but halted when I cast him a warning glare over my shoulder.

"I'm afraid he won't be very... talkative," I warned him as we strode down the hall for the room at the end, the one in which I knew my ancient grandfather would be laying unconscious.

I pushed the door open with a toe and waited as Irim strode inside, staring down at our ailing grandfather, so frail and thin, so unlike the warrior of legend, so unlike the man he had known before. I could tell, from the look on his face, that it unnerved him greatly to see such a powerful man brought so low.

"He's been like this since Gemini broke him out of her court," I said.

Irim did not turn to face me. He kept his grave face on our grandfather.

"So it's true," he said, his voice barely a whisper. "I hadn't believed it. I didn't want to think it could be possible. But she really... drained the magic out of him. She captured his power in that accursed amulet and wore it right under our very noses."

I said nothing. I just stood behind him, letting him come to terms with the state of the man in front of us.

"I should have known," he bellowed then, pounding his fists into the side of the enormous four poster bed.

Rook was at my side in an instant, blade drawn at the raised tone of the Peace Court Prince. But Irim was no threat to us. He was bowed and broken, bent over his grandfather's bed, body shaking in ragged sobs. I reached up to Rook's blade and pushed it slowly down. Rook met my gaze and understood, dropping the dagger to his side but not sheathing it.

Then footsteps were sounding down the hall and suddenly Lark and Cass were behind me, Gemini pushing through to my cousin beyond. She placed a comforting hand on his back and pulled him up straight.

"Come then, boy," she told him, her voice gentler than I'd ever heard it before. "Let's get you settled in."

Irim kept his head down, tears streaming down his pale cheeks, as he let the Morningstar matron lead him out of his grandfather's room and back down the hall to the one that now belonged to him.

"How was Karma?" Cass asked once Gemini and Irim had entered his room, closing the door behind them.

My eyes snapped to Lark, remembering where he had been this morning and how we hadn't gotten to hear about it since Irim had arrived and caused such a commotion. Lark turned down the hall, toward where Irim had disappeared, and then jerked his head toward the stairs. Without a word, we all followed after him down the stairs and into the sitting room where we'd been before. Cass took her seat in front of the fire, still roaring in the grate. The rest of us remained standing.

"Her father has his concerns," Lark said then. "Lord Kabir always does. But he's willing to send us resources while we make our plans and if we can get a few of the other minor lords to join us, he will as well."

"How very brave of him," Cass drawled, unimpressed.

"It's the best we can hope for at this stage. It isn't easy news to deliver. Telling a leader that they're joining a war in which they'd be up against two of the major courts and at least one of the minor."

Cass and Rook frowned, exchanging a glance.

"What are we going to do about the Pride Court Prince?" Rook asked then, turning his attention back to Lark.

Cass frowned.

"Nothing," I said. "We aren't going to do anything about him. He's here, as our guest, as Cass' guest. He's already told you that he wants to see my mother pay for what she's done. He told you what she did to him, to us. What more do you need?"

I could see that it practically physically pained Lark to argue with me about this. I could see how much it pained him to know what my mother had made me do to my cousin, made us both endure, and how I hadn't quite forgiven myself for it despite not having been totally at fault. Still, he opened his mouth to answer me.

"He has every reason to hate us," he spoke, his voice low.

"Why?" I asked. "What really happened with his father? Why did he go to Perseus?"

Lark glanced to his sister and I could have sworn Cass gave an almost imperceptible shake of her head.

"He should tell you," Lark breathed a moment later. "Irim should tell you himself when he's ready. The point is what's done is done and we cannot ignore the bad blood between us. Not when he's staying in the same house. I'll ward the rooms tonight."

"Lark," I started. "I'm trying to make him feel welcome. If you shield him away from us—"

"I'm sorry, Ren, but this is nonnegotiable. I won't risk anyone's safety. Not until he's proven he can be trusted."

I started to argue again but my lips snapped shut at the warning in Lark's eyes. He wouldn't budge on this. And, if I was being honest, it was a compromise I could live with.

"I'm leaving," Gemini spoke suddenly from the doorway and we all looked up to find her standing there, frowning. I wondered how much she had heard, how long she had been standing there, even as Lark crossed his arms and narrowed his gaze. He wasn't done being angry with her then. And she seemed to be in a bad mood herself seeing as she simply turned on her heel and stalked away without so much as a goodbye.

"Gemini," I said her name and hurried after her. I hadn't seen her since that day in the throne room and there was something I wanted to say to her before she vanished and I wasn't sure when I would get the chance again.

She stopped suddenly, frowning as she waited for me to catch up. I didn't hesitate as I threw my arms around her. She tensed, every muscle going perfectly rigid, as I embraced her.

"Thank you for getting him out," I whispered and she relaxed slightly, remembering that command I had given her the last time we had seen one another, my final request. Find my grandfather. Get him out of here. She had. And I would be forever in her debt for doing so.

Her jaw tensed as we separated but she gave a curt nod and then strode to the front door, wrenching it open and vanishing into the streets beyond. I took a deep breath, letting my chest expand and then deflate.

"I told you we'd find a way," a familiar voice said from behind me and I was already chuckling when I turned around to find Rook leaning against the wall beside the stairs, a grin on his face.

"You didn't find anything," I reminded him.

"I didn't say how we'd get you back," he told me with a wink, throwing an arm over my shoulder as he pulled me back toward the sitting room with the others.

I was laughing as we crossed the threshold but that laughter ceased when a glowing piece of paper popped into existence right in front of Lark's face. He reached forward with the arm that had been draped comfortably over the couch and plucked the missive from the air, eyes scanning the page as he pulled it toward him.

"Well?" Rook asked, expectantly.

I could have sworn Lark loosed a breath as he turned. The relief on his face was clear as he faced the rest of us.

"Pack some bags and get some rest," he ordered. "We're leaving for the Court of Scholars in the morning."

PART THREE
HARBINGER

Chapter Twenty-Four
A City of Mist

I awoke to a knock on my door the next morning. I stood, stretching, and padded across the plush dark carpet in my black silk nightgown. I opened the door a moment later to find a very put out looking Cass. She was grumbling under her breath as she pushed into my room and I closed the door behind her.

"I couldn't leave these for you because of Lark's ridiculous wards," she said, handing me a folded outfit.

I took it from her, brow furrowed, and set it on the dresser as I turned back to face her.

"You couldn't get into my room?" I asked, stunned that he would go to such lengths.

"No one can get into your room unless you open the door for them, that's the ward he placed on your room. And only on your room."

Her eyes met mine and I understood. She would have had no issue getting in to see Rook or my cousin or even Lark himself but he had placed more security measures on my room than anyone else's.

"Whatever he's done recognizes fashion as a threat," she grumbled, gesturing toward the clothes she had brought me. I snorted at that, amused by the idea, and reached down to touch the soft black fabric. She watched the motion. "Comfortable and airy but befitting your position."

I nodded slowly, turning toward her.

"Thank you," I said. "For all of this. For helping me feel... at home here. And for your friendship. Even when I turned you away. I don't-I'm not sure I deserve it. Deserve you."

Cass gave me a smile and stepped forward. She wrapped her arms around me and pulled me in close.

"I've always wanted a sister," Cass whispered.

I knew better than to point out that she already had one as we separated, her eyes shining with unshed tears as she stepped away from me.

"My position," I repeated slowly as we separated. I stared down at the black outfit in my hands. "I suppose when I show up at the Court of Scholars wearing black, everyone will know what side I've chosen."

Cass frowned, looking down at the fabric as well.

"That's the idea," she told me, her voice soft. "But if you would rather wear gray—"

"No," I told her. "It's the right thing. I belong in black. I belong with you. But I'm the heir to the Court of Peace and Price so I'm afraid..."

"They'll see you as a traitor?"

I nodded.

"Then we will have to ensure they understand that Ariadne is the traitor here. Not you," she said and I met her eyes again, allowing my gratitude to shine through my expression.

She smiled, reaching out to grasp my arm and squeezing. Then she turned and left me standing in the center of my room, new outfit in hand. Once she was gone, I unfolded the fabric and slid myself into it. Comfortable and airy was a good way to put it. It was a single piece, a jumpsuit, with wide flaring pants and a tight top with a crisscrossed halter neck. A band of silver slimmed my waist and thick bangles adorned my wrists. Earrings and necklace were included. Cass loved nothing more than to accessorize.

When I was ready, I exited my room, feeling the thick, suffocating magic of the wards dissipate as I left them behind. I headed down the stairs to join the others where I could already hear them gathering in the foyer. I paused on the second to last step when I saw a familiar face standing amongst them.

"Gemini," I said in greeting, smiling at the woman with wild gray hair and challenging eyes.

She looked up and her mouth ticked upward in a brief smile before she resumed her brooding.

"Seren," she answered with a nod.

"What are you doing here?"

She exchanged a glance with Lark and the look in her eyes made me remember what she had said about fearing her nephew so long ago. It felt like a lifetime ago now. I looked between them, waiting for one of them to decide to explain whatever was going on to me.

"Aunt Gem is staying here while we're gone to look after your grandfather," Lark explained and I started to argue that the nurse could look after him well enough herself but then Lark's eyes slid pointedly to Irim who was standing nearby, talking to Rook, and I understood.

Despite my assurances that Irim could be trusted, he wasn't willing to leave him alone with the frail old man. I might have been upset if it weren't for the obvious logic of the plan. Irim had shown loyalty to me during the time of my imprisonment with my mother. He had become a true friend for me, helping me through one of the darkest times of my life, but he was a member of the Court of Peace and Pride all the same, and one in line for the throne himself. He couldn't be trusted alone in a house with the incapacitated current king of his home court. Though it sickened me to even admit that it was a possibility, I couldn't fault Lark for wanting someone he could trust around just in case. So I didn't argue.

In fact, I didn't say a word as I strode forward to say goodbye to Irim before joining Lark where he stood in the center of the foyer. I cast a glance in Gemini's direction along the way and she gave me a small, almost imperceptible nod as if to say she could watch after my cousin in my absence. Unable to express the gratitude I felt for her in that moment, I could only nod in reply and then reach for my bonded.

The moment my hand grasped his forearm the world blinked away around us. My chest collapsed and then expanded. My vision dimmed and then brightened. My limbs went numb and then ached. But I was getting used to it all now. I even remained standing and kept my breakfast in tact and inside. Lark patted my arm as the world stopped spinning, a feeling of pride radiating from him along with the effort. I smiled up at him.

Then I caught a glimpse of the world around us and forgot to breathe momentarily.

We stood on top of a lushly forested mountain gazing down at a crystal blue lake below, so transparent that I could see the brightly colored schools of fish swimming just beneath the surface. The mountains ended abruptly all around it, rocky outcroppings jutting out to brush the surface in cliffs so high no mortal would dare leap from them. Waterfalls rose up across from us, enormous, glistening torrents arcing beautifully over the rock and to the lake below, creating misty plumes that rose halfway to the intricately carved white stone bridge above. The bridge itself was a city, so long and so wide that several circular towers and other buildings, all with roofs the color of the bright blue sky above, were built into its sides, creating a bustling city all along the walk from the mountain we stood upon to the mountain across the lake where the true Court of Scholars was.

The entire mountain across the lake was covered by an enormous, towering castle that stretched so high to the sky that its uppermost tips could not be seen in the glare of the sun. It was made of the same pristine white stone and sky blue roofs, stained glass windows depicting various species of birds, mammals, and reptiles filled the entirety of the lower floors. Upper floors had simple openings in the walls where beautiful winged creatures of all shapes and sizes were coming and going constantly. Aviaries, I realized, and messengers as well.

"I never get tired of seeing the look on your face when we bring you to a new court," Rook said with a grin and I turned to find them all smiling at me.

Blushing deeply, I turned away, cheeks burning even hotter at the warm chuckle emanating from my bonded.

A moment later, we were walking. Even high up on these cliffs, the cool mist from where the waterfall crashed into the lake below permeated the air, coating us all with a thin sheen of moisture as we stepped through the trees to a paved road beyond. White and gray stones had been cobbled together to form a street that ran far in either direction and widened past the gate that marked the entrance to the enormous city-bridge to the east.

"This road runs all the way through to the Court of Friends in the North and the Court of Dreams in the South," Lark was explaining as we strode along the path.

It was surprisingly even for how oddly shaped and various the stones that comprised it were.

"It wasn't like this in the Court of Dreams," I replied, staring down in awe of the remarkably flat stones.

"Paving science owned by the Court of Scholars," he replied, lowering his voice as we crossed through the massive white stone gates under the watchful eye of a pair of blue uniformed guards. "You'll find that this court is not as open to a free exchange of knowledge as they claim to be."

I turned to him, raising a brow.

"These nerds and their patents," Rook grumbled from behind me.

"Patents," I repeated, stunned by the mention of such a mundane mortal legal activity. "Are you serious?"

"Geniuses tend to waste a lot of time ensuring other people recognize their genius," Cass intoned from behind us where she and Rook had dropped back at the narrowing of the gate. "That's hard to accomplish when half a dozen scholars are claiming they made your discovery first."

I couldn't help but smile at the academic competition, a friendly reminder of home. But then I remembered the cost of my immortal life being that I could never again set foot in that home and my smile dimmed noticeably. At my side, Lark frowned but I shook my head and made a concentrated effort to smile again, if only for his benefit.

I looked ahead to the shining towers and busy thoroughfare. People ran to and fro, some wearing varying shades of unobtrusive blues, some in softer beige tones. A merchant haggled with a man in wide legged pants and a shirt with billowing sleeves. A woman pulled her child away from a colorful bird, her sky blue dress flapping around her legs in the breeze. An elderly woman leaned against her cane, smiling serenely from an open doorway as we passed. I couldn't help but smile back.

"They seem friendly," I remarked under my breath as we passed beneath another large tower on our way toward the end of the bridge.

"The Bone Court isn't as hated here as we are elsewhere," Lark replied. "Intelligence often recognizes brutality as a necessary means to an end. We make the decisions no one else wants to and they give us some deference in return."

"So that's why we've come here then? You think you can convince them that a war with my mother is inevitable and our victory is a necessary means to an end?"

He nodded.

"It won't be easy though," he told me, lips pulled down in a frown. "The Court of Scholars has always liked the Dawnpaws. Your... cerebral powers strike a kinship with them."

I nodded, considering that as we passed beneath yet another tower. My mother's powers were cerebral. Mine seemed to have far more to do with the heart than the head. Though, I supposed, that was just a matter of phrasing. Emotions came from the mind as surely as thoughts and intentions did. In fact, perhaps even more so as emotions were the result of proven chemical imbalances while thoughts were randomly fired synapses we still didn't truly understand. Yes, that was the scholarly way of looking at it. That was the way this court would look at it and the line of thought I should adopt as well. I was a scholar. Before, I had been a foremost professor at a prestigious university. If there was anywhere in this plane that I could find like-minded individuals it would be here. I was one of them. I would show them that.

"Canis Morningstar?" someone suddenly shouted from nearby.

My group came to a halt and turned to find a woman with neat, short cropped brown hair and wired spectacles stepping forward from a fruit vendor she had been perusing. She wore a royal blue gown embroidered with silver filigree at the sleeves and hem as well as a mesh shopping bag around her wrist that already held several apples, peaches, and a box of mixed berries. She smiled warmly but her bright eyes held ancient depths.

"Phoebe Hollyspeck," Lark drawled as he turned, lips spreading into an easy grin. "A pleasure."

"It's true then. There's to be a war?"

Someone behind her gasped. Several people at the fruit stand began murmuring to one another, wide-eyed. The vendor rushed to calm his patrons while this Phoebe Hollyspeck just planted one hand on her hips and watched Lark, eyebrow raised.

"No sense in lying to me, boy. I'm no fool," she spoke and I could have sworn I heard Gemini's voice when she did, the two of them seemed so much alike. "There's no other reason for one, no two, of the Bone Court's royal family to be visiting my city. You lot do love your wars."

"I hope you aren't referring to the war we all fought thousands of years ago," he replied. "That would be a foolish comparison. And if there's one thing we all know you are not, Phoebe Hollyspeck, it's foolish."

I tensed at the direction the conversation was going, at the condescending and downright insulting tone Lark had used and the way Phoebe Hollyspeck's gaze seemed to narrow further than I ever thought possible in return. I almost reached for my bonded, tugged gently on his sleeve or smacked him across the face, something to remind him that we were guests here, trying to convince them to fight on our side. It wouldn't do well to insult them in their own city. But then Phoebe Hollyspeck's lips spread into a wry grin and she chuckled. I just stared at her, blinking incomprehensibly.

"I've always liked you Canis," she said, turning away and striding up the street. "Come on then. I'll take you to my successor."

Chapter Twenty-Five
An Invocation

The Court of Scholars had an elected leader much like my country had in the mortal plane. But while theirs was elected for their skill, acumen, and intelligence, ours was elected for... well, I wasn't certain but it definitely wasn't any those things.

Phoebe Hollyspeck, who I quickly learned via whispered explanation from Cass was this court's previous President, lead us right up to the palace gates, guards barely even glancing her way as she walked right up and knocked on the front door. Servants and advisors alike greeted her with open arms and did not dare question her presence as she strode through the halls with the air of one who was very much used to commanding them.

"Ah Phoebe. How lovely it is to see you again. Our botanical efforts towards the seeds you brought us before have not yet taken root but, if you wish to visit the greenhouse anyway, you may..."

The beaming man in a fitted blue tunic trailed off at the sight of our retinue. His eyes darted from Phoebe Hollyspeck to Lark, then Cass, then

Rook, before landing, finally, on me. He stiffened noticeably and, though his friendly smile remained firmly affixed to his face, it was a poor imitation of the more genuine expression he'd worn when he believed Phoebe to be his lone visitor. Now, his ice blue gaze hardened, his posture tensed, bronze hair shining in the sunlight streaming in from the unfathomably tall windows as he turned away from them to face us fully.

"Bone Court," he stated. "And the escaped Daughter of Pride. To what do I owe such an illustrious visit?"

Too calmly, he crossed the room and began to pour some tea. He did not order Phoebe away and the way she set herself up leaning against a nearby wall, arms crossed and shrewd gaze narrowed, told me she had no intention of leaving even if he did.

I glanced nervously toward Lark who stepped forward confidently as if completely unbothered by the unexpected audience.

"Lord Falcondew, I come to you in peace," Lark began.

"For now," Phoebe muttered from where she stood and Cass shot her a glare that had her turning away, lips tightening.

"You come to me to request my aid in establishing your floundering coalition," the man in the blue tunic, Lord Falcondew, snapped. It wasn't harsh, per say, but merely impatient. It reminded me of the way other professors would speak to a student when they wished for them to quit dancing around the point and strike to the heart of the matter. "Ariadne means to wage war on the mortal realm and you plan to stand against her, alone if you must, alone as you've always been Canis Morningstar."

"It doesn't have to be that way."

"I fear it might."

Cold dread snaked its way around my heart as the man set the tea kettle down with a sigh.

"Two major courts and one of the larger minor ones have already pledged to her cause," the lord spoke frankly. I liked that about him immediately, even if I didn't like what he was saying.

"A cause that is unjust," Lark countered, passion in his tone.

"Perhaps. Who are we to decide what is and is not just? War costs lives, Prince. It destroys and ruins. It would be illogical for us to join the side which is already so outmatched."

Lark held firm, jaw clenching, but I saw Cass close her eyes, saw the way Rook was shaking his head, irritated and resigned. They were already giving up. They hadn't expected this to work, had anticipated this very argument and, truthfully, who could fault them? This was a court of very wise academics. Of course they would follow logic, of course they would make the decision that seemed most rational in the moment. And the others expected it of them. But Cass and Rook and even Lark didn't understand these people. They couldn't. They weren't scholars. They weren't like us.

Lord Falcondew's words echoed with a ring of finality but his eyes told another story. His gaze remained on the Bone Court Prince, on my bonded, watching, hoping. A reason. That's all he needed. A reason to defy logic. A way to sell his people on taking such a drastic irrational step like joining a losing side in a hypothetically unwinnable war. And doing the right thing wasn't going to be enough. Not when it was his people who would die for it. This wasn't the Court of Justice, after all.

I strode away from Lark, letting my bonded continue his efforts for now, knowing they wouldn't win this man over. I just needed time. I needed him to plant the seeds, to lay out the conflict, and luckily, Canis Morningstar had trained all his life in the way of politics. Even if he wasn't very good at it.

"She will bring war to your door one way or another, Drake," Lark warned, using the lord's first name thereby dropping all pretense of formality. "You know that. You won't be able to remain neutral forever. Not with Ariadne."

"We don't have to throw our lives away in the early throes of this conflict either, Canis," the lord argued.

"If we don't stand together in the beginning we will fall individually."

"You assume we mean to resist."

"We are talking about the enslavement of the entire mortal race."

"Are we? Or is that just your interpretation of Ariadne's intentions?"

"Did you know the Court of Light and Life invented an elixir that grants mortals immortality?" I asked, interrupting the men's argument.

Both of their gazes snapped to me where I now stood at the massive arched windows, peering down at the glorious waterfall only twenty feet below us. Sunlight dappled the current, creating a rainbow haze in the mist as the water flowed over the cliffs to crash into the lake below. It was beautiful. I wondered how often the people of this court acknowledged that.

"Princess?" Lord Falcondew asked after a moment of hesitation.

I tried not to cringe at the title, thankful that I was turned away from him so that he could not see the disgust on my face.

"The Court of Light and Life," I repeated, turning to face him. "They created an elixir that grants immortality."

His eyes widened.

"Impossible," he spat.

"They gave it to her and she gave it to my father. And to me," I told him, making an effort to straighten my spine, clasp my hands primly in front of me, hold my chin high, the way I had learned from, of all people, her. "She stole my father from the mortal realm sixty years ago and yet he looks not a day over thirty. It works. Believe me."

I let my gaze narrow at that, let my eyes darken so he could see the meaning behind them, the implication. He paled.

"But that isn't-she cannot-that is a forbidden field of study," he sputtered, seeming rattled for the first time though he did end his declaration more firmly than it began.

"It is done," I told him. "Sophierial and Ariadne now have the power of a god. The power to grant immortality to those they choose. The power to harness life itself."

He just stared at me, mouth agape.

"It's a volatile little compound," I told him. "Dangerous. I don't think they quite understand what they're playing with. It needs to be contained. It needs to be studied properly."

My gaze flicked from Lord Falcondew to Lark who finally understood what I was doing.

"We cannot risk such knowledge resting in the hands of Ariadne or Sophierial. A discovery of this magnitude, one which has far-reaching implications for the whole plane, should be housed here where it can be studied by our most brilliant minds. Those who hold to a code that will not allow it to be released," Lark spoke and I gave him an almost imperceptible nod as I saw Lord Falcondew wavering.

Appealing to an academic's morality would never work if there was an argument to be made on behalf of the immoral. Appealing to their curiosity, however, or their desire to horde knowledge like a dragon hordes its gold, that was another story.

"Sophierial is aware of the conventions placed on academic study," Lord Falcondew finally said a few moments later. His tone was almost bitter as he spoke. "This is in direct violation of them. She should be held accountable."

Lark and I nodded along, letting him speak.

"I will speak to my advisors about this," he continued thoughtfully, rubbing his chin as he strode away, already heading for the door and, presumably, the advisors waiting beyond. "Such a violation cannot be allowed to stand. We'll be in contact, Prince."

He fled from the room then, guards from hidden corners I hadn't even seen moving to follow after him. I waited for the door to close before turning back to Lark with a wide grin. He was already smiling my way and a feeling of pure, radiant pride beamed from him into my very soul.

"Impressive," someone spoke from the other side of the room and I turned to find Phoebe rising from the wall where she had stood moments before. She approached, eyeing me more curiously than she had before. "This one picked up her mother's political acumen I see."

She may as well have slapped me across the face. I blinked, stunned by how badly such a comparison hurt. Lark noticed, reaching out to covertly squeeze my arm as he addressed the woman.

"Thank you for bringing us to an audience with the lord, Phoebe," he said.

"I wouldn't have missed it," she replied with a shrug. "Strange world-changing things tend to happen around you, Prince. I did not imagine this time would be any different."

"What do you think about our chances?" Cass asked, leaning in and nodding her head toward where Lord Falcondew had departed.

"Well enough, I'd say. Your girl played it beautifully. If there's anything Drake can't resist, it's a challenge. And he's a stickler for the rules. He won't let this new discovery go uncontested. The others might be more hesitant to plunge our court into war over such a thing but Drake didn't get his position without knowing how to be persuasive."

We all nodded at that, thoughtful, as Phoebe led us back through the palace and onto the street outside.

"Even though it might have won you an ally, I'd be careful mentioning that elixir where anyone can hear you, girl," Phoebe was saying as we stepped onto the street. She paused, peering up at the bright blue sky as if she could see something the rest of us didn't. "There's a reason that avenue of study is forbidden. Not just because it's controversial but because it's supposed to be impossible. Whatever god Sophierial convinced to give her that ability might be even more vengeful than your mother."

My brow wrinkled in confusion. God? Impossible? What was she on about?

"I—" I started but Lark grabbed my arm and began pulling me away where I saw Cass and Rook were already walking ahead.

"Thank you again, Phoebe," he said calmly even as he quickened his pace. "Until we meet again."

Phoebe did not even nod, still staring up at the sky as though expecting something to fall from it. Lark released my arm a few feet down the road but kept his hand on my lower back as we walked briskly after Cass and Rook, guiding, protective. I glanced up at him as we strode through the city-bridge and found his jaw clenched, eyes darting side to side, on edge.

"Lark?" I asked, curiosity getting the best of me even as fear clawed its way up my throat, threatening to strangle me in its hold. "What is it?"

"She invoked the old gods," he muttered lowly, teeth gritted.

I blinked, unsure if I had heard him correctly.

"... so?" I asked a moment later.

"It's a warning," he told me. "A dire one. We need to leave."

"What does it mean?"

"The Court of Scholars have long guarded our histories. Dusty old books that speak of wicked deities that ruled over us in ancient times, playing us against one another as a child plays with dolls. No one believes in their existence anymore, least of all the skeptics among the scholars. So if one of them invokes the gods, it's as good as saying we're playing with fire and they fully intend for us to get burned."

"But I don't understand. I thought it went well with Lord Falcondew."

"The lord isn't the only power in the Court of Scholars. Phoebe was reminding us of that in her own way."

"But he controls their army. The people—"

"The Court of Scholars has always had a power structure that is more... unstable than the others. Comes from electing your officials every half-century, I suppose. Falcondew is new to the seat. He isn't fully respected by the others yet. And some, remember, did not vote for his ascension."

"A leader who doesn't have as much power as he thinks," I mused. "Why, Lark, that's almost mortal of you."

He chuckled darkly but then we were approaching the gates of the city and Cass and Rook were stepping through them, the princess gripping the warrior's hand only seconds before they vanished.

"You did well, Ren," Lark said as we stepped through the gate after them. His hand grasped mine and squeezed in a gesture full of meaning as I turned to meet his bright silver gaze. "Will you ever cease to amaze me?"

"I certainly hope not."

He smiled and the world squeezed in around us.

Chapter Twenty-Six
A Disgruntled Lord

Lark and I materialized within the foyer of Cass' Court of Dreams house, still smiling at one another like two heartsick teenagers. But then we heard the shouting.

"How dare you," someone was yelling, heavy footsteps storming into the room as Cass rushed after the madman, trying in vain to calm him. "How dare you come here."

I turned in time to see a shorter man in a vibrant purple pressed suit storming forward. He held up an index finger, pointing it in Lark's chest, his face as red as a tomato, spittle actually flying from his lips.

"I banned the Bone Court, did I not?" he cried, throwing his hands in the air and turning to a man at his back, a solemn muscled guard in a lighter shade of lilac who kept his expression set in a grim scowl as he nodded in reply. "After you broke my daughter's heart, after your sister blamed her for her own failings, after that drunken oaf you call a friend trashed my penthouse, I banished all of you and told you never to come back! And yet here you are, literally risen from the dead to torment me once more. I should have the lot of you strung up for daring to return. What, in the gods' names, have I ever done to deserve your haunting?"

Cass rolled her eyes at the dramatics from behind the man, crossing her arms and frowning. Rook snorted from the corner, leaning casually against the stairs, clearly amused. Gemini took up a more defensive stance, drifting slowly toward her grandson even as Lark glanced down at the man's finger against his chest. One brow arched high as he plucked the finger from his chest and dropped it aside. The man's jaw clenched but he wisely backed away.

"I hope," Lark began easily, tone reverting to that dangerous drawl I knew he reserved for those who believed him to be the monster my mother claimed he was, "you are not threatening me in my sister's home, Kabir."

Kabir stared at Lark for a moment, his anger suddenly dissipating, though his foul mood remained. His lips curled into a sneer as he crossed his arms and slumped like a petulant child.

"What are you doing in my court, Bone Prince?" he spat, vitriol and hatred spewing from him with every word he spoke.

"I am staying with my sister," Lark answered, nodding in Cass' direction.

"This is my home, Kabir," Cass said, taking up the line in conversation, crossing the room to stand between her brother and this intruder. "One which you did not ask to enter."

"This is my court, princess," Kabir spat back, glaring at Cass as he did. "I do not have to seek permission to walk upon my own lands."

"I purchased this home with Bone Court funds. That makes it Bone Court territory."

Kabir paled at that, then began sputtering indignantly, his face turning red once again.

"That isn't how-you cannot just buy-this is the Court of Dreams!"

Cass crossed her arms and smiled at his outburst, satisfied at having made the apparent Lord of the Court of Dreams blubber and shout like a defiant toddler. Rook chortled again from where he stood off to the side. Lark shot him a warning glance, however, and he fell silent.

"I take it you've spoken to your daughter," Lark drawled a moment later, turning his attention back to a wide-eyed Kabir.

"Unfortunately," Kabir snapped. "It seems you've gotten to her once again, Bone Prince."

"I assure you, that title is not the insult you believe it to be, Lord Kabir." Kabir grumbled.

"Perhaps we should sit and discuss?" Lark asked, holding out a hand to indicate the sitting room off to the side of the foyer. "That is, if my sister would be willing to offer her home for our use."

"Of course, brother," Cass replied, beaming. "Anything for the cause."

The cause. The cause of upending my mother's plans, taking up arms against two major courts and one minor, effectively plunging this realm into civil war. I started to feel the same panic, the same anxiety, that was becoming a common occurrence every time this subject was broached but I maintained my composure on the outside, following after the others as they made their way into the sitting room off the foyer. Lark peered back at me once, lips pursed in silent examination as though he had felt that sudden twinge of anxiety. I offered him a placating smile but we were far too connected for him to have truly believed it.

Still, we all settled down into seats in the next room. Cass lounged casually across her chosen chaise as Rook sat at the base of it, leaning back on his arms and not even flinching when Cass placed her feet upon his lap. Lark took up a more appropriate position on the couch, crossing one ankle over a knee and draping his arm over the back of the sofa with a pointed glance in my direction. I filled the space offered, doing my best not to turn into him at the intoxicating scent wafting off of him. Gemini stood in the doorway, frowning and sizing up the single guard Kabir had brought with him who stood, with his arms crossed, on the other side of her.

"What did Karma tell you?" Lark asked carefully but confidently.

"The same dramatic bullshit she always spews whenever you're around," Kabir muttered. "The world is ending and Ariadne is the cause of it. We should all take action now or fall to her hidden might. Blah, blah, blah."

I bristled but Lark's lips spread into a grin.

"You do a good impression of me, Lord of Dreams," Lark mused.

Kabir straightened, surprised.

"I admit I was rather dramatic the last time I came to you," Lark continued with a shrug. "What a pity I turned out to be right."

Kabir's gaze snapped to me and he shook his head.

"The world has gone mad," Kabir said with a sigh, all of the fight seemingly gone out of him as he slumped into himself. "And Ariadne does seem to be the cause of it. What she did to you, princess, was unconscionable."

I blinked at him, stunned by the sudden change in attitude.

"You did not believe me when I came to you before," Lark reminded him grimly. "Do you believe me now?"

Kabir sighed.

"I suppose I have no choice, do I?" he asked, seeming more tired than before.

"You'll join us," Lark said but it wasn't a question.

"I'm afraid I've never had much choice in that either, Bone Prince."

Lark nodded. And that was it. I stared between the men, shocked. I had anticipated, from this man's attitude upon entering Cass' home, that this would take far more convincing, negotiating, perhaps even pleading. But the man had agreed without any fanfare at all. I could see the reason why in their eyes. There was history between these men. Hatred and anger, perhaps, but a respect as well. A memory of a long lost camaraderie. I wondered how long those memories would hold sway over the fury.

"Karma has already begun assembling our armies," Kabir began and Lark nodded, hardly even moving, as though he had expected this all along. Across the room, however, I noticed Rook and Cass release a breath and relax, relieved. "Kismet has gone to convince the Court of Blessings. You're aware of her... connection to them. I expect you can handle Rivals, Wanderers, and Scholars."

"Scholars has been taken care of thanks to the political maneuvering of my bonded," Lark replied, nodding proudly in my direction.

Kabir's gaze snapped to me once more but the fury did not return. Instead he nodded with something akin to exhausted resignation.

"That bit of news made it to me as well," Kabir spoke softly. "My daughter clings to it as an excuse for why it didn't work out between you two. Thank you for giving her that."

Lark nodded curtly.

"I will need to revisit Taurus before approaching Rivals," Lark continued with the strategic planning as though no discussion of his ex-girlfriend with her father had ever taken place. "They will have a far better opinion of him than they do of me. Wanderers will be harder. Wispa can be rather... erratic."

Kabir snorted.

"That's one word for it," he muttered. "Very well. It seems we have our assignments. You'll have my men, Bone Prince. You'll have full access to and the utilization of my court."

"Thank you, Kabir," Lark said, reaching out to take the hand that Kabir offered in a firm shake. "Truly."

Kabir nodded absently, already rising from his seat. He made his way toward the door as Cass and Rook beamed from where they sat upon the chaise nearby. Gemini stepped to the side to allow the Lord of the Court of Dreams to pass, her arms still crossed and gaze still narrowed as his guard strode ahead of him, posture more relaxed now that he was now among official allies.

"One more thing," Kabir said suddenly from the doorway, turning back to peer back at us. "Perseus wrote to me. It seems he is rather... perturbed by his dead son's ability to take command of his court and start a civil war without his permission. I took the fact that he wrote to me rather than popped up in the middle of my study to mean that the rumors are true. His power is gone, isn't it?"

Lark's jaw clenched but, after a moment, he nodded. Kabir sighed, shaking his head as he turned back toward the door.

"World's gone mad, indeed," he muttered as his guard wrenched open the door and they both stepped out into his court beyond.

Chapter Twenty-Seven
A Bigger Picture

Rook and Cass erupted into conversation the moment Kabir was gone, both of them leaping from their seat to hurl ideas and suggestions at Lark who took it all in stride, nodding and considering. I extricated myself from his side, letting the rest of them plan our next steps. Suddenly overwhelmed with exhaustion, I made my way up the steps, intending to retire to my room for a bit of well-deserved rest. But I stopped at the landing when I saw the slender beam of light emanating from my grandfather's open doorway.

Slowly, I inched forward, peering inside. Alban was still laying atop the bed he had been given, skin a warmer shade than it had been but still appearing unnaturally thin. I could still see the bones of his face and didn't even want to look at the rest of him, knowing what I would see. My grandfather was little more than a skeleton these days, his withered chest rising and falling in shallow breaths as the only indication that he still lived. Beside him, however, was a man I knew was living and breathing.

Irim sat in a plush cushioned chair next to Alban's bed. His head was hung low, hair that had grown much longer than it had been when we'd first met obscuring his eyes. One hand rubbed at his temples as he sighed then rubbed his face as he shifted and raised his gaze. Our eyes met and he stilled.

"Seren," he said. His voice was hoarse, rougher than I remembered. My vision flashed with images of him crying out, writhing and screaming. I shuddered, closing my eyes and turning away. "Seren, please. Look at me."

With effort, I did.

"I know it wasn't you," he told me, rising. "I know it was her. I don't blame you."

"I—" I started but my voice cracked. I couldn't. I just... couldn't.

He crossed the room in a few easy strides and then took me by the shoulders, gaze boring into me.

"She manipulated you," he said. "It's what she does. You cannot fall into the trap she set. You cannot believe the manipulations were your own actions. They weren't. I know it. You need to believe it too."

"But I let her manipulate me. I couldn't stop her. I couldn't—"

"Very few can stop Ariadne Dawnpaw when she sets her mind to something, cousin. That's why I... fear for what your friends intend."

"War," I whispered.

"It will be brutal."

"But necessary."

"Is it?"

I blinked at him, utterly shocked at what he was suggesting. He was the one she had nearly destroyed outside of the library in her palace weeks ago. He was the one who she had used my power against, invading my mind and holding my magic against him until there was nothing I could do but watch. And now he was here, advocating peace?

"Irim," I started slowly.

"I know, Seren. I know what she's doing," he replied, voice dropping low as he hung his head with something that seemed strangely like shame. "Believe me, I know better than anyone what she's done. But a civil war would cost thousands of lives, not to mention place mortals in positions of danger. If she really seeks to enslave them, you don't think it's possible she might attempt to use them as well. Against us? Against you?"

My lips parted in surprise. I hadn't thought of that. Not exactly. I knew my mother was powerful but was she capable of holding so many minds at once? Was she capable of the sort of debauchery that Irim seemed to fear?

Yes. I knew the answer the moment my mind formed the question. Yes, she was capable of all of that and more. I knew because of what she did to me and what she had done to my father for years. I knew from first hand witnessing of her terror. My mother would do anything she could, anything she had to, to meet her goal. Suddenly, there was far more to fear.

"I heard Lord Kabir downstairs," Irim said, lowering his voice even further, this time to avoid being heard by the others downstairs. "I'm sure Lark convinced him. And I know you went to the Court of Scholars yesterday. I would never ask you to turn against your bonded, Seren. I couldn't possibly make that sort of request. But you need to understand what you're doing here, what you're putting at risk. Because it isn't just your life you're gambling with."

With that, he pushed past me and into the hall, strolling down until he reached the door that belonged to the room Cass had provided him. He did not so much as glance back at me as he opened the door and slipped inside. I watched, unable to move after him.

He was right. We were starting a war. Sure, one could argue that my mother had been the one to truly take steps toward escalating a conflict of this magnitude but we were standing against her. We were the ones initiating the fighting. Even if we were doing it because it was right. Even if we were the good guys. Then again, was either side in a war truly the good side?

I closed my eyes and shook my head. This was wrong. We were approaching this all wrong.

Part of me belonged to Lark and, because of that part and the weeks I spent pretending to be the cold, aloof princess that my mother made me to be, I had allowed myself to become desensitized to the magnitude of the decisions we were making. People were going to die. Immortal, magical, incredible fae were going to die. Innocent mortals were likely going to die as well. The Divide would inevitably be ripped apart and monsters and myths would descend upon the world I loved so much, the realm that raised me, and destroy anything in their paths. And I wasn't even sure I could stop it. Not with the Court of Scholars and the Court of Dreams at our side. Not even with the might of the Bone Court at our backs. I had been following Lark's lead in dealing with this situation. I had been thinking of this like a politician. But I wasn't a politician. I was an academic.

I spun on my heel and stormed back down the stairs, entering the sitting room below once more to frenzied plans and conversation. Lark was leaning against the back of the long sofa, staring into the crackling fire as Cass and Rook argued about whether they should approach the Court of Rivals or the Court of Wanderers next.

"We're doing this wrong," I announced from the threshold and all eyes turned to face me.

Lark released his hold on the couch and rose slightly, watching me carefully as I stepped into the room and took up a position in the center of it. I held my head high, attempting to use that firm, commanding tone I had worked so hard on during my days of captivity.

"We're rushing to collect pieces of the puzzle before my mother can but we haven't even taken a look at the picture on the box," I said, shaking my head and blowing out a breath. How had I not seen this before? How had

I allowed myself to be so captivated by my curiosity for their world, by my faith in this glorious man? How had I lost myself in this plane?

Rook cocked his head, confused. Cass blinked at me. Lark just watched, lips quirking up slightly in the beginnings of a grin. His eyes sparkled as if to say *there she is.* I averted my gaze, heat rushing to my cheeks.

"Yes, my mother has managed to convince the Court of Light and Life as well as the Court of Friends to join her," I spoke, rushing now that a plan was beginning to form in my mind. "That's an unfortunate advantage, I won't lie. But we've already been thinking militarily. Sheer force and numbers won't matter if the conflict never escalates to warfare."

"Ren—" Lark started, softening. But I held up a hand and he fell silent.

"Just listen," I barked. "My mother has been tearing holes into the sky between this realm and the mortal one. I'm assuming she's doing this in an effort to learn how to pierce the Divide."

"I thought she was doing it to find you," Cass said, brow furrowed in confusion.

"Partially," I replied. "But Ariadne is not the type to let a power so great go unused. She will use it again. It's only a matter of time. And every time she does, she weakens the Divide. If it falls... well, I suppose that is when we will have no other choice but to go to war. For now, however, we have options. Lark, you should continue to make every alliance you can in preparation. Maybe other courts will have better ideas of how to thwart her so that it does not come to bloodshed. But I think it's a better idea right now to focus on how she is controlling the rifts and to find a way to stop her from destroying the Divide."

They all watched me for a second. Then Lark gave a sharp nod and the others began nodding as well.

"Lark, you were able to close one of the rifts while on the mortal side," I reminded him. "And you closed another when we were in Hellscape. If you could explain how you managed to do such a thing, perhaps we could replicate it on a larger scale, create a magical shield of sorts around the Divide itself."

Lark exchanged a glance with both Rook and Cass.

"I... don't think that will be possible," Lark confessed.

"Why not?" I asked, looking between them, clearly unaware of some valuable aspect of this conversation.

"The power of the Void, as we call it, is passed down through our family, generation after generation, to only one heir," Lark explained. "My father has it and now I do as well. This time, however, the power chose two heirs, further confusing the succession process. Taurus has it as well. But the three of us are the only ones, in all the realm, and we won't be enough to erect an entire shield around the Divide. Particularly with my father's ongoing... ailment."

"What is it?" I asked, even as more pieces of the puzzle began to fall into place.

"The Void allows the wielder to negate all magical effects. It acts as a black hole for magic, sucking it in and destroying it. The others call it 'The Death' or 'The Decay' and their fear for it is so great that my father, Taurus, and I never dare to use it unless absolutely necessary. Perseus used it while creating the first Divide and doing so nearly killed him. Now... now, your mother has the power. She is using it via the magic she stole from my father. How she's harnessing it through that little amulet hung around her neck, I'll never know. But that's what she's doing. And my sister is allowing it."

He spat out this last part and I could see how much it hurt him that Ursa would dare use such a thing against her own family.

I blinked at him, stunned.

"It... kills magic," I said. "This Void destroys magic itself?"

"And all things which function by or are made of magic," Cass whispered, looking down at her feet.

"Why didn't you use it against her before?" I asked. "We could use this to negate her power. We could—"

"If you'll recall," Lark drawled, his tone seemingly unbothered but I could see the tension in his shoulders at being forced to remember what we all wished we could forget. "I was held captive by my own mind at the time, paralyzed. She knew what she was doing, choosing to incapacitate me before the others. She knew that if I couldn't move, if I couldn't access the Void, she could practically do as she wished. Gemini is powerful and Rook is strong but even they can't fight against countless guards and iron chains. Cass is no warrior. She knew all of that. She planned for it."

He was growling, angry. I strode toward him and placed a comforting hand on his arm. After a moment, his raised a hand to cover it. He gave me a nod of gratitude and I gave him one of understanding.

"Can we use the Void against her now?" I asked. "If we could incapacitate her the same way she's managed to incapacitate Alban and Perseus—"

"No one knows how she stole their magic," Cass said, shaking her head. "No one understands what power of transference she used to collect their power into those amulets, much less how she actually manages to wield it. It's a mystery to all but Ariadne, I'm afraid."

"It isn't a mystery," I told her. "It's science. And if we can figure out how it's done, we can replicate and reverse the process. We can get Alban and Perseus their magic back. If we cannot shield the Divide, then we can at least rescue the last of the ones who erected it in the first place. With the two of them returned and Gemini by our side, we'll have the best chance of protecting the mortal realm from Ariadne's invasion."

"But how do we do it?" Rook asked. "How can you study the amulets if you don't have them?"

I frowned.

"This part... you aren't going to like."

Chapter Twenty-Eight
A Choice

Cass had been right. Ursa, it seemed, was choosing to nurse her wounded pride at the Evening Starr, a tavern in her home court, a court that Lark was no longer welcome in mainly because they had executed him the last time he came home. But Rook and Cass could come and go as they pleased.

I thought we were going to have to sedate Lark to get him to allow us all to leave together to face one of his most tenacious foes. But I had simply reminded him that Ursa had never truly intended to hurt me, nor had she ever sought to lay a hand on Cass or Rook, and he had yielded. Though perhaps I had also mentioned that I was a grown woman and could make whatever choices I wished. He had actually smiled at that before demanding we return by midnight or he would "tear that whole court to pieces looking for us". Since I believed him, I made sure to continuously check the time as we went about our business.

So here we were, stepping into the raucous bar named in parody of the ruling family of this court. Surely, they knew that same family had members who frequented this establishment as well. I would have claimed it bold to name a tavern in such a mocking way so near to the Bone Court palace itself but I knew that was how things were here. The rougher, the ruder, the cleverer, the better.

"You've come to finish me off then?" Ursa muttered as she turned and narrowed her gaze into a glare as the three of us approached. Her eyes flicked over Rook and I before landing on Cass. "I'm assuming the Pride Princess told you all about my complicity regarding Ariadne's schemes."

"She did," Cass admitted, arms crossed. "Which is why we've come to offer you terms."

Ursa started, clearly surprised.

"Terms?" she asked, blinking up at us from her stool. "For what?"

"For making your way back into this family's good graces, Ursa," Cass spoke though every word was clipped when she did. "You've betrayed us, sure. But lucky for you that puts you in a unique position to right your wrongs."

Ursa's gaze narrowed again.

"What do you want?" she asked, warily.

"Get the amulet back," Cass commanded. "And bring it to us."

Ursa hesitated for a moment before bursting out into a fit of laughter, startling one of the barmaids who rushed by with a full pitcher and averted gaze.

"Right. I'll just go and fetch it then," Ursa replied, actually wiping her eyes as she turned away from us and took another sip of her drink.

"I suggest you find a way to do so," Cass said. "We haven't told father yet but we can. Sick as he is, he's still the patriarch of this family and your King. He can order your execution as easily as he did Lark's or, even worse for you, remove you from the running in the succession."

Ursa gaped at her sister.

"He wouldn't," she snapped.

"Would you like to see?" Cass asked, standing firm. "If there's one thing father respects, it's power. You took that from him. You stole that which was most precious away and gave it to our enemy. You did that, Ursa. And you will not escape culpability but you can make amends so that your punishment is lighter than it should be."

"I can't," Ursa replied, though she had been considering it, I could tell. "Ariadne has taken it away. She says she needs it now. She won't give it back."

"Come up with something. You're good at thinking on your feet and you're great at lying. Give her a reason to believe you'll be using father's power to further her cause."

"She'll see right through that. She can see through any lie, Casseiopia. She can read minds."

Perhaps it was my imagination but a chill seemed to shoot through the air at her declaration. Ursa, for her part, certainly shivered.

"Then don't give her any reason to suspect it's a lie," Cass snapped. "This is it, Ursa. This is your one and only chance. You've done something unforgivable but still, I'm here, offering you this forgiveness. I suggest you take it."

With that, Cass turned on her heel and strode toward the exit of the bar. Rook and I followed after her and I noticed gazes darting our way from various seats in the bar as well. Wide-eyed fae stared at their princess as she passed, head held high and black gown shimmering.

"We don't betray our own, Ursa," Cass called back once she reached the door. Her voice, though low and soft with the pain clearly held within it, still managed to carry through the small dimly lit tavern to her sister sitting at the bar beyond. "We fight and kill each other but we do that, sister. We don't allow others to."

Her voice cracked in the same way I imagined her heart was as she pulled open the door and stepped out into the frigid night air. She strode across the street, making tracks in the light dusting of snow on the cobblestones, before stopping abruptly and turning back to face us. Tears were frozen on her cheeks as she reached out her hands to ours.

"Cass," I started, concern etched plainly on both mine and Rook's expressions.

But Cass only shook her head before grabbing our hands. The world squeezed in around us and I couldn't breathe.

A moment later, we separated. I coughed, sputtering back into existence in the sitting room of Cass' home back in the Court of Dreams. I turned in time to see the hem of Cass' gown vanishing up the steps where she had fled. Rook stared after her, jaw clenched and expression grim. I took a step forward as if to go after her, but nearly stumbled as my world spun. I was still trying to right myself after shadow stepping once more. A firm hand was at my elbow, steadying me, as Lark's warm voice called out from my back.

"Well?" he asked.

"We'll see," Rook replied as he made eye contact with the towering fae male behind me.

I felt, more than saw, Lark nod and then Rook was making his way up the stairs as well.

"I shouldn't have made her do that," I whispered, feeling the guilt at the realization wash over me at the same time. "I can't imagine how hard that was for her, facing Ursa like that after what she did to you all. And it's my fault she had to offer her forgiveness like that. She deserved the right to withhold it. She deserves the right to hate her forever but I made her do it. I—"

Lark spun me around before I could fall too deep into my own pity.

"Cass made the choice to go along with this plan, Ren," he reminded me, tone firm as his eyes, flashing silver, stared into mine. "We all did."

"But you didn't see her face," I groaned, allowing him to gather me into his arms. I leaned my head against his chest and sighed into the soft fabric of his shirt. "You didn't hear how much it hurt her to face what Ursa did."

"But Ursa did it, Ren. Not you. It isn't your fault."

I pulled away from him, taking care to make sure that it wasn't too obvious I was inhaling his scent as I did, and looked up to meet his eyes.

"I'll figure it out, Lark," I told him, nearly breathless. "I'll get Perseus' power back. Then I'll find a way to restore Alban's. With them, she can't possibly stand against us. Can she?"

The last question was a whisper. The truth was, I was still so new to this. I didn't know how any of this worked, not really. I knew she had stolen these men's power and that there must be a way to get it back. But I didn't have half the confidence I claimed to that I could find a way to restore it myself. And I wasn't even sure it would matter if I did. Whatever my mother's plans were, they were already in motion. We were behind the ball on this and we didn't even have a good look at the court. In reality, I didn't know what she had planned. But it couldn't hurt to have two of the strongest fae alive's power returned to them just in case.

"I'm starting to think," Lark replied then, smiling as he did, "that nothing and no one could get in your way if you didn't let them, Seren Belling."

I drew in a breath, not just for the sentiment he had given me, that utter confidence in my ability, but because he had called me by my real name, my chosen name. When everyone else had been intent on forcing me to accept the role I'd never known I held, the princess of the Pride Court, a Dawnpaw and an heir, he was giving me a choice. He was allowing me to remain that simple mortal professor he first stumbled upon in the hallowed halls of Hadley University, that no one who lived a life I would never be allowed to claim again. Seren Belling the academic. The curious professor who got so lost in how things worked she often forgot to ruminate on whether or not they should. The determined young woman who had carved a place for herself into a world that didn't know what she really was. The happy little child raised by a man who hadn't made the choice to do so but stepped up when the time came on behalf of a brother that he loved more than anything. And now, here, on the edge of a potentially realm-shattering war brought on by my narcissistic, relentless mother, Lark was giving me this gift. A reminder that I could still be that woman, that Belling, that I'd been before. A promise that I didn't have to let this world change me if I didn't want it to. And a vow that he would back me up, no matter what I chose.

Emotion rushed through me, bold and swift, and at the crescendo, I pulled him close and pressed my lips against his.

Choice. Lark had always given me a choice. Even when, in doing so, he took away his own. He stole me away at the request of my father to place me somewhere safe where I could grow into whatever person I wanted to become without her influence even though he knew it would result in his exile. He defended me against a fae who sought to do me harm even knowing it would bring about his capture and therefore execution. He fought to free me from my mother's clutches once again even though it required him to seek assistance from some dangerous man named Nyx that I still had yet to learn why he was such a terrible option. Regardless, Lark had always gone out of his way to assure I had a choice. And wasn't the chance to make your own decisions just the biggest privilege in the world?

Lark moved against me now, pushing closer, his hands dropping to my waist and holding me there in a touch both firm and gentle as if keeping me there but simultaneously giving me the option to go. Even now, this was my choice. And I chose him. I would always choose him. He still seemed to doubt that but I had a new plan now. A plan to kiss him until he no longer did.

I pulled away from him suddenly, breathless, and he stared down at me with eyes flashing silver.

"Can we go to your room?" I asked, tentative but firm.

He blinked at me, breath coming in raggedly. His chest rose and fall as those piercing eyes searched my face. The muscles in his jaw ticked as his lips parted slightly.

"You've had an emotional day," he said, so slowly. "An emotional week, actually. I would never want to take advantage of—"

I blew out a breath that caused my blonde hair to flip up and out of my face.

"For the gods' sake, Lark, take me to bed."

His lips spread into a grin that revealed every one of his pristine white teeth.

"I thought you'd never ask, Belling," he retorted.

Then he bent and lifted me off of my feet. I let out a cry of delight as he carried me, easily, up the stairs, planting kisses all along my neck and jaw as he did.

Maybe this was wrong. A war was brewing, evil was plotting, powerful fae were having their magic drained from them, the light court was creating illicit immortality serums, and there was so very much pain in the world. But for a moment, just for a night, Lark and I could shirk the responsibility of fixing that pain. We could revel in our bond, allow our love to grow, and finally celebrate our return to one another in a way we'd never had the chance to before. So maybe it was wrong. Maybe it was selfish to want this, to allow ourselves this. But we would. If only for tonight.

His door flew open on some phantom breeze that I wasn't sure who created between us and then he was striding in, kicking the door shut behind him with his heel as he carried me to his bed as requested.

This was new and fragile. He seemed to realize that at the same moment I did. He slowed before placing me carefully upon his bed, almost reverently. He pulled away slightly, stroking my hair with his hand, and stood up straight, peering down at me with a gaze that seemed apologetically possessive.

I held my breath at the sight of him standing before me like a god. His chiseled features were somehow even more beautiful in the dim, flickering candlelight of his room. His eyes, again flashing silver as they so often did when he looked at me, were endless chasms of adoration. Every muscle was taut and tense as though it was taking every ounce of willpower he had to resist pouncing on me all at once. That dark hair fell haphazardly over his eyes which remained hooded, lowered to watch me intently. And there was awe in the way he looked at me, in the way his gaze flicked over the entire length of my body, delving deep within me until I nearly squirmed beneath it.

"Gods, you're beautiful," he breathed. "I never thought I'd be lucky enough to have a soul bond, never thought I'd live long enough to find love like this. When you were gone, when she had you…"

He trailed off, jaw tensing as his fists clenched at his sides. I lifted myself up onto my knees and scooted forward until I was face to face with him on the raised bed. I lifted my hands, cupping his face in them as I stared into his eyes with meaning. I knew the hurt of that separation. I'd felt it myself. A physical pain, like a knife excising a limb, like you were missing a part of you that you might never get back. It had shocked me, how agonizing it was, and I realized I'd never really known how much I loved this man until he was taken from me. I vowed to never lose him again. Never.

"I know," I whispered softly and then kissed him again, gentler this time.

He shook in my arms for only a moment before his hands were on my waist again and he was pulling me up, lifting me so that I could wrap my legs around him. He deepened the kiss and my lips opened gladly, eagerly. When we both came up for air, his silver gaze met mine.

"I've done things," he confessed, his voice so soft I almost couldn't hear him even this close. "Because of who I am, because of what I'm capable of, I... I don't deserve you, Ren. You're good. You're exceptional and brilliant and radiant and I'm... I'm not worthy. You have to understand. I'll never be worthy. I—"

I placed a finger on his lips.

"You are my bonded," I told him, a note of finality in my tone. "I choose you, Lark. Because you've given me choice. Because you've given me love. I choose you. Now and always. And I will never let her pull us apart again. I swear it."

His next kiss devoured me. It set me aflame, burning away my doubt, my fear, my pain. It drowned me in passion and devotion and that feeling of knowing I was finally, irrevocably, whole. It possessed me in a way that left me as me, pulled me into the present in a way that reminded me I was here, not there. Never there. Whatever he'd done, whatever I did, whatever she would make us do, it didn't matter. None of it mattered. Because there was this and there was us and we would stand together until the end even if the world burned and dissolved around us.

His hands were at my back now, insistent but also hesitant. I reached one hand to the fabric in his hands and gave a firm tug. The halter at my neck unraveled and the shirt dipped low, exposing the swell of my breasts. He bent and kissed them before setting me gently onto my feet so that the rest of the jumpsuit could fall as well and pool around my ankles. His eyes flashed silver once again as his gaze dipped to my nearly naked form standing in front of him. I reached out and pressed one hand upon his chest, pushing him a step back as I took a step forward out of the jumpsuit. We left it sitting behind.

The hand I had on his chest drifted to the buttons of his shirt and I bit my lip, looking up at him through my lashes, seeking permission. He nodded, a lazy grin stretching over his lips. I took my time, kissing every inch of skin that became exposed as I unbuttoned his shirt and tossed it aside. Once it was gone, I couldn't help but run my hands along the sculpted muscles of his chest and abdomen, trailing a finger up his shoulder and down his arm. He smirked.

"It's all about the muscles for you, huh?" he asked, eyes twinkling with mischief.

I shrugged, keeping my eyes on the finger I was trailing over his bicep.

"And the eyes," I informed him. "Then there's your smile and your hair and—"

"Do you always talk so much?" he interrupted, seizing me by my hips and throwing me onto the bed behind us.

I giggled as I fell amongst the pillows, bouncing slightly before coming to rest just below the headboard.

"You know I do," I answered and he grinned as he crawled over me.

Yes, this was right. I thought it as he prowled toward me, smiling, eyes flashing silver, chiseled planes of face and chest shimmering in the candlelight. It may be selfish but it was also right. Why shouldn't we banish the pain for an evening? Why shouldn't we take a moment to breathe, to remember what exactly it was we were fighting for?

"I love it when you talk," he told me, stilling once he was finally hovering over me, his face just inches from mine, the padding of my bra the only barrier between our bare chests. "But for now, princess, I'm going to do my best to render you speechless."

"A fine goal, prince," I replied, feigning a sneer, and his grin broadened as he kissed me again and all of that pain, the fear of war, the guilt of this selfishness, was forgotten.

His hands roamed my body, seeking out every bit of exposed flesh, before coming to cup one breast, then the other. I wriggled free of my undergarments and he removed the remainder of his clothes as well. Then there was nothing between us but warm air and soul-crushing desire. I could feel his breath on my neck as he kissed me there, then on my breasts, then my abdomen, until...

I gasped, feeling his lips stretching into a grin against my core. His tongue darted out again and I lost myself in the throes of pleasure as he stroked and touched and groaned against me. The pressure within built and built until my hips bucked off of the bed and I cried his name in a guttural way that I might have been embarrassed of had I had the presence of mind to feel such a thing.

He was smiling when he rose and climbed back up the bed toward me. My heart was racing, my legs felt like jelly, but I didn't give him a chance to say whatever it was he had opened his mouth to say before I wrapped my legs around him and flipped us so that he was laying flat on his back and I was straddling him. He raised his arms in surrender, laughing as he peered up at me, silver eyes flashing in the flickering light.

"If you wanted control, all you had to do was ask, princess," he replied, his tone deep as he chuckled.

His laughter died off when I lowered myself onto him. His breath hitched as I rolled my hips forward and that silver which so often flashed in his eyes seemed permanent now.

It was so much and not enough at the same time. It was like a high, the feeling of him inside me, and I chased after it, faster and faster, until we were both panting and moaning. Until my skin was coated with a thin sheen of sweat that seemed to glow. Or maybe I was glowing. It could be so hard to tell.

We found our release together, his hands on my hips, mine pressed against his chest, and then I fell beside him, falling upon the smooth black silk, our chests rising and falling in tandem as we stared up at the mahogany ceiling.

"That was..." I started, trailing off.

After a moment of silence in which I did not finish my sentence, he grinned.

"Couldn't have said it better myself, princess."

Chapter Twenty-Nine
A Change In Course

I did not sneak this time. I absolutely refused to do any sort of walk of shame in this house. Lark was my bonded. We had torn apart the very fabric of the universe to find each other again. Honestly, what did the others think would happen?

So I stepped out of Lark's room that morning with my head held high to find no one waiting for me in the hall. Lark himself had slipped out sometime in the early morning hours while I had dozed in his unreasonably cozy bed. I made my way to my room and into the shower. There was something about wearing the same clothes as the day before that made one feel dirty in all the wrong ways.

So I washed myself off and slipped into a new set of clothes, a pair of black leggings and soft, oversized shirt that drooped off of the shoulders which Cass must have left for me sometime in the last few hours. Fixing the angle the shirt set upon my shoulders, I made my way out of my room and down the hall. I didn't hear the talking and clatter of forks until I reached the top of the landing.

I found them all sitting at the table off of the kitchen, laughing and chatting over a spread of seasoned eggs, bacon, sausage, toast, and roasted tomatoes. Gemini was there, along with Irim. I blinked, stunned.

"Irim?" I questioned to Rook who was passing by the doorway with another plate of toast for the table.

"Lark invited him," he muttered in reply, mischievous grin splitting his lips. "Guess the prince was in a good mood this morning. I wonder why."

I punched him in the shoulder and he howled with laughter, drawing the attention of the others in the room. Cass grinned up at me, knowingly, and even Gemini seemed pleased, though also relatively disgusted. Irim just met my gaze and gave me a nod. I didn't yet have the energy to dissect what that meant.

"Coffee?" I asked as I stepped forward to take my seat between Lark and Rook, across from Cass.

"Brewing," Cass promised.

"Sleep well?" Lark asked, resting his hand over mine and giving it a squeeze. I turned mine so that our fingers were intertwined and beamed up at him, grinning like a fool. He smiled back at me, silver gaze sparkling.

"Marvelously," I replied. "If you kick me out, I'm taking the sheets."

"We'll split them in the divorce."

"I get Cass."

"I'll take Rook."

"I—"

"You two are weird," Rook interrupted and we grinned as Cass laughed and Rook beamed.

"If we're done with the infatuated chatter," Gemini began, clearing her throat in true Gemini fashion, "I believe we have some items to discuss which have nothing to do with the state of your bedroom, nephew."

Despite being chastened, Lark retained his smile as he turned to Gemini.

"You have my full attention, aunt," he assured her, still holding my hand.

I couldn't help but grin as I lifted my fork and took a bite of my eggs.

"Apparently, Ursa has been claiming that there is a way to turn the Void against its user," Gemini said. "I've a spy in the peace court that confirms this. She has been telling Ariadne that Perseus' power can be used to destroy your own but only if wielded by one who can use the Void as well."

Lark sat back, steepling his fingers together in front of him, thoughtful.

"Taurus," he replied.

"So that's how she's going about it," Cass added, nodding. "Interesting."

Gemini looked between her niece and nephew, surprised.

"You knew of this?" she asked, her voice accusatory.

"I fear we may have facilitated it, dear aunt," Lark drawled and then proceeded to explain my revelation and what our new plan of attack was. Gemini's eyes widened as he spoke, her expression growing more incredulous. I could tell, by the tension in her muscles as he explained, that she did not agree on the new course we had charted to deal with my mother's ambitions.

"You risk being ill prepared for a war that you are already not favored to win so that you can attempt to reverse magic which has never been performed before and which we have absolutely no knowledge of ourselves?" she asked when he was finished.

"Ren believes that we should take every possible avenue to avoid bloodshed before plunging ourselves into a war which, by your own admission, we are not favored to win," Lark answered calmly, having apparently anticipated his aunt's resistance.

"And it just so happens that you've undergone this drastic change in strategy right after climbing into bed with the girl?"

Lark was on his feet in an instant. Mist rose from the floor around us, coming in through the windows and doors and coalescing at our feet like a thick, threatening smoke. Tendrils of it broke off to veer in Gemini's direction. To her credit, the ancient fae did not flinch but rather held her head high as black smoke, in direct contradiction of his white, rose from her body in wisps, ready to strike.

"Apologize," Lark growled through clenched teeth as his eyes blazed silver.

Gemini sighed but turned toward me.

"I am sorry, Seren," she said. "I know you well enough to know that the two are not connected but I cannot help my suspicions of you. You are her daughter, after all."

Something in my chest caved in. It was true. I was her daughter and nothing I ever said or did would change that fact. No one would ever believe that I truly wanted to stand against her because of the blood we shared. There would always be that doubt, that suspicion, against me. That I would turn to her when all else failed, that I would leave this all behind to join her and claim my rightful place upon the throne of her court.

"Gemini—" Lark started, rage in every clipped word.

"Aunt, please," Cass plead.

"I am a child of rape, Gemini Morningstar," I said, turning my gaze to her and addressing her by her full name so that she might understand the truth I spoke. "I am the daughter of a man who was invaded in every conceivable way; mind, body, and soul. I am the daughter of a prisoner held hostage within the Pride Court. I am the daughter of a gentle soul who sought to teach me how to resist her abilities even when it seemed impossible, even when we both knew she would find us eventually and would punish him far worse than me. I am his daughter, not hers. There isn't an ounce of my being that can be attributed to the monster who stole her own father's magic, crippling him and casting him aside, who forced herself upon an unwilling and innocent mortal, who rips holes in the Divide itself simply because she feels she is owed possession of someone she never truly loved. So do not speak of suspicions to me. No one has more reason to hate Ariadne Dawnpaw than me. Except, perhaps, my father."

Her shoulders dropped at that, her gaze shuttered, and I watched as some of the fight went out of that ancient fae, replaced entirely by obvious pity. Gemini wasn't one to willingly show emotion, especially in front of so many people. The fact that she did made me aware of how sorry she really was.

"I know, kid, I know," she told me, nodding. "But my family has fallen to betrayal from more surprising sources than yourself. I simply have to be sure."

"We are bonded, aunt," Lark reminded her, tone firm. "Hurting me is akin to hurting herself. Besides, we haven't ceased our diplomatic efforts. In fact, I've invited Irim down to breakfast this morning in that very vein."

Irim glanced up at that, still chewing on a mouthful of eggs. Slowly, he swallowed, gaze flickering from Lark to Cass and Rook, to Gemini, and then resting finally on me.

"If you're expecting me to have any sort of sway within my home court, I imagine you'll be sorely disappointed," he spoke a moment later, dabbing at the corners of his mouth with a napkin in a show of propriety before he did. "Ariadne was successful in cutting my family off from the rest of the nobility a long time ago. And ever since my father's death, she's been sending me on more and more expeditions outside of the court so that I would not be seen as a credible threat to her claim. I hardly know anything at all of the prominent members of our court anymore."

"It isn't the prominent members I'm concerned with, Irim," Lark drawled, lips spreading slowly into a grin.

Irim's brows furrowed.

"These expeditions that Ariadne has been sending you on," Lark began, leaning back in his chair and eyeing my cousin as he spoke. "They have to do with solving the common problems that Ariadne does not wish to waste her own time on, yes? My bonded has informed me of a particular issue you were investigating which brought you to the palace where you met her. A drought in the east, I believe?"

Irim's gaze flicked to me briefly before he nodded.

"And did you solve that problem?" Lark asked.

"I did," Irim answered, head held high, proud. "It was a simple malfunction of their aqueduct system. It took some repairing. The stone structure had been damaged in a sandstorm. Then there was the more difficult matter of bringing back the rain."

"And these people were eternally grateful that a member of the royal family should stoop so low as to help poor, simple farming folk regain access to their water systems. Just as I'm sure the farmers in the west appreciated your gift of thousands of seeds when a petulance corrupted their stores and the people of the south appreciated your requisition of thousands of pairs of snow shoes when they suffered a particularly brutal blizzard this winter. Or when those in the north survived an infamous heat wave two years ago because you bottled water from those same aqueducts in the east you fixed just this year and sent it to those in the hot desert sands. Your court is immense, Irim. It covers every biome in our plane. Your people are diverse and innumerable. And yet you have gained their trust over the years."

"You want me to turn the common people against their Queen?"

"She isn't their Queen. I simply want you to remind them of that."

"She'll come after me. She'll kill me. She—"

"If ever you feel your life is in danger, flee to the Court of Rivals. As I recall, you have influence there as well. Perhaps you can join my brother in convincing them to lend us their aid while you're there."

Irim blinked rapidly, looking from Lark to me and back again. He opened his mouth but no words came out.

"If you do this for our cause," Lark continued, "I can promise you the best of Bone Court protection. Ariadne will not be able to reach you short of facing you herself on that battlefield, should it come to that."

"How can you be sure?" he asked.

Lark's eyes darkened even as his grin widened.

"She hasn't found her way around one of my wards yet," he answered. Cass' eyes shot to her brother but Lark maintained eye contact with my cousin who was glancing between us once more, seeming to consider.

"Seren," Irim said my name and I looked up to find him watching me, tense. "Can I trust him?"

I nodded.

"You can trust me, Irim," I told him. "And I trust him. He will do as he says."

On the table, Lark squeezed my hand in appreciation. I ran a finger along his palm in response and watched the corners of his smirking lips quirk even higher.

"You think Taurus can be convinced to help?" Irim asked.

"I think my brother is not the traitor that my sister is," Lark replied easily, as though discussing his siblings did not pain him as much as I knew it did. "If there's one thing we have always agreed upon, it is that we do not stand for attacks from outside of our family. We love one another, in our own way. We will defend our court and its members from all but each other. As ridiculous as that sounds."

"I don't think it sounds ridiculous at all," Irim muttered under his breath and Rook's brows rose in surprise.

"It is," Cass grumbled and I saw Gemini offer her niece an encouraging pat on the back.

"That's it, then? You'll have the Bone Court and Kabir's Court of Dreams. With Taurus and I, you may have Rivals and the weaponless common folk of Peace and Pride. Not much of a fighting force, if I'm honest, Canis."

"We're awaiting the results of a committee hearing in the Court of Scholars as well, though Ren here made an excellent case, and I'm heading to Wanderers tomorrow."

"They won't join you," Irim said, shaking his head. "Wanderers has been proudly neutral for almost as long as Blessings."

"As eccentric as she is, Wispa won't be happy about losing the monopoly on inter dimensional travel that her court held prior to Ariadne's rifts. As for Blessings, we have an in there as well."

Cass' jaw clenched. It was almost imperceptible but I noticed. Irim looked from Cass to Rook before going slack jawed.

"Kismet," he breathed. "What have you offered her?"

"A shot at Rook," Lark replied with a shrug.

A loud scraping sound suddenly emanated from the room as Cass shoved her chair back from the table and rose. Without a word, she stormed from the room and could be heard a moment later making her way back up the stairs. Gemini shook her head at the outburst but Rook just sat perfectly still, expression blank. Irim was nodding slowly.

"Very well," he said, rising. "I will visit my people. I will ask that you continue caring for my grandfather as you have. He is not your enemy, nor your hostage. He is simply a father who loved his daughter so much that it blinded him."

Lark did not reply to that but nodded. Irim took his agreement in stride and left, off to the fringes of the pride court and, likely, Rivals as well. After a shared glance, Rook rose and left as well. Only when he was gone, the front door shut firmly behind him, did Gemini speak.

"That was poorly done, lad," she said. Her tone was calm but I knew her well enough by now to hear the undercurrent of anger in it just the same.

Lark sighed, leaning back in his chair and rubbing his temples as though all of the politicking he had just done had physically pained him.

"I didn't offer a proposal on Rook's behalf," he quipped, annoyed. "It's one date."

"But there's a history there," Gemini argued. "You know that. How would you feel if Seren was arranged one date with Taurus? Just one date for the good of the realm?"

She cocked an eyebrow as Lark frowned back at her.

"Point taken," he replied. "I will speak with Cass."

"Take care that you do. I know what it is to lose one's closest confidante to petty scheming," she said and then frowned, thinking. "It's a good thing that you're doing here, nephew. Trying to restore your father's power is a worthy ambition and one that, I must admit, would help the war effort considerably. Despite the bad blood between us, I do hate to see Perseus suffer."

Lark nodded and then Gemini vanished in a flash of shadow.

I turned my gaze to my bonded who seemed suddenly thoughtful and, perhaps, even remorseful. Questions about all I had just witnessed filled me to the brim but one rose above them all, one that repeated itself again and again after each step in this process.

"What now?" I asked.

"Now," he began, looking even more annoyed than he had before, "we visit Taurus."

Chapter Thirty

A Temporary Truce

A visit to the Court of Rivals was not what I had been expecting and, if I were honest, I wasn't sure it was the best idea for Lark to visit the brother who would inevitably try to kill him alone. But perhaps that's why he did it. If he could speak to Taurus, one on one, without the threatening presence of Rook or the mocking glare of Cass, perhaps the prince would agree to help. Or so I assumed he was thinking. I hadn't had the chance to ask him until we made our way out of the house to shadow step back to the sprawling desert just outside the Court of Rivals.

"Why don't you just shadow step right into your brother's rooms?" I asked, sighing as I lifted my foot to watch endless grains of sand run out of my shoe.

Lark chuckled beside me, reaching out a hand for me to take as we made our way into the city.

"It's considered rude to shadow step into another territory," he explained as we walked. "Bypassing the security at the gates is considered a high offense. It won't do well to offend this court before we even get the chance to attempt to win them to our cause."

I nodded. That made sense.

"Lark," I began then, prepared to begin my onslaught of questions, "why hasn't your father come for us? He must have heard that you're alive by now, that you bypassed his ordered execution. Why wouldn't he send men to capture you like he did before?"

"Perseus is dealing with rumors of the court, rumors that claim he must have been involved in my deception, all while trying to continue to hide the fact that he is weakening without his magic. Of course, he would never have aided in my escape. Such a simple paternal instinct would be viewed as weakness in the King of the Bone Court."

Lark gave me a pointed glance at the end and my jaw dropped in surprise.

"Do you mean to say your father knew of your plans to escape and that he helped you do so?" I asked, stunned.

"I would never say such a thing," he replied but the pointed glance was there and the implication was as good as verification.

"And I said such horrible things to him," I muttered, ashamed.

But Lark merely laughed.

"Perseus Morningstar has heard the worst of what others have to say about him," Lark assured me. "I'm sure whatever you said appeared to affect him more than it did. He's quite good at making you feel guilty for speaking the truth."

I considered that for a moment and then spoke again.

"Cass and Rook?" I asked and Lark's amused smile vanished.

"Best not to get into that," he grumbled.

"Gemini said there was a history there."

"There was. Rook and Cass had always been close. They were... together for a time. Sort of. But they had a falling out shortly before our exile and, well, neither of them handled the fifty years apart very well at all."

"How were they 'sort of' together?"

"I tried very hard not to know of the details before and I certainly haven't asked since. There's definitely some affection between them but neither seems willing to admit it. So they dance around the idea but never truly act upon it."

"How long has this been going on?"

"Oh, two hundred years or so," he said it with a shrug but my eyes widened in a very mortal way.

Two hundred years of repressing your feelings, of lying to yourself about what someone meant to you, of missing out on what it was to be close to that person you love so dearly. How had they done it? And why?

"I can see you thinking, Princess," Lark mused, grin splitting his lips. "Don't meddle."

"But—"

"It won't be appreciated. Trust me."

I folded my arms and stuck out my bottom lip in a pout but fell silent as we approached the arena. We split off from the main thoroughfare just before reaching the doors and turned down a side street lined with sturdy brick townhouses that all looked the same. I was stunned, momentarily, by the modern simplicity of them. I suppose I had suspected a brutal warrior like Taurus Morningstar to live in a hut somewhere in the desert, not in a perfectly accommodating warm and cozy townhouse. I was further stunned when Lark led me up the front steps and simply knocked on the front door.

He glanced at me out of the corner of his eye and sighed.

"Rude to shadow step into someone's living room, remember?" he said.

"But this is Taurus," I argued.

"Even more reason not to surprise him."

Before I could say anything in response to that, the door swung open to reveal an already frowning Taurus. Lark's older brother looked much like him with the same black hair that probably would have been wavy as well had Taurus not made a habit of keeping it cut so short, the same dark eyes and bronzed skin. But where Lark was lean and sculpted, Taurus was a bulging mass of muscles and irregular angles.

"Come to admonish me further for losing the key to Hellscape?" he grumbled, turning and marching back into his own home, leaving the door open so that we could join him.

Lark glanced my way, one eyebrow raised, as if he were wondering the same thing I was. This was an awfully cavalier way to treat a sibling you were destined to fight to the death. But Taurus showed us his back as though he knew he had nothing to fear from us. I supposed it made sense. If we had come to kill him, we wouldn't have simply knocked on his front door.

"We got it back," Lark informed him, closing the door behind us as we stepped inside. "If you're at all concerned."

Taurus grunted and I found myself staring at our surroundings in awe. What had appeared to be a soft and cozy townhouse from the outside truly was a soft and cozy townhouse. The furnishings were all about half a century out of date but appeared to be worn with love, rather than carelessly. The spines of the books on the shelves were all cracked, indicating that they had, in fact, been read, and he even had a steaming pot of tea placed beside a delicately chipped teacup on the table in the barely visible kitchen.

"I'm sure father was thrilled," Taurus grunted, practically ignoring us as he made his way back to his tea, setting the pot back on the stove and coming into the living room with the cup. It looked amusingly tiny in his enormous hands and he pointedly did not ask us if we would like to partake as he took an exaggerated sip.

"Father is never thrilled," Lark said and his brother snorted at that, the only hint of amusement I'd ever seen from him.

Taurus' eyes flicked to me and I tensed without meaning to.

"It's true, then?" he asked, looking between us with interest. "You're bonded?"

"You know it isn't polite to ask—"

"Lark."

"Yes. We are bonded."

Taurus made a sound that seemed more like a scoff before pushing past us to settle into the faded maroon couch in his living room.

"What do you want?" he asked gruffly.

"You have influence here," Lark began.

"You want me to convince Echo to join your asinine war."

Lark's jaw tensed but he maintained his composure. I'd never seen anyone get to Lark as much as his siblings did.

"We are attempting to avoid bloodshed," Lark answered slowly, diplomatically. "But if all other measures fail, yes. We intend to know whether or not Lord Stormflight is on our side."

"He won't be," Taurus said simply and then held up a finger to stop Lark before he could speak again. "But he won't be on hers either. Echo likes how things are now. He likes profiting from the vices of the fae. He's created an entire economy based off of the Court of Rivals' history as a bloodthirsty, immoral tribe, yes. But he's comfortable now and old. He won't be quick to jump back into warfare."

"How can I make it worth it to him?"

"I'm not sure that you can. Your defense of the humans is admirable, Canis. But there are those who believe it to be a weakness as well. Many of them live here."

"If we get formal acknowledgments from Dreams and Scholars—"

"You'll still be up against Friends and Light."

Taurus stood, setting aside his tea cup as he shook his head.

"I'm sorry, Lark," he said with a sigh. "Maybe, when the battle comes, he won't be able to resist it. But I can't promise you which side he will join."

"And you, brother?" Lark asked, voice quieter but no less firm. "Which side will you join?"

Taurus watched us for a moment, frowning, and then spoke again.

"Did you know Ursa came to see me again?" he asked, seeming thoughtful as he turned away to grab his tea cup and take it back into the kitchen. "Scared me half to death. I nearly killed her before she could get a word out. She said she was going back to Ariadne but not really. She said it was a ploy, that she was going to claim she needed me, along with our father's power, to destroy you but really it was all just to get her hands on the amulet again. She said I was supposed to lie if anyone from the Pride Court came to check. I was supposed to say I'd agreed to help her defeat you."

Lark waited in silence. We had already known all of this. Taurus watched him for a moment and then nodded, apparently pleased with the verification of his suspicions that Lark had been involved in this from the start.

"If Ursa is on your side, you know I am too," Taurus said then, more determined than resigned now that a course had been set. "We agree to a temporary truce to handle things outside of our court before dealing with the succession."

"There is no dealing with the succession if father lives," Lark replied.

"I will stand by your side," Taurus vowed, ignoring his brother's entirely rational argument regarding the succession, "until I begin to expect a knife will find its way into my back."

"I wouldn't—"

"Power corrupts everyone, little brother. Even you."

Lark frowned but did not argue again. Taurus, however, was grinning as he extended a hand. Lark took it and the brothers shook their agreement.

"I will speak to Echo Stormflight," Taurus said as they let go. "Perhaps he can be convinced. The man does love his bloodshed and you know I can be quite persuasive."

Lark smiled at that.

"If anyone can do it, dear brother, it's you."

Chapter Thirty-One
A Voyage Into The Unknown

Though I thought the meeting with Taurus had gone well, I couldn't ignore just how tightly Lark gripped my hand as we made our way back through the sandy streets to outside of the court. He only relaxed his hold on me after we shadow stepped back to Cass' home in the Court of Dreams, leaving Rivals well behind us.

"I thought it went well," I said, confused as we popped into existence inside of Cass' foyer, my head still spinning from the strange method of travel that was becoming more and more familiar as of late.

"It did," he agreed, already striding toward the sitting room. "Better than expected if I'm being honest."

"So why did we practically run out of there?"

"For the first time in over half a century, my siblings and I are at peace. Whenever that happens, my father inevitably gets involved. Considering how he chose to summon me home last time, I thought it best we get behind the wards here as soon as possible."

My eyes widened at the implication behind his words. That his father would not hesitate to snatch him off the streets again, dragging him home for another lecture or worse, seemed inconceivable after all we had accomplished. Of course, we had done all of those things in his name without his permission. I was starting to see why avoiding Perseus Morningstar might be best for the moment.

"Will he pull his support if things turn violent?" I asked, suddenly worried. "You've been speaking on behalf of your court but your father is still king. Would he withhold his armies if Ariadne attacked?"

"No," Lark said, certain. "My father would not let Ariadne win just to teach me a lesson. But I'm sure he is displeased by the way I've handled things."

"Why? How could he be? You've nearly united every minor court, except for the Court of Friends, to stand against her."

"He would argue that we should have tried a different way first. That we should have sought peace and negotiated. He still doesn't believe the worst of what she's done. And he will fear for his own power, which she still has in her clutches. He will fear the fact that he may never have it returned if we take up arms against her."

"But you have already considered this option?"

"Ariadne is not the sort to relinquish power once she has it. And you've seen what she's done to your father, what she did to you, to Irim. How can one negotiate with a woman who can not only read minds but control them? If there were a way, I would try but..."

He trailed off with a sigh. I nodded in understanding and then moved up behind him, wrapping my arms around his waist and leaning my head against his powerful back. He relaxed and turned until he was holding me to him, cradling me in his arms as my face pressed against his chest.

"Tomorrow, I will go to Wanderers," he said, his voice barely above a whisper. "After that, Blessings. And we'll need to check back in with Scholars. They've had their time to discuss. We need an answer."

I nodded against him, letting his warmth and the solid form of his body strengthen me. We could do this. We could win this. She could be beaten. It was possible. I had to believe that. I had to.

"You should get some rest," Lark said slowly and I extricated myself by sheer force of will. He smiled softly down at me, running his fingers through my hair as those dark eyes flashed silver. "I should visit Kabir, see how he's faring with the tasks I assigned him."

"And check up on Rook and Kismet?" I asked, raising a brow.

Lark smirked, one corner of his mouth lifting.

"Can't get anything past you, can I?" he teased but leaned forward to kiss my head softly, diminishing the effect of his taunting.

"Never," I replied. "We're bonded now, Lark. Two halves of a whole."

"I've never felt so whole in my life, princess."

Then, with a final kiss upon my lips, he took one step back and vanished.

I allowed my hands to drop to my sides before turning and glancing at the stairs. Cass would be up there, still locked away in her room, upset. I should go to her. In fact, I was a terrible friend for not considering it earlier. But there had been things to do, places to go, and I let our friendship fall to the wayside. I'd been doing that more and more lately, pushing Cass aside for later in favor of something new, something more pressing. When had we last simply sat and talked the way we used to? Well, I would rectify that.

I made my way up the stairs and to her room. The door was closed, as I expected, but I knocked softly and pressed an ear against the wood, expecting to hear the call to come inside. It did not come.

"Cass?" I called out, knocking again.

The silence that greeted me, however, was not as intriguing as the light spilling through the hallway from an open door just a little way down from this one. Assuming that Cass must have gone out while we were gone, I crept away from her door and down the hall toward the other one.

Alban Dawnpaw was laying in precisely the same place he had been put upon his arrival in this house. As far as I knew, he had never moved nor been moved, except for whatever the healer from the Court of Blessings did for him when she visited. He wasn't as frail as he had seemed before. His skin was healthier, warmer rather than that nearly translucent papery pale that he had displayed for so long. His chest rose and fell with deeper breaths now and he did not appear to be so emaciated.

I frowned, stepping into the room. My mother had allowed her own father to wither to such a state. Lark was right. What mercy could she possibly show the rest of us?

I settled into the seat beside his bed, watching him as he breathed. His eyes were closed but the lids flickered as if he weren't truly sleeping or, if he was, he was plagued by endless dreams which drew his attention and restricted his rest. I leaned forward, watching more closely. He wasn't conscious. He hadn't opened his eyes or said a word in all the time he had been here. But my power did not have to do with the conscious world. Nor did his, little that he might have remaining.

I looked down at my hands, curious, and then raised them. I closed my eyes, focusing as I fled to that place of emotion, that realm between reality and feeling. Then I held his hand.

The sensation of emotion, the vibrant angry reds and somber blues, muted somewhat. I sensed another presence immediately. It wasn't dark like the bone court's high obsidian walls or vast like my infinite shoreline. It was soft and firm at the same time. Loose soil under my feet, the heads of wheat stalks ticking my fingertips, a bright blue sky above. I turned my face toward the imagined sun and thought, perhaps, I could feel its heat.

"Who are you?" a strong male voice commanded and I turned back to my surroundings to see him approach.

Alban Dawnpaw looked far better in his youth. He had golden hair that waved despite being cropped closely to his head and chocolate eyes that sparkled in the midday sun. His body was not the frail, withered thing awaiting him in the realm of reality but was solid, sturdy. He wore beige linen, a softly wrinkled shirt and pants, as he stepped toward me through the endless field of wheat.

"I'm Seren," I told him, my voice taking on an ethereal quality in this realm so that I sounded far more serene than I intended. "I'm your grand-daughter."

His steps faltered as he stared at me, wide-eyed. His lips parted in surprise.

"You're-I'm dead, then?" he asked and I couldn't help the chill that shot down my spine at how easily he had accepted such an idea.

"No, King Dawnpaw," I told him. "You live."

"But you're dead. She said..." he trailed off, pressing a hand to his head and stumbling.

"I assure you I am very much alive. Your daughter lied to you. She has been lying to you for years."

He stared at me for a moment and I swore I could see his heart breaking. The wheat around us began to wither and die, all but the stalks that surrounded me. They remained bright and golden, vibrant.

"I suppose I shouldn't be surprised," he said then. "Ariadne has been keeping a great deal from me. Her ambition... but you were taken so long ago. I suppose I thought her betrayal had been more recent. Or, rather, I wanted to."

I nodded, agreeing with this conclusion.

"I wish we had first met in a better way, granddaughter," he spoke and his voice sounded fainter, weaker. The decay of the wheat that had spread from him was beginning to encroach upon my own, killing around the edges of my impenetrable sphere. "But how are you here now?"

"I imagine it has something to do with the nature of our powers and the connection within our blood," I told him. "I cannot speak to others like this."

He nodded, thoughtful.

"We do not have much time," I told him as the decay swept closer. Somehow I knew, inherently, that I would need to abandon this place before it reached me. "Ariadne was keeping you locked away, hidden, claiming that you were sick with age. Gemini Morningstar freed you and now you rest in her niece's home. Ariadne has formed a coalition between your court, the Court of Light and Life, and the Court of Friends. It seems they seek to tear down the Divide. They've made an elixir that grants immortal life through great pain and they've forced it upon my father and upon... upon me."

Alban started, horrified.

"We are trying to figure out a way to bring your power back but if you could wake up, if you could find your way back to the realm of reality, perhaps you can help to destabilize her claim on your throne."

"I-I can't," he said, glancing wildly about in panic. "I cannot find the way. I have been trying. I've been walking through this field for ages. It never ends, never changes. You are the first I have seen among the wheat. Wait, no. There was another. A man. Or... perhaps a god? I cannot be certain. My mind plays tricks on me here. Sometimes I hear things, people speaking, and sometimes I feel the weight of my body in the physical plane but I cannot reach it. The healers try. I can feel their work on the fringes of my mind, like a tingling sensation in my limbs, but they aren't strong enough. I'm trapped here, in my own mind. She made sure of that."

I was certain I wasn't mistaking his bitter tone as he finished. I watched him for a moment, horrified. How terrible it must be to be trapped in one's own mind, to be unable to trust your own thoughts for they had become a prison to you. I shuddered to think of it.

There had to be a way out. Maybe I could help him find it, through this connection. I was running out of time now. The decay was nearly inches from my feet. But I could return. I could help him. We could find the way out together and then, maybe, we could find a way to return his power.

"I have to leave now," I told him, inching back away from the decay but it was approaching from all sides. Only seconds now. "I will return, grandfather. We will find a way to free you."

"She isn't a monster," he called out but I was already pulling away, already retreating back to reality. His voice trailed after me, growing quieter the farther I went. "It is fear that controls her, not evil."

I wasn't certain I agreed with him but I did not say as much. He would not have heard me anyway. I was already back inside my own mind, my own body, the aura of my own emotions swirling and raging like a violent sea around me. I took in a deep breath as I pulled my hand from the old man's grasp, gasping as if breathing for the first time. I turned wildly about but we were alone and the room was dark. I blinked, letting my vision adjust to the lack of light in here. The moon shone in through the window opposite me, the night breeze blowing the curtains about. The candle on the dresser had long been lit and burnt out. And standing in the doorway, arms crossed, was Gemini Morningstar.

"I told the boy you'd be fine," she muttered, shifting so that she stood up straight in the threshold. She pretended to be relaxing, getting more comfortable, but I saw the way her gaze flicked over me in examination and I understood why. Lark and I had visited Taurus in the morning. How long had I been sitting here in a trance-like state? It had felt like only moments in the other realm, the realm of thoughts and emotions, but the deep night outside of that window said otherwise.

"How long have I been here?" I asked, rising. Every muscle groaned in protest and I nearly stumbled, surprised by the soreness that had developed in what seemed to be a very short time to me.

"Hours," she said. "I don't know how many. I wasn't here when you started. Lark wanted to rouse you but I told him to let you be. I wasn't even sure he could pull you out of that place, much less if he should. Did you find him?"

I nodded and her shoulders slumped in relief.

"Must have been a shock for him," she added. "Meeting his supposedly dead granddaughter."

"He knows the truth now," I replied, nodding in the old man's direction. My eyes drooped and I snapped to attention to remain awake. I was so tired. When had that happened? "He knows what she's done and what we're doing to stop her. He's been trying to come back but... he can't find the way. He can hear us though, sometimes. So it might help to talk to him. I think he understands. Although..."

"Although?" Gemini encouraged, raising a brow.

"I think it's possible that he's starting to lose himself. His mind, that is."

"Why do you think that?"

"He mentioned seeing someone else in that place. He said he saw a man. He said it might have been a god."

"Don't take that derisive tone, little scholar. You're so certain god does not exist?"

I stared at her, unsure if she was kidding.

"There is no empirical evidence—" I began.

"Of anything contradicting a theory of creation," Gemini finished. "I'm two thousand years old, girl. And in all that time, I've seen more evidence in favor of divinity than I've seen against it."

I sighed.

"I'm too tired to engage in theological debate with you tonight, Gemini," I said, rubbing my temples as a headache began to form from my exhaustion. I needed sleep. I wouldn't be able to think properly until I slept. But before I did, there was something I needed to do, something I had been trying to do when I'd gotten distracted and come to visit Alban. "I need to see Cass."

"That... isn't a good idea, I'm afraid," Gemini replied and her tone had my gaze shooting back up to her. Suddenly wide awake, I frantically searched Gemini's expression for what that could mean. My lips parted in question but the old general was already explaining. "My niece made some... questionable choices after the events of this morning. She and Lark have had a little talk and now she's back in her room recovering. She's requested to be alone. I think we should give her that. For tonight, at least."

I nodded. It wasn't enough information. What had Cass done? She wasn't one to want to be alone. She wasn't one to shut us out and make poor snap decisions. If she was truly so affected by Rook's involvement with Kismet, that was something she needed a friend to talk to about, wasn't it? I would give her the night because she asked for it and because I was so utterly, completely exhausted. But I would be at her door at the crack of dawn and she had better open it this time or I would blow it right off the hinges.

"You were watching me, weren't you?" I asked, changing the course of the conversation, allowing some exhaustion to seep into my tone.

Gemini noticed, her eyes narrowing.

"Only so he wouldn't pace right through these nice mahogany floors," she grumbled and I gave her a tired smile. "Off to bed with you now, girl. You've done well here. Get some rest."

I nodded, too tired to argue, and slid out into the hallway. I plodded along, fighting a yawn as I made my way toward my door. I reached for the handle and paused. If I concentrated hard enough, I could sense the extra wards Lark had placed upon this room. I knew a warm, empty bed waited beyond as well as a glorious shower and some fresh clothes. But those comforts weren't what I needed right now. So I turned away and shuffled across the hall. My room didn't feel like mine anymore anyway.

I knocked on the dark door and waited, practically leaning upon it in my exhausted state.

"You don't have to knock, princess," that familiar drawl called from within. "What's mine is yours, remember?"

I twisted the knob and nearly tumbled onto the soft carpet below. Tired, so tired. My eyes drooped and I stumbled. Strong arms were there to catch me. Lark muttered a curse but lifted me easily, carrying me to his bed. My eyes opened just long enough to spot Rook seated on one of the plush velvet armchairs on the other side of the room and then silk sheets were around me and a fluffy pillow was under my head and the world was no more.

Chapter Thirty-Two

A Moment

I heard their voices first. Before any of my other senses returned, before I opened my eyes or fully regain consciousness, I heard them.

"It isn't a good idea, Lark," Rook was saying.

I blinked awake but remained perfectly still, staring at the candles burning on the dresser across from me.

"It's probably a trap," Rook said.

"Perhaps," Lark agreed, thoughtfully. "But I don't see that we have much choice. Whoever controls the healers will have an enormous advantage in this conflict. If this is the condition that Kismet claims they require, then we must meet it. No matter what it is."

"It won't work. You know that. Ariadne is not one for negotiations. She's gone too far to agree to peace now."

"I know. We all know that. But the healers seem to need proof. So we will try it their way. We will meet with her, discuss what it would take to have peace in the realm again, and let them see how rooted she is in her beliefs and just how far she's willing to go to see them realized."

"No," I said.

I hadn't necessarily meant to speak. I had determined to remain silent, eavesdropping on their conversation in a way that I should probably be ashamed of. But I wasn't. Lark was my bonded. We were two halves of a whole. I knew he wouldn't have withheld this from me. Still, I wanted them to have the peace to speak to one another openly, the way they did before I was around. Especially since I was intruding upon a room that wasn't truly mine.

Now, they both looked my way. Rook seemed surprised to find me awake. Lark only met my gaze knowingly. He had known I was awake. He could sense it in the same way that I sensed him. But he had allowed me to listen as I knew he would.

"You cannot go to her again," I said, sitting up so that the silk sheets slipped and fell to pool in my lap. I let some of my fear show in my expression, in my voice. "She will hurt you again. She will capture me. She—"

"The Court of Blessings will not allow that," Lark told me. "They have mechanisms in place to prevent either party from striking at the other during negotiations. Peace talks have been held in their court for centuries. It's the safest place we could meet your mother."

"There is no place safe from Ariadne Dawnpaw," I replied, my gaze narrowing as I dug in my heels.

"I'm inclined to agree," Rook added. "With your father's power dangling around her neck in addition to the already potent magic of her own, we have no idea what she's capable of. She can call the Void. She can read minds and influence them. She can use other's magic against them. Is that someone you really want to face again?"

"We will be better prepared this time," Lark argued and I could see that there was no shaking him from this course. I sighed, closing my eyes and turning away. "And we will have the entire Court of Blessings at our defense should she seek to upend centuries worth of tradition for some foolish attack on us. Besides, I can call the Void as well. And I have far more practice with it."

His words seemed to burn into the air around him. I could hear the barely restrained rage underlying his tone and knew he would not hesitate, if necessary, to use his most deadly magic against our sworn enemy, against my mother.

"I will tell Kismet we agree," Rook said with a sigh, rising.

"Make sure that is all you tell Kismet," Lark warned, his voice so low that Rook turned back to look at him. "We do what we must but my sister's heart means nearly as much to me as the fate of the realm, old friend."

Rook watched his prince for a moment longer before nodding and striding through the door into the hallway beyond. Once it was shut behind the warrior, Lark turned to me and his gaze softened.

"Ren—" he started.

"I will not be captured again, Canis Morningstar," I snapped, using his full name to show my displeasure. It worked. He winced but continued to approach me, sitting on the edge of the bed next to me.

"She will have to kill me to take you from me again," he vowed.

I couldn't help but melt at that, at the devotion in his tone, the way his eyes flashed silver as if to put a finer point on the matter. I sighed and reached for him, wrapping my arms around him and leaning my head on his shoulder as he wrapped one enormous hand around my thigh and squeezed.

"She won't agree to peace," I whispered, my exhaustion returning as the fight left me. "She's already gone too far, crossed too many lines, to go back now. And she's promised something to Koa and Sophierial. I don't know what but she will have no choice but to deliver, to repay Sophierial for the elixir and the support."

"I can't help but wonder, though, why Sophierial allowed us to claim refuge with her all those months ago, why she didn't turn us over to Ariadne the moment we arrived at her gates," Lark mused, thinking.

I looked up at him, brow furrowed.

"They were already working together by then," he continued. "They had to have been since your father had already taken the elixir. And yet Sophierial allowed us to stay in her palace, treated us as guests, and kept our presence a secret from her supposed ally. I wonder why that is."

I blinked, stunned by the fact that I had never considered this before. And finally the realization struck. It had been so obvious. How had we never seen it before? I pulled back from Lark, staring at him with pure shock.

"Because she knew Ariadne would stop the rifts once she found me," I whispered, in awe at this revelation. "She needed my mother frantic, unstable. She needed Ariadne tearing holes in the Divide in some reckless search to find me. This isn't about profiting off of the elixir. Sophierial has her own motives for seeing the Divide fall."

Lark nodded as I spoke.

"We need to figure out what those motivations are," I finished, determined.

"I doubt she will tell us," he replied. "But it isn't too difficult to figure out if you know the history of the Court of Light and Life. They fancy themselves some sort of missionaries. You saw how they made us pray to their gods while we stayed with them. They will want to 'spread the light', as they call it, to mortals, converting them to their belief in Lemnus and Rhene and Cylon and whatever other gods they can force upon them."

Gods...

"Lark," I started, my mind attempting to make connections that I wasn't entirely sure were there, "is there a history of divinity in this plane? Do you follow a religion here?"

"Not anymore," he replied, shaking his head. "But the fae used to. They claimed there was a pantheon of gods who granted our power. Our courts are modeled after them, in a way. Lemnus, the god of Light, was the example for the Court of Light and Life. Dryas, of Valor, for Rivals. I think both Wanderers and Blessings claim Iphitheme, goddess of fertility. Friends follows either Macar, of the hunt, or Bisaltes, god of the harvest. I can't remember. Scholars claimed Pherusa, the goddess of wisdom, though they were the first to abandon her. Dreams has Siculus, god of dreams. The Bone Court took Alkiphron, the god of night. And, ironically, the Peace Court was modeled after Theoros, the god of justice. But the Court of Light is the only one who still worships any of the gods and they choose their own, Lemnus, as well as Cylon, god of time, and Rhene, goddess of prophecy. I'm not convinced Sophierial actually believes in the gods anymore but religion is always an easy method of control over one's people."

"Did these gods ever... interact with the fae?"

Lark scratched his chin, thoughtful.

"There are ancient legends of them doing so. Some claim the amulets were a gift from the gods in exchange for excellent service from the twins. And there are other artifacts and stories attributed to them. But they're all hundreds of years old. If the gods still live, they do not do so here."

"Are you sure?" I asked. "Could something have happened to send them away? Could they simply be hiding or refusing to show themselves again?"

He cocked his head to the side.

"I thought you didn't believe in such things," he said.

"I didn't," I told him. "But there are many mortals who don't believe in minotaurs or magical powers and yet here we are. I'm only curious because this is the second mention of gods I've overheard in the last twenty four hours and I wouldn't be a proper scientist if I were confronted with a repeating theory and did not evaluate it for merit."

Lark grinned. He loved when I got academic. That was refreshing. So many men I had dated in the past had been positively bored to tears when I started hypothesizing.

"A war is brewing," Lark reminded me as if that were explanation enough. "People get more religious when there's an imminent threat of death. We all want to believe there's a life after this one when we begin to approach it."

I nodded. That was a rational explanation. Only the man who had claimed to see a god hadn't known there was a war. Then again, Alban Dawnpaw's sanity was not something to assume was stable at the moment.

"I spoke to my grandfather," I told him and his eyes widened.

"You did?" he asked. "It worked then? Whatever you did to put yourself into that trance? Which was terrifying, by the way. A little heads up would have been nice."

I snorted.

"I would have told you if I could," I promised. "I didn't even know I was capable of it myself until I was doing it."

"But you spoke to him. How was he?"

"A little stunned to find that I was alive. Even more so to hear about all his daughter has done. He's trying to find a way back but he needs help. He can't do it alone. The problem is, I don't know how to help him. He said it would take a healer stronger than those that have been coming around lately. Maybe, when we go to the Court of Blessings to speak with my mother, we can request the services of a more powerful healer? If he wakes, he won't have his magic, but he'll regain his faculties. He will be able to function, as your father can. I'd like to give him that, at least, if I can."

Lark smiled again, this one warmer than the last, and reached between us to grip my hand in his.

"You are an incredible person, Seren Belling," he announced. "And I'm a better man for having met you."

"Likewise, prince," I replied and he chuckled, that deep mirth that reverberated in my chest.

Then I was moving toward him, pulling him closer, the sheets sliding further away from me. He kissed me and I forgot about the war, about the gods and Sophierial's machinations. For a moment, I was just Seren and he was just Lark and those names had no meanings, no duties, no responsibilities. For a moment we were two become one, we were bonded, we were lovers who worshiped each other rather than long forgotten gods. We lost ourselves in hands and lips and exposed skin as the candles burned low and eyes glowed silver in the night. It was only a moment. But it was enough.

Chapter Thirty-Three
A Mistake

I knocked tentatively on Cass' door.

I'd waited until the very first beams of sunlight shone in through the window. Then I had tossed off my blankets, to the grumpy tune of a much annoyed Lark, and padded down the hall to the princess' room. I knew she would probably try to turn me away but I was prepared to stand my ground, remaining out here in the hallway and talking to her through this door if I had to. So I was surprised when a weak voice called out for me to enter and the door creaked open by some gentle magic.

"Cass?" I asked as I stepped forward and peered into the darkness.

Her curtains were drawn so that the room was pitch black. Not a single beam of light found its way through those thick drapes. I gave myself a moment to allow my eyes to adjust, stepping inside and shutting the door behind me so that we were plunged into a complete darkness. After a moment, I could make out a faint lump upon the middle of the bed. She laid horizontally rather than vertically, one pillow under her head and back to the door. Her long black hair was unbound and fell in waves to the mattress below. Her bare shoulder peeked out over a slouchy shirt that she didn't bother to adjust.

"Cass, it's me," I said, stupidly, as I perched upon the edge of her bed. I reached out to touch her but wasn't sure it would be appreciated and withdrew. "I fear I haven't been a very good friend."

That got her attention. She moved, slowly but surely, to face me, turning so that her hair fell to frame her face as she peered up at me from where she lay.

"I hope you're wrong," she groaned. Her voice was rough, raspy, as though she had been up all night crying. My heart clenched in my chest to think it and I, again, resisted the urge to reach for her. "Because you're the best friend I've ever had so if you're shit at it that says quite a bit about me."

I snorted and her lips quirked briefly into a slight smirk.

"Do you want to talk about it?" I asked, gently, frowning to see that smile fade away.

She sighed and turned so that she was laying flat on her back staring up at the ceiling.

"I'm an idiot," she said. "An idiot with too high of expectations for everyone around her. I expect my siblings to defy thousands of years of tradition and not fight each other to the death. I expect my father to make the choice not to be an asshole for once in his unending life. And I expect a man to still love me after over half a century apart."

She sighed again and I finally allowed myself to reach out. I gripped her hand in mine and allowed her to speak freely, the way one would when confiding in a friend.

"I knew things would be different when they returned," she continued. "I knew he would have changed. Almost sixty years in exile would do that to a person. But I didn't expect him to barely look at me, barely talk to me at all, while smiling and making jokes like my heart wasn't shattering to pieces. And then this thing with Kismet. He knew. He has known how badly she wants him for centuries now. He toys with her when its convenient for him, when it aligns with Lark's plans, but it was never anything serious and I thought he would stop when... when we... but now here we are again. Lark issues a command and he follows without question. Never mind that it's my heart he's breaking. Never mind that I'm the one left to pick up the pieces again. Never mind that neither of them spoke to me about this at all before the decision was made."

I nodded along. Now that I knew the history, I found myself agreeing with everything she was saying and, what's more, growing angry with Lark because of his role in this. Sure, Rook should have told her, should not have agreed to go along with this plan so easily. But it was Lark's plan. And he should have known how this would affect his sister. He could have at least warned her.

"I'm always the one who has to put us back together again," she whispered in the darkness, still staring up at the ceiling. "Lark makes decisions, Rook follows them, and then things fall apart. And I'm always the one that has to fix them. Always."

She sounded so... tired.

"I wanted to be the one who got to fall apart," she said and her voice was now so quiet that I had to lean in to hear her. A tear caught some light I didn't see as it leaked from her eyes and ran down her beautiful face. Something in me cracked at seeing Cass cry. "Just once, I wanted to be the one who got to mess everything up, who got to make a mistake. And I did, Ren. I made a big mistake."

I gulped at the gravity in her tone.

"What did you do, Cass?" I asked, whispering to match her soft tone.

"I knew Kismet would find a way to win over Blessings," she replied, her voice taking on a note of bitterness as she spoke. "She's always been close with the healers ever since she had that accident as a child. Taurus and Irim would get us Rivals. You and Lark got us Scholars. I wanted to help. I wanted to be the one to form a plan for once. So I... I went to Wanderers."

My hand on hers tightened. I couldn't help it. If she noticed the sudden tension, she did not mention it, perhaps too lost in her story to break from it now.

"Wispa Amberberry has a son," Cass said and my heart began to race. No. No, Cass. Not that. "I thought I could convince him. But she was there, his mother, and she wanted... assurances."

I tried not to gape at her.

"I cut Lark off at the knees because I thought I could win the alliance first," she told me and I could hear the despair in her tone now, the devastation. "I thought I was smart enough to politic my way into convincing them to join our side like he did, like you did. But I... I didn't see the trap until it was too late. I was willing to give him my body. I thought I could secure the alliance while pissing off Rook in the process. And yes, I know how childish that sounds. But I wasn't offering my future, never that. And yet..."

"Wispa proposed a betrothal," I said, knowing where this was going before she finished.

Cass nodded with a finality that felt like the final nail in a coffin.

Despite my heart aching, I could see the genius in Lady Amberberry's ploy. She could align her court, a minor court, with a princess of a major court. Her grandchildren would be in line for both thrones, even if Cass had already passed on her succession rites, her family's status would elevate considerably. And, as she had seemed to have found her son and Cass in a compromising situation, what argument could the princess have made against the arrangement?

"Oh, Cass," I murmured and the bed shook as tears flowed freely down her cheeks and onto the soft mattress below.

"I have until the war is ended," she said. "Then Wispa will see us married. She's already reached out to my father for his approval."

"Could he—"

"Perseus will not get me out of this. Our father is a stickler for ensuring we suffer the consequences of our own actions. He will call this a learning experience for me."

I frowned. There was a way around this. There had to be. Of course, I was thinking along those lines for a great number of problems lately and I was becoming more and more certain that there, in fact, did not have to be solutions for them all. Still, looking at Cass, I couldn't help but believe there was a way out.

"Does Rook know?" I asked softly, carefully.

She shook her head.

"Lark promised not to tell him," she said. "Yet. He agreed to allow me to be the one to break the news. But I-I don't know how-I can't—"

She broke off into a sob and I laid down next to her, wrapping my arms around her and pulling her in close, comforting her as she cried.

"I've made a mess of everything," she wept. "I was angry and I was jealous and I turned what would have been a few dates between Rook and Kismet to forever between myself and Quinn."

I patted her head, stroking her hair while she mourned for a love lost. It hurt more than I thought it would, seeing a friend in so much pain. I wanted to take it from her and, for a moment, I toyed with the idea, wondering if I could. I closed my eyes and reached out with my senses.

I felt it there, her pain, her sadness, her despair. It was right on the surface where she could feel it, where she could express it. I could reach for it, gather it up and lock it away somewhere it could not hurt her. But that wouldn't be true healing, would it? That would be avoidance. And they wouldn't stay locked away forever. Better to feel them properly now than to risk their exploding at a later date. No matter how badly it hurt us both.

So I pulled back and simply held her as she cried.

Some time later, her sniffling subsided and she looked up at me with red-rimmed eyes. The sun had risen so high in the sky that even her thick drapes could not keep out the light and I saw her face, wet with tears, as she wiped her eyes with her sleeves and met my gaze.

"Did he do it, at least?" she asked, her voice broken and raw. "Do we have the Court of Blessings?"

I bit my lip.

"Almost."

"Canis Morningstar!"

Cass' shout rang through the halls of her Court of Dreams home. If there had been anyone who wasn't yet awake, they certainly were now. For a moment, I thought I might check on my grandfather in the coma to see if she'd woken him as well. Instead, I could do nothing but follow after her as she stormed down the stairs and into the sitting room.

Rook was already gone on some errand. That, at least, was a blessing I had to note as she blew into the room, glare narrowed into a point at her brother who glanced lazily up from his cup of coffee as she strode in.

"Yes, Casseiopia?" he drawled, using her formal name as she had used his.

Cass was far too angry to notice.

"You've agreed to meet with her?" she questioned, furious. "The woman who nearly broke you on the sentient floor of that gaudy throne room? The one who captured Ren and held her for weeks? The one who abducted a mortal from his realm, brought him here, fed him some immortality elixir, and chained him to her side for all eternity? This is the woman you're wasting your time trying to reason with?"

"It would be hard to make the argument of superior morality if we don't at least attempt to make peace, sister," Lark said calmly.

"So you risk your life for argument's sake? You risk your life, again, so that others cannot accuse you of evil?"

"We need every minor court. We need Alban and Perseus returned to their power. We need the people of the Pride Court to revolt. I will risk my life to ensure the Divide stands. I stood against Ariadne alone before and was given exile as a result. I hope, this time, I will not be alone."

At the ferocity in his words, I couldn't help but cross the room to stand behind him, reaching over the back of the chair and placing my hands on his shoulders in a steady display of support, of comfort. Cass looked from him to me and slumped.

"You're both going," she said, sounding defeated. "Aren't you?"

Lark gave a firm nod and I swore Casseiopia Morningstar crumpled.

"And if she captures you?" Cass asked. "If she takes you back to her palace for torture or worse? Are Rook and I expected to save you?"

"We leave that room free or we do not leave at all," I spoke, teeth gritted.

Cass stared at me, horrified, but Lark simply nodded in agreement, patting my hand with his own.

"We do this to earn the Court of Blessing's trust. We do this so that no one has to die for a war that could have been resolved before it began," Lark vowed. "We have to know, Cass. We have to be sure."

She hesitated but then nodded.

"And what are we to do?" she asked with a sigh.

"Rook will go to the Court of Blessings with us," Lark answered, though he spoke slower every time he mentioned the warrior's name, clearly gauging his sister's reaction at every utterance. "He will act as our guard, waiting for when the negotiations end. I need you to stay here with Alban. I can't trust that Ariadne wouldn't make a move to retrieve him once she knows Ren and I are otherwise occupied. Guard the King of the Pride Court. I'm certain Ursa, Taurus, or Gemini would come to help if you wished it."

"I will be fine on my own. I'll probably know they're coming before they even make it anywhere near the house."

He nodded.

"We leave as soon as Rook returns from his visit with Kismet. They are setting up the meeting at the Court of Blessings now," he told her. "If we don't return by nightfall, contact father and tell him what happened."

"So soon?" she asked, looking from Lark to me, wide-eyed and afraid.

"We will be fine, Cass," Lark told her, finally rising to place a comforting hand on her arm. "The Court of Blessings has managed this sort of thing for centuries."

She nodded but she didn't seem convinced. I couldn't help but share in the feeling.

I had learned, from experience, that Ariadne was a master at circumventing boundaries. And she knew far more than she should. She was capable of far more than she should be and she loved nothing more than to flaunt that fact in the face of anyone who opposed her. If she had agreed to peace talks so quickly, she must have reason to. Perhaps it was to take a shot at retrieving her father while she knew Lark and I were away but I did not think that likely. She would know we had others guarding him. There was something we were missing here. Something important...

"It's ready," someone spoke and we all turned to see Rook standing in the threshold, nodding to Lark.

We stepped forward, following after the warrior toward the door and, beyond, the Court of Blessings.

I couldn't help the dread that pooled in my stomach as we did.

Chapter Thirty-Four
A Betrayal

Something was wrong.

It was a prevalent thought in my mind as Lark and I shadow stepped to the Court of Blessings, bringing Rook along with us. Nothing seemed amiss. This was all standard wartime procedure even in the mortal realm. One side requested peace negotiations, the other accepted, a neutral third party was selected as the location for the discussions, both sides arrived tense but hopeful. So why did it feel so wrong? Why did it feel like we were missing something?

"Ren?" Lark asked, his voice pitched low so that the Blessings guards wouldn't hear him as we passed and they nodded in greeting. "Are you alright?"

"I'm—" I started to lie, started to assure him that I was fine, but he raised a brow and I knew he was aware of the truth. This was Lark, after all. He knew my heart better than I did sometimes. I couldn't lie to him. "I feel like we're missing something."

He cocked his head to the side.

"Like what?" he asked, curious.

"I don't know," I confessed, fidgeting a bit as we waited for the guards to open the gate for our entrance. "It just feels like this was all... too easy. What do you know of this court? Could they be traitors? You say that the Court of Blessings has been managing peace negotiations for centuries but we're asking them to pick a side. What if she did first? What if they aren't neutral? What if this is a trap?"

"And what if the gods smite us all for daring to war in their realm in the first place?" Lark mused, shaking his head. "There are endless possibilities, Ren. We have to trust what we know and what is most likely. What I know is that the Court of Blessings has not once, in its entire existence, upended tradition or the roles of hospitality. We will not face danger from the healers, princess. It's only your mother we have to look out for."

"Right. But you said she might make a move for Alban. What if it isn't him? What if it's something else? What if she attacks the Bone Court?"

"That would be foolish. My father is well garrisoned and our home has defenses even Ariadne Dawnpaw would be a fool to test."

"Not that then. But what if—"

"Ren, trust me. You will drive yourself crazy trying to imagine every possible scenario that could take place while we are locked in that room with your mother. Do yourself a favor and focus on the conversation, on the negotiations. I need that brilliant mind in there, okay?"

I nodded.

"Of course," I said. "But I-wait, what do you mean locked in?"

He frowned as we reached a building and two healers in long yellow robes approached, clinking manacles of iron gathered in their hands. My eyes widened and I turned to Lark in a panic.

"It's procedure," he explained, far too calmly. "They take your weapons and bind your hands. Iron suppresses magic. The walls of the room are made of it as well. No one that enters will be able to wield and the bindings keep us from physically fighting one another. There will be guards inside, unbound, but we must wear the chains if we wish to enter."

I froze, staring at the dark metal, anxiety ratcheting up within me. I couldn't do it. I couldn't wear these chains. I couldn't allow myself to be bound. Not again. I shook my head, taking a step back, but Lark was there, a solid mass behind me.

"I'll be beside you the entire time," his voice ghosted over the shell of my ear and I inhaled the scent of him. "No one will hurt you, princess. I promise."

Hands shaking, I nodded, stepping forward to accept my chains. I tried not to wince when they clanked shut around my wrists, the healer assigned to me pocketing the key and gesturing me forward. I joined Lark who looked so at ease even bound as he was by the door.

A moment later, the guards opened the door and we stepped through to find ourselves in a brightly lit iron room beyond. I immediately tried to reach out for the emotions of those around me and couldn't. My senses were dulled. I could sense the power, the magic, but I couldn't access it. I had a brief moment of panic before I saw her.

Standing on the other side of the room, my father trailing in after her through the door that had been opened for them across from us, was my mother. She looked the exact same as she had before, golden hair flowing, wicked eyes gleaming, dressed head to toe in bronze so that she shimmered in the lights flickering above. Her painted lips spread into a mischievous grin when she saw us but I looked right past her to my father. He stood, silent and stoic, behind her but his eyes were pinned to me, widened and imploring like he was trying to tell me something, like he was trying to communicate something he couldn't say aloud. Why had she brought him?

"Canis," my mother said tersely, lips pursed in disgust as her gaze flicked over Lark.

"Ariadne," Lark drawled easily, reverting to that charming politician I had seen him become so often lately. Then he did the unthinkable. He turned to the mortal man at my mother's back and smiled. "Richard. Good to see you again."

My father dipped his head but did not speak. Why didn't he say anything? Could he? My gaze flicked to my mother.

"What have you done to him?" I spat, glaring.

Ariadne immediately rolled her eyes, inspecting her nails in that vain, disinterested way of hers, despite the chains clinking with her every movement.

"Honestly, Seren. Don't be so dramatic," she said with a sigh. "He's fine. I have, however, taken his voice for a time. Wouldn't want him revealing state secrets and all that."

My eyes widened.

"How?" I breathed with awe that I was not able to suppress.

She grinned wickedly.

"My own power comes with its perks," she admitted. "And you'd be surprised how well it pairs with the Bone Court King's."

Lark kept a placid expression on his face though she glanced his way to check if her barb had stung as expected.

"Well, you've got me here," she announced then, moving on once she realized that Lark wasn't going to give her the satisfaction of appearing wounded. "What do you want?"

"The Court of Blessings has advised us that it would be most prudent to attempt negotiations prior to this escalating into a conflict that neither of us wants."

"Very good, Bone Prince. But I suppose you did learn politics from the best. Perseus always was skilled at making his lies seem like his opponent's fault. I have to admit I'm curious. What did you promise them to join you?

Kabir was no surprise. You do have a very... intimate connection with that court. Does my daughter know of your past with Karma?"

"I do," I interrupted, doing my best to remain as calm and collected as Lark. It was clear that my mother was trying to rattle us. I refused to let her.

"Very well," she said, waving me off as if nothing I said was worth her time. "Scholars then. I've been trying to convince them for years. Yet you did it in a matter of weeks. How?"

"Actually, your daughter accomplished that one, Ariadne," Lark said, always giving me credit whenever he could. "And the answer to that question, as will be the same for all of the other courts, is you. No one wants to live in the world you're trying to create."

"Cute. And noble. But a lie. I know what you promised Wispa. The elusive princess' hand in marriage. How could she possibly refuse? And Echo has always been a blowhard but he adores your bloody brother. And this court. Well, it's fairly obvious that's what we're doing here, isn't it? Let me guess, they wouldn't agree to join you unless you attempted peace first. You don't actually expect anything to come of this meeting but you're going through the motions and checking all the boxes just to say you did, so that they will join you when the time comes?"

I clenched my fists at my sides. How did she know? How did she always know?

"So why did you come?" Lark asked. "If you know all of this, and if you have no intention of negotiating for peace, why did you agree to speak with us?"

My mother's lips curled into a very slow, wicked smile and my stomach bottomed out.

This is wrong. Something is wrong.

"Lark—" I started, reaching for him, forgetting I was bound.

Then the door opened, so suddenly that I jumped. Ariadne did not take her eyes off of us as Lark and I both peered to their side where a familiar figure was entering. Familiar blonde hair, almond eyes, tall, wearing brown with a glowing amulet around his neck.

"Irim?" I asked, brow furrowed, confused. What was this? Why was he here?

"You bastard," Lark swore suddenly, leaping to his feet.

I understood why a moment later. Irim was wearing an amulet around his neck but it wasn't the only one in the room. There was one around my mother's neck as well.

"Two…" I said slowly, my brain working overtime to understand what had happened. "Who—"

Ariadne was grinning broadly now, the amulet around her neck growing brighter despite the fact that she could not wield any of its magic in this room. It made no sense. I had shattered the amulet holding my grandfather's magic. She hadn't been able to recapture it as it was slowly returning to him bit by bit even now. And yet they stood before us with two glowing amulets hanging from their necks.

"Gemini," Lark hissed.

My mother did not reply but my father gave a solemn nod before dropping his eyes to the floor. Every muscle in my body locked up in shock. My heart rate sped up rapidly, my lips parted, my eyes widened. Not Gemini. It couldn't be Gemini. Gemini was strong. She was defended. They couldn't have possibly—

Irim. We had trusted him. She had trusted him. Suddenly I knew with stunning clarity exactly what had happened. I whirled on my cousin.

"I'll kill you," I growled, lunging for him.

The guards were on me in an instant, pulling me back, off of him, and I couldn't fight back because my hands were bound together and my magic was inoperable. I growled at him, actually physically growled like an animal, as they pulled me backward by my chains. Lark held up a hand when I neared him again and they released me to him. He touched my shoulder and I stopped snarling, stopped fighting, but kept my glare on Irim, breathing heavily, seething.

"Seren, please," he started and he had the audacity to look hurt. "I didn't—"

"I. Will. Kill. You."

"Well! That ends peace negotiations then," my mother announced loudly, tossing her hair over her shoulder as she turned and made her way toward the door. "Thank you, Irim. Let's go, shall we?"

Irim cast me one last glance but my responding growl chased him into the corridor after my departing mother. My father lingered for only a moment, gazing at us, apologetically. I softened slightly.

"I'll get you out," I vowed before I could think of what I was promising. "I'll get you away from her. I swear it."

He smiled but it didn't reach his eyes. Then his gaze flicked to Lark and his lips opened. No sound came out but he mouthed the words in an exaggerated fashion that was hard to miss.

Hurry.

Lark's brow furrowed in confusion.

"Hurry?" he asked, uncertain. "Hurry for what?"

"Richard!" my mother shouted from the hall.

My father's gaze flicked from Lark to me.

Hurry. Go. Save them.

"Save who?" I asked.

The urgency from my father was telling. I knew why as he turned and shuffled out after my mother. This betrayal wasn't over. Not by a long shot. Stealing Gemini's power wasn't the only arrangement my mother had made to take place while we were busy with these doomed peace negotiations.

"Come on," I said urgently, grabbing Lark's arm and turning. "We have to go."

Lark did not question me. I could see the confusion and concern warring in his features but he did not argue. Instead he pushed forward, through the Blessings guards, as quickly as he could. But when we emerged in the open foyer beyond, something had changed. It was... empty. No more healers in robes, no guards. No one awaited us but Rook. And he looked panicked.

"We have to go," he spat, rushing over to us as soon as the guards unlocked our chains and took them away. "Now."

Chapter Thirty-Five
A Field of Carnage

We landed in the middle of a battle.

No longer reeling from the shadow stepping as I had before, there was nothing to distract me from the abject carnage taking place before my eyes. Lark and Rook wasted no time, turning and nodding to one another while Rook drew his blade and took up a defensive stance.

Men and women alike were screaming as blades swung through the air, piercing flesh and bone. Civilians dressed in garish orange ran quickly through the chaos, keeping their heads low to show they were not a threat. Nearby, a familiar portal buzzed louder than it ever had before. Wanderers. We were in the Court of Wanderers.

We had landed near the portal where it seemed the heaviest of the fighting was taking place. Soldiers in brown and green screamed as they slashed and fought their way inward. The defensive orange lines had broken and red and purple were rushing to fill the void but the sheer numbers of the Pride Court soldiers overwhelmed them ten to one.

Because Irim never went to recruit the common folk, I realized, the betrayal burying itself deeper into my soul, burrowing so deep that I knew I would never be rid of it.

On the other side of the battle, Sophierial was standing on a small rise, surveying the carnage with a shrewd eye. She was surrounded by a line of men and women in white robes who stood beside her, intermittently throwing bolts of white hot lightening toward any of our soldiers that managed to veer close enough. As I watched, the Court of Scholars soldiers began to arrive. Yellow robed healers ran about on both sides, though there were more on ours. And then, out of the corner of my eye, black.

"Where have you been?" someone was shouting over the loud scrape of metal on metal and concussive magical blasts.

I turned to see Taurus approaching. Blood splattered nearly every inch of him already. The shield he carried was dented beyond repair. He tossed it to the ground as he strode forward, wiping the sweat from his brow in a way that left behind yet another streak of blood.

"Peace negotiations," Lark growled and Taurus raised a brow.

"Assuming they didn't go well."

"That's an understatement."

"Clear out this section for us? We're nearly overwhelmed here and if they get to the portal—"

Lark gave a curt nod and then turned to me.

"Look away, princess," he said, so softly that it was amazing I could hear him in this cacophony.

"Why?" I asked but he had already turned away.

I watched him, curious. How could one man clear out an entire section? Taurus was right. They were already getting overwhelmed here. Vines were wrapped around the Wanderers guards, holding them in place as soldiers in green fought their way forward. Lark stepped into the chaos without a weapon.

"No!" I cried as he reached toward the nearest soldier, a hulking brute in green who was plunging a gleaming blade straight toward Lark's uunguarded face.

But then Lark stepped forward and ducked, reaching with one hand at the same time. The moment he simply touched the soldier's side, the man simply... disintegrated. All that was left of him was a pile of bones so pristine white that one might have thought they were polished. Lark moved again, raising an arm and the bones lifted into the air, just in time for the skull to block an oncoming blow. Lark spun and the discarded femur flew through the air straight through the man who had struck at him.

I gaped, amazed, as Lark spun and struck and blocked using the bones and when he ran out he simply made more, his touch turning living, breathing soldiers into nothing more than a pile of bones, a new round of weapons for him to use as he pleased. Rook followed at his back, fending off attacks he couldn't see. It was a whirling dance of death and destruction, equal parts terrible and beautiful. I simply couldn't pull my gaze away. Until I became aware that Taurus was still shouting at me. I blinked and turned to face him.

"What?" I cried back over the noise.

"I said can you fight?" he shouted.

"Oh, um. I don't. I can't—"

"I've got her," another voice cried and I turned to find Ursa approaching, obsidian blades twirling at her sides.

Taurus hesitated, glancing between us, but then must have decided he didn't have time for this and stepped into the fray. I watched him as he slashed one man's neck and the blood that sprayed stopped and hung in the air around him.

I gaped.

"Court of Blood and Bone," Ursa reminded me. "You thought the title was just because it sounded so delightful?"

"But you—" I started, glancing down at her spinning blades.

"We have a Bone Prince and a Blood Prince," she said and I thought she sounded quite bitter at the admission. "Mine are a gift from the god of night. My sister's are... well, something else. Now, if you're done inquiring about my family history, we have a battle to fight."

I nodded, chastened.

"What do I do?" I asked, turning toward the soldiers in brown who were advancing upon Rook and Lark despite the bone dust now permeating the air around them, making it thick, like a fog. And I realized all at once that it had never been mist surrounding Lark when he summoned his magic... it was bone.

"Target the soldiers," Ursa commanded. "Emotions run high on a battlefield. Use that. I'll cover you."

I nodded again, turning. Though I wasn't quite certain what I was doing, I closed my eyes. It felt foolish, to close your eyes in the middle of a battlefield where hundreds of soldiers likely had orders to target you specifically, but I wasn't skilled enough with my abilities to use them without focusing yet. So I closed my eyes and felt. Then I stumbled back.

I heard the whir of blades through the air as Ursa defended me on all sides, the sound of steel on steel and bone crunching as Lark and Rook fought nearby, and a chilling war cry echoing from Taurus somewhere farther off than I'd thought. But I couldn't focus on any of that because Ursa had been right. Emotions did run high on the battlefield and the aura of them was nearly overwhelming. Anger, fear, anxiety, and pain pulsed all around me, it rose higher and higher until it practically suffocated me with its presence. What I did next was simply instinctual. I reached out towards those pulsing threads, grasped them, and pulled.

Ursa gasped and I opened my eyes to find that at least two dozens soldiers around us had fallen to their knees. They had no discernible injuries but had become blubbering, crying messes on the bloodstained ground in front of us. They had become a slave to their own emotions, drowned in them until they were unable to surface again, to rise above them and fight. I had rendered them incapable of wielding their swords.

Ursa stepped forward, knife forming in her hand, and pressed her weapon against the first man's throat.

"No," I said, my voice rough.

She looked up at me.

"If we don't kill them today, they will return to kill us tomorrow," she replied, her tone somber.

"We cannot kill those who cannot defend themselves," I told her, shaking my head. "If we do, we're no better than her."

Ursa frowned but stepped away, her blade disintegrating into dust.

"That honor will get you killed, princess," she warned. "And they can defend themselves. I could."

"Don't pretend to believe these common soldiers have the same magical capacity as a Bone Court Princess, Ursa," I said.

She just shook her head and stepped away.

"We should go to the portal," she told me, looking in that direction. "Someone needs to get in close and defend it. Maybe you can clear out enough soldiers to—"

A loud wail pierced the silence and Ursa and I both turned to see Irim standing at the opening of an alleyway nearby. An amulet glowed softly against his chest and in his hand was Cass, bound and gagged.

"Bastard," Ursa growled and lunged.

Irim and Cass disappeared only to reappear a few feet away.

"This shadow stepping thing has its perks," he mused, grinning. "I'll give it to you, Bone Court. This might be one of the most practical abilities any of us have."

"Let her go," I said, stepping forward.

"Or what?" he asked, raising a brow and peering at the soldiers behind me. "You'll make me cry? Come on, Seren. We both know you can't do much more than that. I promise you, I won't be as easy to conquer as those men."

"Why did you do it?" I couldn't help but ask. "Why did you join her? She killed your father. She drove your mother insane. You hated her."

"Ariadne has a vision for the world that I find enticing," he answered with a shrug. "And my father would have told me to choose the winning side."

Without warning, Ursa threw one of her obsidian blades but Irim just vanished again, reappearing a few feet further down the road. In the seconds he was away, I turned in an attempt to locate Lark. He and Rook had fought their way so far into the battle that it would be impossible to call for him. My gaze flicked back to Ursa who was seething.

"Get Lark," I told her.

Her eyes flew from Irim to me and she hesitated.

"Ursa. Now."

She muttered a curse but then disappeared as well. I reached for the blade at my waist. I had seconds, only seconds.

"Let her go, Irim," I commanded.

"For what it's worth, cousin, I did like you," he said, ignoring the threat of my blade entirely. "At least, I did before you got his Bone Court stench all over you. Bonded to a Bone Prince. How awful."

I threw my blade. As expected, Irim blinked from existence. I ran.

He had been moving three feet to the left every time, consistently. So I aimed for where I expected him to reappear. Then he did, exactly where I had planned. He blinked into existence and, because he was so new to shadow stepping, was too busy reorienting himself to notice me. I slammed into him only a second after he materialized. The impact forced him to release Cass who stumbled away, mumbling something in shock that I couldn't hear through her gag.

Irim and I rolled through the dust, wrestling for control. He had a sword at his belt and I was weaponless, having tossed my knife to force him to shadow step. I had to keep his hands away from that steel. I gripped his wrists as we rolled, holding on with all my might so he couldn't reach for his belt. He grunted and then I felt it, the prodding presence of an invader into my mind. I slammed down my walls and reached for his fear. It had to be there, somewhere.

"Ren!"

I heard Lark as if he were far away. Adrenaline compelled me to keep rolling, keep fighting, keep my focus on my cousin as he snarled and growled and tried to pull out of my hold. Out of the corner of my eye, Rook stepped forward. A strong breeze blew him back.

Mine, I thought, gritting my teeth. This kill is mine.

But then Irim smiled and that insistent prodding force in my mind eased. I only relaxed for a moment before I saw the reason he had retreated. Nearby, Rook moved forward, raising his blade. I tried to blow him back again but he batted the wind aside with the blade as if the thing could simply cleave through my magic. He approached, face stoic, emotionless, and Irim began to laugh.

I only had a second to roll before Rook's blade slammed into the sand where I'd been a moment before. I released my cousin's wrists out of necessity, springing to my feet.

"Rook, stop!" Lark was shouting but I could see the vacant expression in the warrior's eyes and knew he couldn't hear him.

"Rook!" Cass cried.

But it wouldn't do any good.

Ursa was calling for Taurus as Lark got in close.

No, no, no.

"Don't hurt him," I said. "He doesn't know what he's doing. He—"

Irim was laughing gleefully now, eyes alight as he watched Rook turn on his closest friends, as he watched the warrior swing his blade at his prince who ducked it as bone dust began to rise around them.

No!

Without thinking, I dove for Irim. I had to disrupt him somehow, had to break his hold on Rook's mind, had to... to... get him away from here.

I squeezed my eyes shut as I leapt, reaching. The moment I made contact with my cousin, I expelled a breath and a little burst of power, not mine. The world squeezed in around us and then expanded again.

"What the Hell?" Irim shouted, gasping as we clattered to a glistening white floor.

He growled, pulling his sword, lunging.

I used my wind to buffet it aside and then ducked out of the way. He advanced still, taking the missed swing in stride and trying again. I turned and ran. I couldn't keep this up, couldn't fight him without a weapon.

I passed enormous marble statues that looked vaguely familiar but didn't spare them a passing glance. My feet slapped against cool white stone as I ran, glancing in every direction for a weapon. Anything would do. I felt that invasion into my mind and slammed my walls tight yet again, passing by empty corridor after empty corridor. What was this place? It looked familiar and yet...

"There is nowhere you can run that I will not find you, Seren," Irim called from behind me.

I knew he was right. I could shadow step again but where? If I returned to the battle, he would too, and then he would regain control of one of my friends, use them against us. No, I needed to keep him here, away from the true fight at the portal.

"You cannot stop this," he cried out from behind me. So close. He was too close. "Ariadne has plans for the mortals, plans to unite our realms once again. This was, after all, our world originally. Why should we have to divide ourselves and give up so much of what was ours? Especially for such inferiority. That will change, though. For the ones who are worthy, at least."

I nearly stumbled. That will change? The ones who are worthy? Suddenly, I knew the full extent of my mother's plans and shuddered. They won't have to enslave the mortals, I realized. All they have to do is offer a few key players immortality and those will sell out the rest. They won't have to rule over the mortals because the mortals will rule themselves. There will be rebellions, bloody civil wars, genocides. But my mother was counting on that. Why destroy a people who could be so easily convinced to destroy themselves? My mother didn't want to rule the mortals. She wanted to ruin them.

I can't let that happen.

I skidded to a stop in front of a particularly large statue and realized, suddenly, where I was. This was Lemnus, god of light. I was in Sophierial's court.

My first thought should have been panic. But it wasn't. A plan was beginning to form in my mind, one that I should have thought about the moment I began to make the connections I had started to see in this realm. But I didn't have much time to consider it. I simply had to keep moving and hope it worked.

Without much more thought than that, I took a breath, and shadow stepped right into the Court of Light and Life's throne room.

Chapter Thirty-Six
A Last Hope

Semyaza gasped.

I knew Sophierial herself wouldn't be here. I had seen her on the battlefield with my own eyes. That was fine. I didn't need her to be. In fact, this might work even better if she wasn't. I wasn't entirely sure what Sophierial herself was capable of and I would rather not find out like this.

"Traitor!" Semyaza screamed immediately. "Guards!"

All around me, white-robed knights blinked into existence, their strange staffs pointed at me.

"Where are the elixirs, Semyaza?" I asked, my voice low but loud enough for her to hear.

She blinked at me, stunned by my request.

"I will not tell you," she sneered. "How dare you come here! How dare you use that vulgar Bone Court power to enter our dwelling uninvited! How—"

Irim was somewhere in these halls, searching for me. The fuss that Semyaza was making was bound to draw him quickly enough. I was running out of time.

"Where are the elixirs, Semyaza?" I repeated.

She scoffed, crossing her arms and glaring at me.

"Very well," I replied and then lifted my hands.

I reached toward the guards all around me, toward their fear, and pulled. They collapsed immediately, falling to the floor, silent. Perhaps I had pulled a bit too hard. I was still getting used to these abilities after all. It had the desired affect, however. Semyaza's jaw dropped and she stared at me in awe. She didn't know these men weren't dead. In her mind, I had merely raised a hand and killed a dozen armed men. My mother herself had taught me the power of perception. I would use it now. I could feel the fear radiating off of her, stronger now than her anger, her defiance. I could use that.

I took a step forward, stepping over the slumped body of one of her men.

"Take me to the elixirs," I repeated. "Now."

Despite her nearly overwhelming fear, Semyaza raised her chin, though it wobbled, and stood her ground.

I sighed and clenched my fist.

She gasped, collapsing to the stone below. She whimpered, fighting the fear encasing her heart.

I strode forward and leaned down beside her.

"The bulk of your forces are in the Court of Wanderers fighting some ill-advised battle against my side. Sophierial is there. I saw her myself. You are alone and undefended," I said, giving a pointed glance at the fallen guards below. "I have the time to search this place myself, find them on my own, after I kill you. Or you could be helpful. And survive."

She whimpered again. I released my hold on her slightly and it was enough. She raised a shaking finger, pointing, to a door behind the throne.

I nodded.

"Good," I told her. "Now sleep."

I clenched my fist and she fell unconscious like the others.

Hurrying, I made my way across the stones and wrenched open the door she had pointed to. I stepped into an unlit hallway so dark I couldn't see my hand in front of my face. I could hear nothing but the sound of my own breathing as I stepped forward, one foot after another, until the way began to slope downward. Then there were steps. I took them, going lower and lower until I was certain I was well beneath the palace itself.

I paused for a moment but couldn't hear Irim above. Nor had Semyaza or any of her guards awakened to sound the alarm. I still had time. Not much but some. If this didn't work, though...

I took a breath and kept moving. Faith. That was why they called it that, right? Believing in something even when you had practically no evidence of its existence? I had to have faith. For the first time in my life, I had to believe in stories and legends rather than science and proven theory. Because if I was wrong...

Suddenly, the floor leveled out and I stepped into an enormous open space. There were shelves as far as I could see and, upon them, were thousands of little vials, all glowing softly in the dark. Elixirs. And so many of them.

This would do it. This would destroy mortal society. This would end the world of mankind.

I raised my hands and let my anger build and build. It rose higher when I thought of my mother, how she had enslaved my father, all that she had done to him and then, to me. When I thought of Irim and his complete and utter betrayal. When I thought of Wispa Amberberry who had trapped Cass into a betrothal contract with her son. When I thought of the Court of Blessings who had forced us into peace negotiations that distracted us long enough for my mother to steal Gemini's magic. When I thought of

Lord Koa Oaksky and his smug, undeserving smile. It rose like a violent, formidable wave.

Then I released it.

The harsh sound of shattering glass filled the air around me and I fell to the floor, exhausted, utterly spent. I couldn't raise my arms, couldn't lift a finger to call my magic. It was there still, I felt it faintly stirring within me, but so used up that it nearly pulled me into the world of the unconscious like those I'd left quivering above.

The light of the elixir, a swirling gold, rose off of the floor like mist, twisting and whirling around me, illuminating the stone floor. I watched, entranced, wondering if it was going to happen, wondering if my risk had paid off. If not, at least I'd destroyed them. At least I—

"Seren Dawnpaw," a familiar voice spoke and I turned to find the elixir looking back at me as the same vision of my uncle, drifting in the air. "Or is it Ren Belling?"

"Cylon," I replied.

And the god of time smiled.

About the Author

My name is A. N. Horton. I am a two-time award-winning author living in Nashville, TN with my husband, children, and moderately chunky Corgi. When I'm not writing, I'm reading, baking more cookies than my family can eat, and plotting crimes against my characters. I'm best known for crafting characters that steal my readers' hearts as much as they shatter them. I am a cross-genre writer focused mainly on fantasy and romance.

Award-Winning Author of the Divinaxy Saga.

Aspiring Writer. Avid Reader. Lover of Literature.

See my LinkTree for all things social and creative!

https://linktr.ee/ANHorton

http://authoranhorton.com/

Also by A. N. Horton

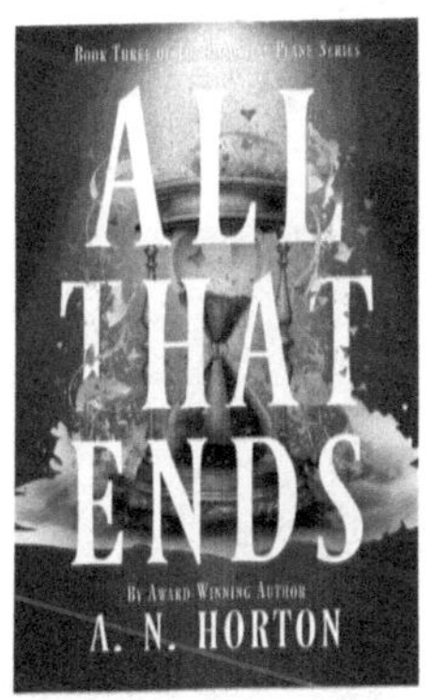

All That Ends — Book Three of The Immortal Plane Trilogy

War has arrived.

With cryptic gods and ancient beasts in play, no one is safe.

It turns out freeing the god of time has consequences and Ren Belling is dealing with them. But fighting a war to guard the Divide and protect the mortal plane from her mother takes precedence. As court politics shift, Ren finds herself unsure of who she can trust. Sometimes, being on the same side of a battlefield doesn't mean you're allies.

As she learns her world is much more affected by the forgotten deities than she thought, Ren comes face to face with a power that no one has ever held; a power that should have remained buried.

Despite her best efforts to save her people, Ren has to admit that the more she learns of the Immortal Plane, the more she realizes...

Secrets can kill.

Buy All That Ends

Want to know what court you would belong to? Take the official quiz here.

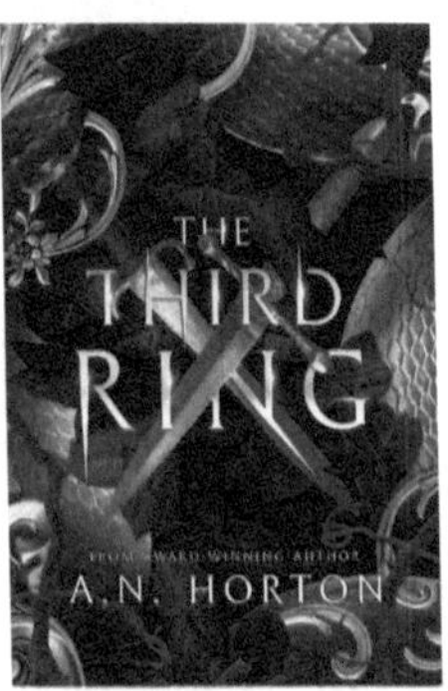

The Third Ring — Book One of The Sanctum Series
Ten Trials. Two Oaths. One Chance.

To Adrian, the gods were never anything to be worshipped, just tolerated. But in the walled city of Sanctuary, whether through the religious fervor of the elite or the quaking fear of the poor, the Geist have always been served. And now it's Adrian's turn.

Born into power and raised for greatness, Dante stands for everything Adrian has come to despise, but he may be her only hope of survival. When the two of them are bonded against their will and forced to compete together in the Trials, the god's ancient gauntlet of physical brutality and psychological torture, they have no choice but to set aside old prejudices and work together. Navigating religious zealots, a patriarch intent on breeding the pair for power, and the increasingly obvious cruelty of the gods, Adrian must come to terms with the fact that, whether Culled or Championed, we all serve the gods in the end. And, for her, betrayal has always been waiting just around the corner.

Buy The Third Ring